Praise for *Bitter*

'*Bitter* **is just wonderful.** It's a very painful story but told with a kind of lightness and grace. It's so well-written, with such deceptive directness and simplicity, so well-organised and well-paced. Francesca Jakobi completely inhabits Gilda, in all her pain and obsession, all her self-deception and self-sabotage. **An absolutely astonishing first novel**'        Michael Frayn, author of *Spies*

'Stormingly good, deliciously addictive, **as gripping as Zoë Heller's *Notes On A Scandal.*** It's got to be the beach read of 2018!'        Peter Bradshaw, Guardian Film Critic

'I bloody loved this book. **It was emotionally so intense, so addictive, I tore through it,** unable to stop. Buy it. Read it.'
        Susie Steiner, author of *Persons Unknown*

'Bitter, yes, but also sweet – and moving, and searching, and quietly devastating: a novel to detonate the heart. Steep yourself in this exquisite story. You won't regret it, and you won't forget it. **Fans of Gail Honeyman and Joanna Cannon will love *Bitter***'
        A.J. Finn, author of *The Woman in the Window*

'**Provocative and skilful** . . . The results are as hilarious as they are unsettling as Jakobi exploits the stereotype of the needy Jewish mother and we are drawn against our better judgment to side with out-of-control Gilda'        Barry Forshaw, *Guardian*

'Brilliantly paced, **moving, thoughtful and sharp.** Loved it'
        Renée Knight, author of *Disclaimer*

'**Gloriously sinister** and yet, when you least expect it, quietly heartbreaking.        *Man*

**Francesca Jakobi** studied Psychology at the University of Sussex, followed by a stint teaching English in Turkey and the Czech Republic. On returning to her native London she got a job as a reporter on a local paper and has worked in journalism ever since. She's currently a layout editor at the *Financial Times*.

*Bitter* is her first novel and was inspired by her grandmother, who was sued for divorce in the 1940s.

# BITTER

FRANCESCA JAKOBI

WEIDENFELD & NICOLSON

First published in Great Britain in 2018
by Weidenfeld & Nicolson
This paperback edition published in Great Britain in 2018
by Weidenfeld & Nicolson
an imprint of the Orion Publishing Group Ltd
Carmelite House, 50 Victoria Embankment
London EC4Y ODZ

An Hachette UK Company

1 3 5 7 9 10 8 6 4 2

Copyright © Francesca Jakobi 2018

A CIP catalogue record for this book is
available from the British Library.

ISBN (Mass Market Paperback) 978 1 4746 0758 2
ISBN (eBook) 978 1 4746 0759 9

Typeset by Input Data Services Ltd, Somerset

Printed in Great Britain by Clays Ltd, Elcograf S.p.A.

MIX
Paper from
responsible sources
FSC® C104740
FSC
www.fsc.org

www.orionbooks.co.uk

For my grandmother, with love

# I

She's childishly small, my freshly baked daughter-in-law, despite that blonde beehive stuck on her head. Light blue eyes, either innocent or she's rather dim, and a tiny shiksa nose that belongs on a toddler.

All morning, strangers have been coming up to tell me how charming she is. I nod my head and bite my tongue and I keep what I think to myself.

I wonder if my Reuben did it on purpose: searched far and wide for the opposite of me. He hasn't married a Jew – so what? – but why not a dark woman? Why not a tall woman? Why not a woman with a bit more shape?

The truth is I've been dreading this wedding: seeing my ex-husband, being here alone. I planned this outfit months ago but this tight, white suit is too tight and too white. And this hat, all the netting, what possessed me? I thought I looked so smart when I left the flat this morning but I've come to my own son's wedding in a white suit and a veil.

The day feels endless. Five hours in and the speeches are only just starting. I look round the reception room at all Reuben's friends and I don't recognise a single one. The girls are dolly birds in shrunken outfits – legs in pale tights like limp sticks of celery.

The boys slouch beside them in garish cravats. Patchouli oil mingles with cigar smoke.

It's a brand new hotel, frightfully with-it: champagne and canapés, thirty shillings a head. For the money, I thought they'd have a sit-down meal but that's not the fashion, they say. I shift my weight from foot to foot. A sit-down for a minute would be nice. I force down a couple of salty chicken vol-au-vents despite the knot in my stomach.

My ex-husband, Frank, and his beloved Berta are chatting away right next to me. We're all terribly civilised these days, you see. Only, I can't help noticing that Berta's hair looks slightly brassy – red is such a difficult shade, unflattering with ageing skin. Frank looks well. Was he really that short when we were married?

'So lovely to see you,' I say.

Yes, we're all so very civilised these days, Frank, Berta and I. I don't think they saw me wince when Reuben's silly friend came over and congratulated Berta on her 'brilliant son'. *She's not his mother*. I stuffed my mouth with a devilled egg.

The best man's speech goes on, and on, and on. Finally we're asked to toast the happy couple. Fizzy acid burns my throat.

Berta tries her best, I'm sure, but she's never had much in the way of taste – just look at that dress she's wearing now, those shoes with that dreadful hat.

I remember: it was at the end of the school holidays and Reuben came to visit me at the flat. Berta had dressed him in dark brown shorts with a too-short haircut like a lice-plagued refugee. He had a grubby plaster on his left knee, in the soft spot just below his kneecap. I wondered how he'd fallen over, if she cuddled him before she patched him up.

He came into my room while I was sitting in front of the mirror. I was putting on my earrings for a night out at the theatre.

He held the gift very carefully with both hands and he hesitated before putting it down on the dressing table next to me. He didn't say anything, just waited until I picked it up. I looked at him and he looked down at his feet.

When I opened it I saw six ugly coffee cups nestling in a flimsy cardboard box, Woolworths price tag still on it. They were the cheapest chunky china in dirty yellow.

Insulting, but that's typical of Berta – as if some tacky cups could fix things. A token gesture from a guilty second wife who didn't care enough to take the price off.

So I told my Reuben exactly what I thought of those cups: their cheapness, their chunkiness, their stained-urinal yellow.

And now it's Reuben's turn to give his speech and everyone cheers as he takes to the floor. To me he looks too nervous but his voice is strong and clear. I breathe in deep and smile at him. I want him to know how proud I am. I gesture, try to catch his eye, but he doesn't once look my way.

He tells the room how he met Alice and knew she was the one for him right from the start. He almost stayed at home on his own that night because cocktail parties give him a headache. The music was too loud and he wished he hadn't come; the hostess kept on plying him with lethal dry Martinis. He went to hide in the kitchen and that is where he found her. She was sipping Mateus Rosé from a mug.

He asked her for some wine and that's how they started talking. When the wine ran out they drank lemon squash instead.

He says: 'I fell for her warmth and her radiant smile and seduced her with my paisley kipper tie.'

And everyone laughs, though I can't see what's funny. He knows the room is on his side and he straightens his shoulders and grins.

He tells us about their very first date, how he prattled on for hours about typesetting and fonts. How he tried too hard, spilled soup on his shirt, then forgot where he'd parked his Cortina.

3

He says that he and Alice walked for miles round Hampstead; she didn't grumble once when the rain came pouring down. They were soaking wet and freezing cold and they couldn't find the car but it really didn't matter. They could have gone on walking all night.

And he tells the room that he couldn't quite believe it when despite all his failings she agreed to meet again. He thinks it's more astounding than man on the moon, that she's next to him here as his wife.

And the room falls silent apart from his voice as he tells us just how much he loves this woman. He says she taught him how to love; that she taught him what love could be.

And I can't look at him because he didn't learn about love from me.

## 2

A large manila envelope arrives at my flat, the address typed neat and official on a mean white label. I don't hurry to open it, sure it's a gas bill or a pamphlet from the bank. I sit down, drink my coffee and swallow my grapefruit without any sugar.

Once I've poured myself a second cup of coffee, I look properly at the envelope. It's thicker and stiffer than the average bill and red letters read *Do Not Bend*. The postmark informs me it was sent out last week: *15 Aug '69*. I take my curved grapefruit knife and slit the envelope open in a jagged line. I enjoy the ragged swipe of it.

Inside I find two pictures from the wedding, a photographer's business card and a letter from my son. I lay the items out on the tablecloth. I pick up Reuben's letter and unfold it with trembling hands.

I'm calling it a letter but it doesn't really qualify. It is four words in black ink on thin, white paper. There's no greeting, no pleasantries, just the scrawl of a scratchy fountain pen. Four words in black ink: *From your loving son*.

I know those four words well; they sat at the end of every letter Reuben sent from boarding school. The writing is a little more grown-up now but the content is much the same. Even at their most expansive his letters were only a paragraph.

*The weather is fine here. I am working hard. Yesterday we had crumpets for tea.*
*From your loving son.*

So, they're back from honeymoon, then. I've heard nothing. Not even a quick phone call just to let me know they're safe.

Still. It's good that they found time to get the photographs developed and sent out. It's good that they found time to print these little labels and stick them on the envelopes.

I put on my reading glasses to examine the photographs in detail and the day comes rushing back to me in shades of black and white. I remember the photographer, too old for such tight trousers. He bellowed like a market trader for the parents to join the frame. Disrespectful. He touched bits he shouldn't as he jostled us together and he wiped his smudgy fingers on the arm of my white suit.

I wasn't surprised when Berta muscled in, though she isn't a parent and she didn't belong there. I made sure I was the one standing next to Reuben.

She smiled at me and I saw lipstick on one of her teeth. 'Gilda, darling, I'm glad you're next to your son. You two get to see each other so rarely these days.'

Look at me there, clutching my champagne with both hands in case I throw it at her. She's sucking her stomach in for the camera. I can tell by the way she's holding her shoulders.

Everyone else is enjoying themselves but I'm strained and anxious in the middle of it all. My eyes look tired, dark rings beneath my make-up. It's an ugly photograph. It makes me look ugly.

I gulp down my coffee and pick up the second picture. It's Reuben and Alice outside Chelsea Old Town Hall. The scene is romantic, the two of them on the steps with a flurry of confetti. It's a shame her mascara has smudged.

6

They're so hopeful standing there, so full of fairy tales and happily ever after. They think they're at the start of something, stepping out into the world for the very first time.

Well, I've been married twice, once with Frank and once with Leo – I was more in love with Leo than I ever thought possible. It doesn't last, what they're feeling. It will not last.

And I worry for my Reuben because he looks triumphant. He's holding her hand like it's a trophy he can't believe he's won. This is the son who never touches his mother, not even on the cheek when he kisses me hello. This is the son who never calls me, never visits me unless he knows he has to.

I used to think he was a bit of a cold fish, some people are, you have to accept it. But when I met him and Alice together that first time, I couldn't believe my eyes. The son I saw before me was a loving man, exuding warmth like he'd swallowed a radiator. I couldn't have been more amazed if he'd opened his mouth and started talking Japanese; if he'd grabbed a violin and played flawless Mozart; if he'd flapped his arms and flown around the room.

Something has changed in him. What magic did this young girl use? I study her in the pictures, trying to work it out. She's pretty, yes, but not so very pretty. Intelligent, yes, though no match for my son.

There were girlfriends before her, plenty of girlfriends – that skinny one, Rachel, and Charlotte with the laugh. I remember when Reuben brought Rachel home, I thought they would get engaged. But I never saw him look at her the way he looks at Alice.

I knew that Reuben would marry eventually, prepared for it, even hoped for it. Who doesn't want their son to settle down with someone nice? It's just I want him to love me too, to need me in his life like he needs her. It's just I wasn't prepared for it to hurt so very much.

# 3

I've had to come to terms with living alone. It was hard at the start, I won't deny it. There were times after Leo when I floundered in the empty rooms. The silence and the stillness pulled me down.

But now I've reached a sort of understanding with my flat. After fifteen years of solo living it's part of me, like my skin. Every drawer is full, every surface is in use; I've expanded to fill all the gaps. If Leo were to change his mind and come back, there wouldn't be space for him.

That's not to say I've got rid of him entirely; in some ways he's still all around the place. He's in the mushroomy tones he chose for the living room and the hard-backed Danish sofa he bought when we couldn't afford it. There's a dent midway up the doorframe of the bathroom where he punched it in a temper late at night. He's in the glass of whisky I pour at four when our evenings together once began.

Occasionally I miss him still. Only sometimes, though. Rarely. Not much.

The secret is to keep busy, I've found. One thing a day is what I strive for. Yesterday, I rinsed out my nylons. Today I will purchase a stamp.

I arrive at the Post Office just before two when the queue outside is pleasantly long. I take my place behind a matronly woman who's fanning her face with her letters. 'It's hot for the time of year,' she says. I agree, though it's August so hardly a surprise. 'Feels like there's going to be a storm,' she adds. I look up, but the sky is quite blue.

I turn away to discourage further chit-chat and that's when I see Alice on the other side of the road. She has a basket hanging from the crook of her arm and her blonde hair is swept back in a hairband.

The shock of the sighting slows my reactions. For a second or two I just stare. Her face is free of make-up and I'm struck once again by how young she is. The street is grey but the sunlight catches her. From where I stand she looks golden.

I lift my hand to wave at her but her gaze is firmly fixed on the butcher's window. I open my mouth to call 'Alice'. Before I can, she ducks inside the shop. I am left with the shape of her name on my tongue. I swallow it back like it's a pill. My pulse is pounding in my ears and there's a queasy sort of flicker in my stomach.

I could leave the queue and cross over to Alice. I can see her neat little outline through the shop front. I could tap her on the shoulder; tell her I'm pleased they're home. I just stay standing where I am.

Afterwards, back in my flat, it's that little golden moment I remember. The way she seemed to glow in the afternoon heat. The way the sunlight caught her.

I try to imagine how it feels to be so young and happy and loved. And I ask myself, as I sip my whisky, was I ever golden like that?

# 4

My father always said I was a clumsy child: too tall, too broad, my hands and feet too big. He said it whenever I tripped on a step, dropped a book or knocked over a cup. It was a statement of fact and no one thought to question it. I was a giant goose in a household full of finches.

The truth of the matter is I'm not so very tall, a bit above the average, that's all. Yet my father's comments have lodged in my head so I stoop when I enter a room. He was a proud little man and my height must have rankled. I see that now, but it doesn't make a difference. Daughters remember their father's words, even after forty years have passed.

My mother was the great beauty in our family and loved it when people told her so. She'd wake up late, spend hours getting dressed and then drift through the house, glass in hand. She was vague and unfocused during the day. She dosed herself with vodka and Gauloises cigarettes. She came alive only when guests arrived. She switched on her dazzling hostess smile just as her daughters went to bed.

Sometimes, if the fancy took her, she'd come up to see us late at night. I remember the nervous tightness in my stomach as she stood there, swaying in the doorway.

In her prime she'd been a flapper, skin-deep and feckless – she was not someone to turn to in times of trouble. She'd laugh that tinkling laugh of hers and pat at her pin-curled hair. Our childish concerns were 'simply too tiresome', so she left us to resolve them ourselves. We had a string of nannies who never stayed long; not one lasted more than a year.

They were Hamburg's darlings, those two: the antiques dealer and his beautiful wife. They knew all the right people, went to all the right places. But they were never at the table when my sister and I sat down.

Our house back then was like a mausoleum and, really, I don't miss any of it. It had rooms beyond rooms but nothing that was home. It had high ceilings, panelled walls, deep red carpets and mountains of mahogany. Priceless ornaments we weren't allowed to touch and corridors we weren't allowed to run down.

We were lucky – I do realise we were lucky – safely tucked away in there while the rest of the world fell apart. Outside, people lost everything; starved on the streets after the crash of '29. Inside, we ate *Wiener Schnitzel* for dinner. Inside, it stayed quiet and still.

Lucky. It's such a smothering word. It suffocates my thoughts about that time. I feel I have to whisper it, in case I seem ungrateful. *Lucky is not the same as happy.*

# 5

Margo and I are going to the cinema. It's what we like to do on Saturday afternoons. The film isn't important, we sit through more bad ones than good ones. It's nice for old friends to spend time together without really having to talk.

The usherette shows us to our places in the back row, it has to be the back row because Margo can't see up close. We squeeze past handbags and jackets on knees. Margo leaves a trail of startled faces as she juggles her choc-ice and drink.

Once we're safely ensconced in our corner seats, we wait in silence for the picture to start. Margo has a cold again. She's breathing through her mouth.

I can tell straight away that the film's a dud; it's clear from the opening credits and the 'swinging London' shots. Margo reaches the end of her choc-ice and rustles the wrapper as she licks it clean. The woman in front of us turns round and tuts. I close my eyes and think about my son.

It's been two whole weeks since they came back from honeymoon. Three weeks, now, since the wedding. When I call he's out or busy and he never calls me back. Perhaps I've been ringing too often but I don't know what else I can do. Alice says she's sorry I've missed him. I'm starting to wonder if that's true. She's always just a little too cheerful; her apology a little too pat.

It feels like they've shut the world out, those two. They only need each other. But I'm his mother, shouldn't they let me in?

I sink down a little further in my seat and rest my head against the chair-back. I spread my cardigan over my chest and clutch it to my chin like it's a blanket.

I've been wondering lately if there's still time to mend things. I've tried before without success, it doesn't mean I can't try again. Reuben is married, a fresh start for all of us; I have endless empty hours stretching in front of me.

I picture the past as a sort of Rolodex with thousands of life events marked out on cards. I didn't pay attention when the cards were filed and now they're all in a mess. I need to flick back through and find the cards responsible, then maybe I can sort them out and fix the errors I've made.

The thought of it is comforting. A little tidying up is needed. Nothing here is beyond repair, I'm sure of it.

Margo heads straight for the cafe once the film is over. I'd like to stretch my legs but she wants to sit and drink tea. I let her have her way because she doesn't get many outings these days. I try not to look disapproving when she orders a large slice of cake.

We find ourselves a window table with a view out onto the street. Afternoon sun illuminates the dust motes. I brush some stale crumbs from the sticky gingham oilcloth. The jukebox blares 'Boom Bang-a-Bang'.

Margo doesn't have children of her own but she likes to hear about Reuben. It makes her feel included, I think, like she's part of my family too. She's always asking me how he is and what he's been up to and if he's well. Today she wants to hear about the wedding.

13

'I need you to tell me everything, Gilda. I don't even know what the dress was like. How was Frank? Did Reuben make a speech? What did they give you to eat?'

I shrug. 'It was a lovely occasion. I was sorry I couldn't invite you.'

'Yes, yes, you explained all that. They had to keep the numbers down.'

I say Alice's dress looked more like a nightdress, she chuckles a bit when I describe Berta's hair. I tell her I would have liked a sit-down meal and the canapés had far too much salt in.

But it's not enough, she's hungry for more. She wants to hear it all, who I spoke to, what was said. So I pick up the teapot and top up our tea and I roll out the first of my lies.

I stumble a bit to begin with. It's important to get it right. She likes to hear nice things about my son and I don't want to let her down. I say: 'Alice and Reuben went out of their way to include me. They introduced me to all their young friends.'

I smile, but Margo's expression is anxious. 'I was worried for you on your own.'

I stir my tea. 'Oh no, there was no need. I wasn't left alone for a second. Everyone kept me frightfully busy. It's quite a job being the mother of the groom.'

She bites off a mouthful of Battenberg cake. 'That's nice,' she says through the sponge. 'I thought it might be tricky with Berta and Frank there. I'm sure I would have found it difficult.'

I scratch at a smear on the oilcloth with my thumbnail. It's pale and congealed, maybe salad cream. 'The fact is, Margo, in the end I hardly saw them; they were over on the other side of the room. There were so many guests there, so much going on. We barely exchanged a single word.'

When I look up I see my friend is frowning. Her voice is edged with hurt. 'Oh. But you said it was just a little gathering. They had to keep the numbers down.'

The room is rather airless so I tug off my cardigan. I turn round and drape it on my chair. It slips straight off. I pick it up and rearrange it. 'Silly old thing,' I say.

# 6

Lena was two years older than me but I have never felt like the little sister. She stayed tiny and I couldn't work out how. We ate the same, moved the same, drank the same water. I just kept on growing while she stayed neat and small.

It was a constant source of amusement to people that two sisters could be so different. Lena loved to point it out: 'Look at her hands compared to mine!' I played along, I don't know why. Held out my hands and provided the punchline.

On the evenings when our parents were out, my sister and I would go on adventures. We'd slip through silent corridors while everyone's backs were turned. We'd climb the stairs to the third floor and head straight for Mother's dressing room. We'd creep in, little trespassers, and quietly shut the door.

The room was small by the standards of the house and muffled in cotton-wool softness. The carpet was so thick and deep that you couldn't see the tips of your toes. I always thought it should have smelled sweet, like the Shalimar scent Mother dabbed behind her ears. Instead it surprised you with a windows-shut smell of feet and stale cigarettes.

We didn't talk, my sister and I, as we rifled through all of

Mother's precious things. In silence, we shed our everyday dresses, then struggled into corsets and slips. We helped each other with hooks and eyes, we tightened our straps and straightened our seams. Then we wrapped ourselves in silks and furs and wobbled around in Spanish heels.

Once we'd painted our lips and spritzed ourselves with perfume, we'd sit at Mother's dressing table and stare into her mirror. We were movie stars, the two of us; heartbreakers just like her. We spoke of all the parties we'd go to, the boys we'd dance with, our wedding days. We'd sit there for hours side by side and practise pouting with sucked-in cheeks.

I was twelve when I first noticed that Mother's gowns were tight across my shoulders. I ignored the buttons straining at my chest and the chiffon cutting into my armpits. Lena laughed when she saw it, saying: 'Gilda, you're going to burst out!' She ordered me to stick to the sturdier outfits: winter blouses and hard-wearing skirts.

It wasn't long before Mother's shoes began to pinch. My toes bruised painfully as I tried to jam them in. I told myself my feet were too hot, my toes had swollen, the shoes had shrunk. If I was to be Aschenputtel, then the slipper needed to fit.

When Lena saw me struggling with the shoehorn, she took away the Mary Janes and the mules with marabou trim. After that I wore father's shoes instead, their leather hard and shiny as a beetle's shell.

# 7

Alice has invited me round for coffee, 'just the two of us'. She says it will be a chance for us to get to know each other better. It's a very sweet gesture and I'm sure she's doing her best, but all that I can think of is that Reuben won't be there.

I dress carefully for our meeting, I want her to think well of me, in my dove-grey suit and a lavender silk blouse with a pussy-bow tied at the neck.

When I look in the mirror I see someone in charge: the woman announcing the raffle prizes or the head of the local Conservative association. A little tired, perhaps, but not bad for a woman in her fifties. Nothing a bit of lipstick and some powder won't correct.

One I've fixed my make-up I put on my jacket and give myself a last once-over in the hallway. I straighten my stockings and blot my lips, I want to look just right. Overall, it's fine. I'm pleased with what I see. I am neat and tidy and not to be messed with.

It's the first time I've been to Reuben's house, which, like his marriage, is newly built – part of a little estate just off the Finchley Road. It takes me a while to find it. It's one of several terraces tucked behind a bank of trees. They are small and uniform and rather plain: caravans parked up on a camping site.

I know how much Reuben paid for this place and I'm shocked at how little he's got for his money. Two storeys and neighbours practically on top of you – you pay £5,000 for that? Still, I won't say anything, it's nice to have him near me for once. I'm eager to see what they've done with the decor, to gather some clues about their lives.

I smooth the creases out of my skirt and knock on their blue front door.

When Alice answers she seems a little flustered. 'Gilda, you're early, how lovely.'

My daughter-in-law is wearing a red paisley scarf; she's tied it round her head like she's a fortune-teller. Bohemian I suppose. But I'm glad my own hair is freshly set.

'You look colourful,' I say.

She takes me through a small entrance hall that has wallpaper teeming with black and white spots. The bold print is claustrophobic in such a narrow space.

She offers to take my jacket and hangs it on a hook by the scruff of its neck. The weight of the material droops down like a wilted flower.

The living room smells of new carpets and sawdust. Alice apologises for the packing cases, which are still stacked in the corner. I glance around; there's not much here though they moved in weeks ago, these newlyweds. There's a sofa. It's orange. A shade one rarely sees in furniture. There's an armchair in lime green. I wonder if they're planning to cover it.

There are no ornaments or knick-knacks and the bookshelves are utterly bare. Reuben's always reading something. I can't see any sign of him here.

Next to the only lamp there's a single framed photograph on display; a picture of my daughter-in-law in an English country garden. Her family's all around her: her mother, her father and a sweet-faced younger sister. They are arm in arm the four of them. They are laughing.

It's the frame itself that gets to me, I think. Home-made and gluey in cotton-covered cardboard. It must have been a present from Alice's sister – something she brought home from school. She's done some embroidery across the top, *All you need is love* in clumsy purple cross-stitch.

My Reuben is part of that family now. I want to knock that little picture frame down.

'I think we'll have our coffee in the garden,' Alice says. I follow her through sliding patio doors to a large patch of neatly trimmed lawn. We're not the only ones here – all the houses back onto this shared bit of green. Three children kick a ball in the far corner.

My daughter-in-law drags out a couple of rickety deckchairs and sets one up for me in the shade. I lower myself into its blue stripes with caution but still sink deep into its base. I straighten my clothes and rearrange myself while Alice brings out coffee and cake.

It's not until she's ensconced in a yellow deckchair opposite that I realise this is the first time we've sat down together, alone. I watch her as she serves us coffee. She fills my cup with clumsy inattention. She pours her own drink more carefully, I notice. Her saucer stays dry.

She offers me a slice of sponge cake: 'Do have some, Gilda, I made it specially.' I take a slice to be polite and leave it on the side of my plate.

We sit there for a few seconds and sip our drinks in unison. Then Alice starts to tell me about the honeymoon and I let myself drift off.

She talks about the weather, the sights they saw, the nature. My focus shifts and I find myself studying her mouth, her eyes, her hands. Her fingers outline two marble columns as if she were planning to build a pair. She is very expressive, my son's new wife.

She is talking about an amphitheatre. I do my best to seem

20

interested. The blouse she is wearing looks cool and airy and I like that tangy shade of green. It could be very pretty if it wasn't quite so see-through. It's fortunate she hasn't got much up top, though I'm surprised that Reuben doesn't mind. Her skirt is really far too short. Miniskirts and deckchairs are a risky combination. I think these skirts are beyond the pale. Some girls have the legs for it but—

My focus snaps back when I hear Reuben's name.

'I ate exactly the same and I was perfectly fine.' She raises her shoulders in a what-can-you-do shrug. 'We couldn't understand it. Must have been one bad prawn. Poor thing, he was dreadfully unwell.'

She looks unconcerned as she tops up my coffee, but people can die from food poisoning. People can die from one bad prawn. I remember when he was a baby. My Reuben has never been strong.

The nanny had the evening off so the maid was the one who noticed his fever. She went to call the doctor, though I wanted her to stay. I closed up all the windows to keep my baby warm, coddled him in layers of blankets and turned the heater to full. Then I sat and watched as his face got redder. After a while he wasn't crying any more.

The maid looked so scared when she came back, I knew I'd got it wrong. She pushed me out of the way – pulled the blankets off my son, put him naked in the bath and turned the cold on.

The doctor told me later that Reuben nearly died. For a long time after that I couldn't trust myself with him.

'He's fine, Gilda, don't look so worried.' Alice reaches forward and touches my knee.

This deckchair is hurting my back. I want to go home.

# 8

It's strange, but I know I'm not imagining it, people are often disappointed when I tell them I left Germany in time. They'd never
say it to my face but I think it's only natural. They're a little less
interested, a little less attentive, a little less respectful when I talk.

It's only natural too, though I'd never admit it to anyone, that
sometimes I find myself trying to win my audience back. I trawl
through childhood memories for incidents to satisfy them. Little
scraps of suffering. It's what they want.

At secondary school Lena wouldn't allow me near her. She became
a different person on the other side of those gates. This was long
before the Doris Day dye and that fake American accent that
makes my skin crawl. But she was trying to be someone else, even
then.

Aged fifteen my sister had light brown hair, which she liked
to lighten further with lemon juice in summer. Her brows were
plucked to high thin lines above pale blue eyes and freckles. She
looked fresh-faced, healthy and very Germanic, the poster child
for the Hitler Youth. Strangers never guessed she was Jewish. They
could tell straight away with me.

Lena made me walk a hundred yards behind her on the way

to school. She arrived first and I had to wait outside. I had strict instructions to count to three hundred before I was allowed to enter the gates. I'd stand there waiting, an obedient pet, doing just what the mistress had told me.

I look at parents these days and I'm struck by how much they praise their children; handing out cups and medals for every footstep they take. 'Darling, you clever girl, you ate a biscuit.' 'Just look at you, that's marvellous! You breathed in and out!'

It wasn't like that for us. No one paid us any attention. Father never praised his daughters, especially not me. I should have been a beauty, or I should have been a boy. If I wasn't either of those, what was the point of me?

No pats on the back for us when we'd done well. No fatherly hugs, no comfort when we were ill. Mother was always busy getting dressed or busy with her guests and not to be disturbed.

School was the only time I shone.

I realised early on that I could never be popular like my sister. I would be the clever one who always came out on top. I loved it: the stretch in my arm as I put my hand up higher than the other girls; the excitement as I waited for my homework to come back. It didn't make me any friends, it didn't make me any closer to my sister. But it meant a lot to be the best in the class. Lena could never do that.

The end of school was on a Thursday that year. I'd had top marks all term and was looking forward to the prize-giving, convinced that I'd be getting something – maybe geography, maybe maths.

I was nervous, of course, as they gathered us all together, but I made sure I sat near the aisle so I could get to the stage when I was called. *Gilda Meyer.* I willed the headmaster to say it. Sure he would. Sure my achievements would be recognised. I looked round at my neighbours and knew they felt it too.

Biology, no. Geography, no. Prize after prize went by without a mention of my name. The chair edge cut into my flesh, making ridges on the backs of my thighs. History, no, French, again no. Blonde head after blonde head went trooping up to the stage.

I looked round for my sister who was sitting with an older group several rows behind me. She caught my eye for a second and scowled, then turned back to her friends.

When it came to the maths award I held my breath. I was top of the class, always top in the tests, surely that couldn't be denied? I clamped my hands between my knees so no one could see them shaking.

When they called out that other girl's name I wanted to leap from my chair and punch her. I wanted to stand and shout at the stage. I wanted to kick down the walls. Instead I sat quietly and stared at the floor. The girls beside me didn't look in my direction.

Afterwards, back in the classroom, I hid my tears behind the desk lid. I didn't put my hand up once that afternoon.

At the end of the day, as I packed up my books, a huddle of girls stayed on at the front. I kept my head down but one of them called over to me. 'We've got you a prize,' she said.

For a foolish fraction of a second, I hoped. But when I saw their faces I knew I was wrong. They were whispering and giggling. Their excitement alarmed me. And yet I went over just the same.

It was Greta Braun who made the presentation. She smiled as she handed over a small paper scroll. 'This is for you. Well done, Gilda.'

I said nothing, just took my prize. I unrolled it as their eager eyes watched me.

What I saw was a home-made airline ticket with *Gilda Meyer* scrawled across the top. Below it was the outline of an aircraft drawn in blotchy fountain pen.

The passenger type read: *One Jewess*. The destination: *Away from here*.

*

This is the story I tell when they ask me about my life in Germany. It seems to be the sort of thing that people want to hear.

Worse things happened to me later in England but nobody wants to know about those; I was never made to wear an ugly yellow star.

# 9

Sometimes even now, even after everything, I see something that amuses me and I wonder what Leo would think.

There's a group of them, about twelve I'd say, on the patch of grass beside Swiss Cottage library. They've gathered on the scrub as if it's a beauty spot, unbothered by the passing cars.

One of the boys is strumming a guitar and I listen as I wait for the 31 to Margo's. He has thick black hair curling down past his collar and what might one day be the makings of a beard. What catches my attention, though, is the girl he's with. She's holding a bunch of pink hydrangeas she's picked from a nearby shrub. She's as tall as him and thin, dressed in bleached-out rags that defy description. On top of her head is the most enormous hat.

And what would tickle Leo, I think, is that the young man looks at her with such adoration. He's blind to all the people around him, oblivious to the other girls there. They couldn't be more different those two – a would-be Rasputin and a cocktail umbrella. I want to ask Leo what their offspring will look like, I want to hear what he'd say. Who can I talk to now about such things? There's no one.

I've been staring too long so I take out my library book, Agatha Christie's *Murder at the Vicarage*. It's a little bit dog-eared but I like that in a novel. It's nice to know where others have paused. I'm just about to start Chapter One when I become aware of someone approaching. I look up and the cocktail umbrella is there, so close I can smell her sweat.

I take a step back, unused to such proximity. The face beneath the hat is even younger than Alice's. Warm brown eyes match a smattering of freckles.

'Sorry, I didn't mean to startle you.'

She searches my face for some sort of answer. Then she plucks a pink hydrangea from her bunch and hands it to me.

I'm unsure what to do with it, so I thank her and rest it in my book. She smiles like a child who's just drawn a picture with brand new crayons.

'Remember: all you need is love.'

I smile politely and she gives a little bow. Then she turns and walks back to her friends on the green.

The man behind me mutters: 'Bloody Nancy boy.'

Later, on my return from Margo's, I find the flower in the bottom of my handbag. It's squashed and a little bit brown in places, I sniff it but it doesn't have much scent left.

*All you need is love.* It's the same words I saw on Alice's picture frame. It makes it sound so easy. As if love were simply there for the taking.

# IO

We'd been too much in each other's company that summer. We were fractious and spiky on the way to the tram stop. My sister kept walking at different speeds so I struggled to keep in step. She was teasing me about the brother of a friend who had greasy hair and smelled of pickled herring.

The walk wasn't far, little more than a mile, but time and distance swell when the day is so hot and dry. We meandered down pavements bleached pale by dust. I swung my arms and smelt the sweat. We were going to the swimming pool, Lena and I. Both of us desperate to be cool.

There are many pools in Hamburg but I liked the Kaifu-Bad best. The outdoor pool was long and deep and I could swim a whole length under water. I remember the swimsuit I had back then, it was blue with silver thread and it shimmered like a mermaid's tail. My limbs looked graceful, less gangly, when I wore it. For once my sister looked frumpy in comparison – her swimsuit was sea-monster green.

It wasn't until we were in the tram queue that I realised I'd left my swimsuit behind.

'*Dummkopf.*' Lena told me to go back and fetch it.

One forgotten swimsuit and the whole of my life was changed.

*

The walk took even longer in reverse. It was too hot to hurry so I went slowly, feeling the sun on my head. I dragged my feet and scuffed the soles of my shoes. Past the school, all closed up for the summer. Past the bakers, the waft from the oven stifling.

I was tired and irritable by the time I reached the house and I fumbled with my key in my desire to get inside. Our entrance hall was a cool, dark cave. There was no one around, no servants, no sound. I soaked up the gloom before heading upstairs.

My swimsuit was exactly where I'd left it, laid out neatly on my counterpane. The bed looked fresh and comfortable, I was tempted to sit and read for a minute but I was spurred on by the thought of my sister in the pool without me.

I was walking back downstairs, on my way past Father's study, when I thought I heard something. Some sound, some small movement from inside. I didn't give it a moment's pause, I leant into the heavy door and pushed it.

What I saw made no sense to me – a split-second tableau of a man and a woman. My father was standing grim-faced in his grey serge suit and a woman with blonde hair was kneeling on the floor.

My mind grappled for an explanation. The woman was a seam-stress. She'd dropped her pins and was picking them up. She was measuring him for some trousers. I noticed one of Father's hands was gripping the back of her head. I noticed he still had his hat on but his belt was hanging loose.

I saw so little, a glimpse and no more.

But Father saw me in the doorway and that was enough.

I didn't tell anyone what happened in Father's study. I didn't have the words for it, but that didn't save me. Ten days later my bags were packed for an English boarding school.

Father said it would be good for me: 'You're fortunate to have such a fine opportunity. You can practise your English, learn a few

29

manners. Who knows what it might lead to?'

My sister said I was a lucky dog, a *Glückspilz*. But I knew I was being punished.

On the morning of my departure, I sat on my bed and tried to take it in. I'd finished my German homework and now it would never get marked. I'd sharpened all my pencils and had a new white blouse laid out for the first day of term. But here I was going to a different country with a different school uniform, alone.

Lena appeared in the doorway, frowning. 'What's so special about you? No one's ever offered to send me to boarding school.' She kicked the bed leg. 'Don't think any of us will miss you.'

My family waved goodbye at the door and the chauffeur took me to the station. I cried when I had to leave them all. I don't recall tears from them. I stared out as we drove away and I saw them all turn and walk back inside the house. I saw their lives continue without me; lives I was no longer part of.

I thought of that moment years later – the pain of it. When we had to send Reuben away it brought the memories back. I'd felt pushed out, not good enough, rejected by the people who should love me the most. It's been thirty-seven years since I left Hamburg, I can still feel the pain of it now.

## II

I'm halfway down the Finchley Road when the sight of Alice stops me in my tracks. She's sitting in the full-length salon window for all the world to view. Strands of her hair poke hedgehog-like from a fleshy rubber highlight cap. She's deep in a magazine and doesn't see me. It's a cheap one, not *Harper's* or *Vogue*.

Hair by Raymond isn't far from Freda's where I go for my shampoo and set. But it seems designed for another species. It's a carnival ride of clashing colours and blaring music. Still, my daughter-in-law looks peaceful enough as she waits for her dye to fix.

I go off and have my morning coffee at The Regency but my thoughts stay pinned to Alice. I try the crossword; it isn't any good. I can't think of anything else. I'm curious to know what she's having done – is it simply a trim or a whole new look? Has she told her husband or does she plan to surprise him? I wonder how Reuben will react?

I drink up and leave a shilling on the table so I can walk past the salon a second time. Alice is still sitting there with the same thin magazine. She's slow with it, I notice, gives equal attention to every page. Reuben can read a whole book in a couple of hours.

I trot off to have another coffee and it strikes me that I'm rather enjoying myself. It's nice to have this glimpse into Alice's world.

She's brought a little frisson to a tedious day – made me feel more connected to my son.

The next time I walk past, her hair has been washed and towelled and a young girl with a crooked fringe is going at her with the scissors. Alice's eyes are fixed on the mirror, her expression serious and slightly worried. The hairdresser works quickly. Tufts of blonde hair flutter to the floor.

I go off and have yet another cup of coffee. I'm anxious to know the final result – a little jealous part of me hopes Alice will look a fright.

But when I walk past again someone else is in her chair. I feel cheated. I've been back and forth past here all morning, it feels like she's been wasting my time.

I'm about to move on when Alice comes out of the salon door. Her hair is sculpted to perfection in a honey-shaded bob. She takes me by surprise. I blush and hope my make-up is hiding it. I trip over my tongue as I praise her new hairstyle. 'It's lovely. Just lovely,' I say.

She touches one side of it, a gentle caress, a woman stroking her sleeping lover. 'I hope Reuben likes it.' A modest shrug. It makes me hope Reuben will hate it.

She suggests we go for a coffee. 'Such a nice coincidence to run into you, Gilda.'

I nod my enthusiasm, though I've had three coffees already this morning. 'I was passing. How lucky you caught me.'

We walk together in large strides down the street and every few seconds she touches her new hair. She is tentative with it. Delicate. She's worried about displacing something. My fingers twitch to reach and mess it up.

Fortunately Alice has chosen a different cafe from the one I've been frequenting. Her choice has tables without any cloths and little poufs where there should be chairs.

We sit near the back of the room and look around awkwardly while we wait to give our order. Alice asks the waitress for a camomile tea. I hate the stuff but I do the same.

'How is Reuben?' I ask. I haven't spoken to my son since the wedding.

My daughter-in-law smiles. 'He's really well. He's working very hard but he seems to be enjoying himself. He's full of funny stories when he comes home.'

My son is a sub-editor at the *Financial Times* – people are often impressed when I tell them that. They want to know what the office is like, what the editor's like, the hours he works. I don't know how to answer them. Reuben tells me nothing. When I ask him how he's getting on he says, 'It's fine,' as if that's enough. For a man of letters, he has very few words.

I don't recognise this effusive Reuben who comes home from work full of tales for his wife. I want to ask her more but the questions catch in my throat. How does she get him to talk like that? She makes it sound so easy. I've known my Reuben all his life – she's known him less than a year.

The camomile tea arrives in a large metal pot. I let Alice do the pouring and lift my cup to take a sip. It's weak as dishwater and scalds my tongue. I won't warn her to wait for it to cool.

She tells me it's Reuben's birthday next month, as if I didn't know that, as if I'd forget. She wants to take him to dinner somewhere. Do I have any ideas? For a giddy second I think she's including me. She reddens and makes it clear that's not the case. She wants a quiet evening. Romantic, just the two of them.

'I'm sorry, we've been so busy since the wedding. I do hope you don't mind.'

I swallow my disappointment and suggest she tries Luigi's restaurant. It's local, it's Italian, and the food was always nice. I used to go there often with Leo. We had some happy times there, Leo and I.

She says: 'That sounds perfect, Gilda. I'll book us a table. Perhaps you can join us there next time?'

'Yes, next time. Lovely.' I won't hold my breath. I smile. 'Have you chosen him a present yet?'

'No, not yet, I thought perhaps a shirt. He could do with something smart, all his old ones are terribly scruffy.'

She asks for the bill and I let her pay. She chats away to the waitress as if she's a personal friend.

I study her as she digs in her purse and decide that her hair is definitely an improvement. It gives her face angles she was missing. It frames her jaw, lengthens her neck, makes her look less of a child. I like the colour too, it's warmer than it was. Still blonde, but buttery blonde. Much softer than that over-bleached haystack.

Later, at home, in front of the mirror, I scoop up my own hair and play with the style. I hold up the back and let the shorter strands come down and frame my face. I turn my head from side to side. I hold up a second mirror to catch it from a different angle.

I think a jaw-length bob might suit me.

# 12

Father's cousin drove me to the school from London. Gothic red brick and mullioned windows reached up like a cathedral in the afternoon shadows.

The headmistress rushed out to greet us at the gate. She called: 'Welcome! Welcome!' But I wasn't welcome.

We passed a group of girls in the entrance hall and I heard someone whisper: 'That's the Hun.'

Father's cousin wished me good luck. He said he had to work and couldn't linger. I watched his back as he walked down the driveway, watched his car disappear through the gates. I stood beside my little trunk in the hallway and pinched my hand hard to stop the tears. I bit my lip – it didn't work. I stared up at the ceiling. When the headmistress offered me tea I couldn't answer her.

Right from the start, everything was wrong with me: my Heidi hairstyle, the way I spoke, the words I used, my shoes. I was the only German girl and the only Jew and the only foreigner in a large Surrey school. Imagine the looks I got, imagine the jibes – they dug in their fingernails and gouged.

I'd thought my English accent was good, I soon realised I was wrong. The teachers acted like they couldn't understand me and the pupils did so too. If I made a mistake, they'd collapse into giggles. 'Vorter? Vorter? Gilda vants some vorter!' I simply stopped speaking, it just seemed easier, learnt not to put my hand up in class.

The taunts got worse towards the end of term when I fell into a daydream during maths. I was thinking about my old school, trying to remember which books they'd been set – I was struggling to recall the name of an author.

When the teacher addressed me, it didn't register at first. 'Gilda? Are you with us? Gilda?'

I snapped to attention. All the other pupils were staring at me. I said the first thing in my head. '*Verzeihung, Madame. Wie bitte.*'

I realised my mistake as soon as it was out. I covered my mouth with my hand.

The teacher raised an eyebrow. 'Bitter? Well, you may be. How's that going to help with your maths?'

Bitter. For weeks the word followed me around – in the dining hall, on the hockey pitch, in the library, the corridor. It wasn't just the girls in my year, it made its way down through the school. The younger ones would murmur it, if I looked in their direction they'd stop. But when I turned away the whisper would start up again. *Bitter, bitter, bitter, Gilda, bitter.*

I know that all schools are a hunting ground and I know I wasn't the only prey. The fat girl, the short girl, the spotty girl, all of us took our turn. We didn't cry or mope about it, our generation knew not to complain. We kept stiff upper lips like good soldiers' daughters and waited for the torment to pass.

The other pupil they picked on that year was Margaret, a big bovine hulk of a girl. She sat next to me in maths and was so slow she drove me to despair. I noticed she had to move the desks aside in order to squeeze down the classroom gangway, I noticed how her thighs spilled over the edge of the classroom chair. She didn't walk like a normal girl, she lumbered. One side went down, then the other went down, with no sense of ease in between. She always seemed to be out of breath. Even when sitting, she was huffing and panting.

Margaret wanted to be friends with me and didn't try to hide her loneliness. She reeked of desperation in a way that made me cringe. She'd stay to talk to me after class – her brown eyes followed me like a hopeful puppy. In Hamburg I'd been the top of the school, now here I was stuck with the classroom dunce. I thought I was better off without her. I thought I'd rather be on my own.

# 13

The bird is small and dappled brown and it is, quite definitely, dead. Its ruffled feathers are moist with saliva and its legs look stiff and snapable like twigs. The cat stares up, then back at the bird. It prods the body with a paw. When I fail to react, it turns and stalks away. *Bloody woman. What are you waiting for?*

It upsets me to see the bird cold and rigid on my doorstep. There's something about its downy chest that reminds me of the last time I ate quail. I decide I need to speak to next door because it's unhygienic if nothing else. She can't just let her cat roam freely in the corridors. We can't have little corpses on the carpet.

I've seen my neighbour a handful of times and we've nodded hello, but that's all. She's about my age, though she doesn't seem to bother much with make-up. I'm slightly nervous as I knock on her door because it's a boundary I'd rather keep in place.

I tap quietly at first but no one answers. I can hear her movements inside. I knock again, louder. Eventually the door cracks open. There's a waft of warm air and the scent of pine bath salts, my neighbour is there in her bath towel.

'Gosh, I don't know where this morning's gone!' Her smile creases crescent eyes and turns her wrinkles into neat, white stitches. 'You're Mrs Meyer, aren't you? We haven't met properly.' She thrusts out a damp hand for me to shake. 'I'm Lizzie.'

I turn and point to the bird. 'I think that was meant for you.'

'Oh God, how awful! I hate it when he does that.' The cat slinks past us and into her flat. 'Bad boy. Naughty boy.' But she looks more proud than disapproving and she strokes him as he brushes past her leg.

'If it's any comfort, it's a sign he likes you. If you get a rat? Well, that's true love.' She laughs as if she's made a joke. But it isn't funny. I don't find it funny.

She adjusts her bath towel, which is starting to slip. I have to look away to preserve her decency. She says: 'Why don't you come in for a coffee? It would be nice for us to get to know each other. We've been neighbours for almost a year now.'

I accept to be polite, though I tell her I can't stay long.

Her flat is the mirror image of mine. Everything exactly the same, only just the wrong way round. She leaves me in the living room while she goes to put the kettle on and dress.

'I won't be a minute. Make yourself at home.'

Her cat is, mercifully, absent from the room, though its little grey hairs are everywhere. I pick a few of them off my skirt but I can feel them still clinging to my nylons. Her walls are lined with abstract paintings – not my sort of thing but each to their own. A Persian rug covers most of the floor and looks like it could do with a Hoover.

Over next to the far wall where I have my bookshelf, Lizzie has a table with a forest of photographs. I assume they are her family: Victorians stiff and formal, a young man proud in his RAF uniform, a chubby little boy in his school cap. Those near the front are more recently taken, a man and a woman aged somewhere in their twenties. I pick one up for closer inspection when Lizzie comes back with our mugs.

She looks at the picture over my shoulder. 'That's Eric, my son, and Sophie, my new daughter-in-law.'

Sophie is lumpy in a halter-neck wedding dress, her face is rather masculine, 'handsome' is the word that springs to mind. Eric is plump with the same crescent eyes as his mother. They're a sweet pair, nothing special. I put the picture back down.

Lizzie asks me if I have children and I tell her about Reuben, that he's a newlywed too. I start to tell her about his job but she wants to talk about Eric.

'I was nervous when they first got married – you know how it can be with sons. I've been lucky with Sophie though, she's brought us all closer. Eric gets very caught up in his work. She makes sure he remembers to call me.'

She smiles her crinkly smile. 'Do you see much of your son?'

'Oh yes.' I nod. 'He's always popping by.'

Afterwards, back in my flat, I take Reuben's wedding photograph out of my desk drawer. I should have it on display; put it in a frame. I don't know why I haven't done so already.

As I study Alice's beaming face, my shoulders tense with irritation. I think how much easier my life would be if only she were more like Sophie.

# 14

Perhaps it was an accident. The school gave me pork by accident. Perhaps one of the teachers wasn't fully briefed, or didn't understand Jewish laws. More likely is that they did it to test me, like they tried to make the fat girl climb the rope in gym class. That seems far more probable to me, more in keeping with the boarding school way.

Nowadays I don't worry about pork; there was ham in the canapés at Reuben's wedding. Frank was upset, said he found it disrespectful but I ate three or four just the same. Now I don't think twice about such things, but that first time pork appeared on my plate it might as well have been a lump of human flesh.

The dining room was a high-windowed hall with ranks of tables under stiff white cloths. The food was revolting even at its best and all of it had to be eaten: every lump of gristle, every cauliflower stalk, the skin on the custard, the slug-black potato.

I remember the pork chop exactly: a pale grey slab with a sweaty border of fat, the gravy congealed into a waxy mask with little lumps of flour like warts. I should have spoken up and said I couldn't eat it. I should have made more of a fuss. But I didn't

41

want to draw attention to myself; to be more foreign than I already was.

I cut off a piece of the chop and sniffed it. I put it in my mouth and let it rest there on my tongue. Finally I bit down – sank my teeth into pig meat.

The dining room walls were lined with wooden boards carved with the names of pupils past. I read the names of every one of those girls but I couldn't swallow that meat. I tried not to think about snouts and trotters. I tried not to think about bristles and tails. I tried not to notice the globules of grease that slid down my throat like phlegm. I chewed and I chewed until my eyes were watering. I chewed and I chewed, but I couldn't swallow.

I started to gag, small spasms and hiccups. I could feel my stomach convulsing, a reflex about to kick in. In desperation I took out my handkerchief and coughed the lot into clean, white cotton. Then I quickly slid the rest of the chop off my plate and put that in my handkerchief too.

I stuffed the bundle in the pocket of my gym slip and carried on eating cabbage as if nothing had happened. Margaret saw me do it. All of it. But she didn't say a thing.

I felt the meat there for the rest of the day, heavy and warm like a dead bird next to my hipbone. I felt it there through my English class. I felt it there through maths.

At the end of lessons, I hid in the toilets and took the parcel from my pocket. I went into a cubicle and dropped it into the bowl. I held my breath and prayed as I yanked the metal chain. Water thundered through the cistern, it rattled and it gurgled and the pipework shook. But when I looked back in, the meat was still there, solid and obscene against a dark brown crust of limescale.

Twenty minutes later, when Margaret came to find me, I was still standing in the cubicle, flushing and flushing in vain.

Soon the whole school would know what I'd done. Soon the headmistress would telephone my family. Soon my father would find out.

I imagined the call. *'Your daughter's disgraced herself. Apparently our English meat's not good enough for her.'*

Margaret knocked on the cubicle. 'Gilda, are you all right?' I could hear her heavy breathing. 'You might as well let me in.'

I unlocked the door, red-faced and hot with panic. The sight of Margaret's anxious eyes was enough to make my own spill over.

'Come on, old thing, it can't be that bad.'

I shook my head. 'It is.'

She pushed me gently aside so she could enter. Her bulk filled the space and I was pressed against the wall. She didn't hesitate, she rolled up her shirt-sleeve, reached into the toilet bowl and pulled the pork chop out. Then she held it aloft with a look of triumph, as if she'd just landed a fish.

I watched dumbly as she carried the dripping parcel to the sink. She ran the handkerchief under the tap and scrubbed it with the grey school soap.

She didn't ask me any questions, just took the chop away. The following day, she gave me back my handkerchief. It was clean and neatly pressed and smelled of pork fat.

We weren't exactly soulmates after that, I didn't find her any less annoying. Her bulkiness, her breathing, her slowness; all those things still drive me mad. But I realised then that we needed each other. She was the only one who ever stood up for me at school. So I sat on my irritation and swallowed my pride and Margo and I became pals.

In time I realised she wasn't so stupid, just lacking in confidence and afraid to make mistakes. It turned out the two of us had rather a lot in common – both of us were outcasts, both of us lonely and shy.

In some ways, we're still stuck with each other, Margo and I. I often think we're more like security blankets than friends. Many's the time I've tried to shake her off but she's a fixture in my life and I need her there to anchor me.

Neither of us is blessed with many other friends to choose from.

# 15

I'm his mother, so it's not so strange that I might drop round on a Sunday evening. Other mothers go round to see their children all the time. 'I just thought I'd take a chance and see if you're in.' That's what I'll say. Bright and breezy; spur of the moment. I'm his mother, so it's fine.

It's good to have a walk after a day spent stuck inside. The early evening air feels nicely cooling on my skin. A pleasant visit with my son is just what I need to soothe my anxious thoughts. 'I'm not stopping long,' that's what I'll say. 'Really. I'm just passing by.'

I haven't seen or spoken to Reuben since the wedding and that was over a month ago. I realise he's been busy at work but a phone call isn't any trouble. There's a tight little knot in the pit of my stomach that makes me think something's really wrong. I bet Lizzie talks for hours to her son. I bet she sees her Eric every weekend.

I try to tell myself Reuben's always been different – not the sort of boy to stay close to friends and family. He's independent, the strong and silent type. He's not the sort to show how much he cares.

But I've seen how he is with Alice now, so I know he has it in him. He said she taught him how to love, I hoped he might have softened somehow.

When I get to their street, I see their car parked on the corner. They've left it an angle, too far from the kerb. It makes me feel uneasy because the front is sticking out where anyone could hit it. They've obviously parked it in a hurry – too eager to get back home.

I go up to the house and knock on their blue front door. A light is on upstairs behind half-drawn curtains. I knock on the door again but no one answers. It's quiet and it appears there's no one in.

At first I'm limp with disappointment, silly to get my hopes up. I knock on their door one last time just in case they didn't hear me.

I'm unsure what to do with myself, it seems wrong to go back to my flat. I've walked all this way to see my son. I need to know he's well, that he's happy.

The door has a panel of textured glass so I press my face against it. I squint past the blur of black and white wallpaper. I can see the outline of some coats on coat hooks. I can see Reuben's briefcase on the floor.

I sidestep off the path and into the flowerbed. My suede shoes sink deep into the soil. I bend to brush it off but only spread it to my stocking. There's a thick streak of mud on my inside leg, when I rub at it the nylon stretches.

It takes three more steps to reach the kitchen window. I lean forward and peer inside. The place looks much the same as the last time I was here: like they still haven't really unpacked. Next to the sink I count eight empty wine bottles. There are a couple of plates on the draining rack, plus a saucepan, a bread knife and a red enamel colander. There's a white apron hanging on the back of the door for the sweet little housewife to wear. It is frilly and feminine. Impractical. Too clean. Not the sort of apron a proper wife would wear.

Yes, I can picture Alice in that silly, frilly apron with her butter-blonde hair and her dainty little hands. She's stirring a pot of stew she's made for Reuben's supper. I imagine my son likes to watch her in the kitchen. I bet he sips his wine as she stirs and chops and hums. I bet he draws her close to him sometimes. Kisses his wife on the back of the neck.

I stumble and lose my footing in the flowerbed. I reach to the window for support. I steady my hand against the smooth, clean glass. It leaves a smear of mud behind by accident.

The light is fading fast and I probably should be going, but I might just have a quick look round the back of the house while I'm here. I enter the narrow side-return where there's a filthy little window up high. If I stand on tiptoe I can just about see in.

I'm confronted by a view of the downstairs loo. There's a copy of *Private Eye* on the cistern. Reuben has left the seat up.

I move further down the passageway to a gate that leads to the communal garden. I try the handle and it opens easily. Careless to leave it unlocked.

I hold my breath as I enter the gardens but there's no one else around. I walk right up to the patio doors and cup my hands against the glass. A geometric rug stretches out in front of me. They've left their big ceramic floor lamp on; you'd think they had money to burn.

The place has changed a lot since my coffee with Alice. Still some boxes in the corner but the bookshelves are now full of books. The ugly orange sofa is heaving with cushions, though they're not nicely placed, it's like someone's been jumping on them. Their gramophone's surrounded by record sleeves. There's an ashtray full of dog-ends on the floor.

I think of the eight empty bottles by the sink and I wonder if they've been entertaining. He's clearly been having fun, my son. Too much fun to call his mother.

Well, I'm glad that Reuben isn't working all the time and I'm glad he's got friends and I'm glad he can relax. Still, it wouldn't hurt Alice to do a little housework.

As I'm walking down the pathway I think, just for a second, I hear a burst of music. Just two loud chords then nothing. It sounds like it's coming from inside. It's one of those things, so quick I can't even be sure I heard it. The buildings are crammed in so tightly round here. I'll bet it came from a neighbour.

I glance back at the house – the place is in darkness. I could have sworn a light was on upstairs when I arrived. Perhaps it was just a reflection in the window. The sunset or a street lamp. When I'm tired like this I sometimes get things wrong.

# 16

My sister lives in New York, in a pokey apartment in a pricey part of town. We've ended up the same, Lena and I, and it's not what either of us thought. Where are the servants? Where is the family? Where is the grand German house we were born to? Here we both are, in two little flats, in two foreign countries, alone.

Lena's husband, Gustav, died almost seven years ago. So much older he was bound to go first, but still it was sad just the same. They didn't have children and I don't know if she wanted them. She's never shown much interest in Reuben.

Gustav left her well-provided for and she spends her days wandering round shops and playing bridge. I go and visit her from time to time but somehow we always end up fighting.

Lena has bright yellow hair now and says she gets mistaken for Doris Day. I think Miss Day would be very alarmed if she ever saw my sister. She looks a bit like her plus several years that haven't been kind; a bit like her plus at least three stone. Let's be honest, she's got yellow hair, that's where her Dorisness ends.

Lena has only been to visit me in London once. She came just after the end of the war and she stayed for less than a week. Britain still had rationing and she couldn't believe how little we got. She kept on about life 'back home in America' where food was still plentiful and cheap.

I remember: we went out to dinner in Knightsbridge, Lena, Gustav and Frank and I. She was wearing her big fur coat even though the night was warm. When she handed it in to the cloakroom boy, she said: 'Do you think I can trust him?'

Her voice was loud, on American volume, and the whole room heard what she said.

She wrote to me only once during my second year of boarding school. I have the letter still and I know its contents well. Her handwriting was large and round – it's smaller and spikier these days. It's grown out of its puppy fat. She wrote on Father's headed paper, he'd have killed her if he ever found out.

It was after breakfast when Matron handed out the post. I'd had so few letters that she pointed out the German stamps. Margo urged me to open it but I wanted to save it, read its contents when I was alone.

I opened it at lunchtime, sat on the bench by the duck pond. It was cold and my gloved hands fumbled with the envelope. Margo hovered, too close, behind me.

Lena began with typical warmth, the loving sister so far away.

> *Hamburg, November 1933.*
> *Dear Gilda,*
> *Sorry I haven't written before, but I didn't have anything worth saying. You should only write when you've actually got some news to impart. Otherwise save your ink.*

It makes me smile now, she hasn't changed at all. I'm lucky if Lena writes to me from one year to the next. She doesn't believe in warmth, she doesn't believe in sisterly sharing. She writes terse little messages when something has happened. Otherwise she saves her ink.

*Well, now it seems I have plenty of news, though none of it is good. Father is making us leave Hamburg and won't say when we'll return.*

*I know we're not the only ones leaving. People are nervous, I understand that. But we're German, Father has the medals to prove it, and we've lived in Germany all our lives. Why should we have to leave everything we love? Why should we run and hide?*

*Of course, Father doesn't listen to me. As usual it's all about his business. He looks like he's enjoying himself; pulling strings and doing deals. He says he's found a little flat for us in Paris but things are strained enough with a mansion's worth of space around us. Father says we'll get our furniture sent, but how will it fit in a flat?*

*Mother is in a panic – she'll have to leave her maid behind. I think she was crying this afternoon. She locked herself away in her dressing room.*

I'd never witnessed my mother in tears – her life was one long cocktail party. The closest I'd seen to her being upset was when a Marcel Wave went wrong and burnt her hair. For a moment I pictured her red-eyed and shaking, damp streaks of grey down her flawless face. I couldn't breathe, I felt dizzy and sick. I had to push the image away.

Instead I tried to picture my old room in Hamburg: the rocking chair, the heavy oak bed. I tried to remember the colour of my curtains, so different from the fawn school blinds. I'd occupied that space for almost sixteen years but now I struggled to recall it. I tried to take in the loss of it but none of it felt like mine.

*As if that wasn't enough of a disaster, Father's determined to find me a husband. He says it's important to have me settled. He's even suggested Gustav Katz! I laughed out loud when he said it – you remember Mr Katz? But even Mother says it's worth considering. I think they've lost their minds.*

Mr Katz was Father's business partner. He was older than our parents, with a paunch and thinning hair. He seemed to have a permanent cold and mopped his nose with revolting thoroughness. He was wealthy and polite enough, but a husband for my sister? She always said she'd marry a film star.

I turned the paper over. There was only one paragraph on the back.

*I hope you realise just how lucky you are, not having to deal with any of this. You're tucked up nice and safe in your grand English boarding school.*
*You've always been spoilt.*
*Lena*

## 17

At last I get my son to pay me a visit at my flat. My bookshelves need fixing so he doesn't have a choice.

It took surprisingly little to break them – I had thought they'd be sturdier. I bought them from Heal's and they didn't come cheap, but so much is shoddy these days. All I had to do was loosen one screw, apply a little weight and the whole lot came crashing down. Wood, books and a figurine from Margo that I've never really liked, strewn across my living room floor. A strip of wallpaper pulled away too, which is annoying but it can't be helped now.

I've spent this morning plumping up cushions and making sure the flat looks neat. I've put lilies on the table so the room feels fresh and light. I've hoovered and I've dusted and I've wiped every surface. The broken shelves are polished to perfection.

I'm wearing the dress I bought for Reuben's graduation; that was almost ten years ago, but he told me he liked it. I'm wearing my favourite necklace too, the one Leo gave me on our first anniversary. He used to say the glass pearls made my skin glow.

I've got a little bowl of the cashew nuts Reuben eats and I've put it on the table by the bookshelves, where he'll see it. Just a few little nuts because you never know, he might be hungry. I always keep some cashews in the cupboard just in case my son drops by.

They've been in my cupboard for a while now. They look a little pallid; I think they're still OK. I put one in my mouth and chew – it's soft but Reuben won't mind. I pour myself the smallest shot of whisky just to wash that little cashew nut down.

The doorbell rings and it makes me start. I feel suddenly unsure that everything's ready. I hear Reuben's voice on the intercom and my stomach flutters with nerves. 'It's me,' he says. He sounds tired, I think. I take a calming breath and buzz him in.

It takes him so long to come up in the lift that I wonder if he's got lost in the building. It's been quite some time since he last paid a visit, but surely he remembers the way?

Just when I'm thinking I'll go out to find him, I hear his voice in the corridor. He says, 'Hello there,' in a warm and loving tone. My heart soars as I open the door.

His words are addressed to next door's cat, which he's holding in his arms as if it were a baby. He looks up, sees me and says: 'Oh. Hello, Mother.'

He sets the cat down with a look of regret and it rubs itself up against his trouser leg.

I pause to take Reuben in: the sight of him, the height of him. I can hardly believe it; my son is really here. I lean in to kiss his cheek and he moves just out of my reach as usual. He always does that; it doesn't mean anything. I kiss the air near his cheek instead.

Once he's inside my flat I see his skin is lightly tanned. He has laughter lines at the corners of his eyes, which I haven't noticed before. His hair's grown too and it's shaggy, almost down to his collar. But the thing that strikes me most about my son is that he's so much thinner than he was four weeks ago. He has shadows under his cheekbones and his jacket seems too big. I remember the little double chin he used to have, it was there in all the wedding photographs. He used to have a little tummy. He had such chubby knees when he was small.

Reuben walks off towards the bookshelves and I can see he wants to get on with it. I notice his trousers are baggy at the rear. I'm sure they never used to hang like that. I remember the food poisoning he had on honeymoon and the fact he's never been strong. I'm hit by a painful panicky feeling.

'Reuben, darling?'

He doesn't answer. He's focusing on the bookshelves. He picks up a piece of wood and studies it. He looks at the wall where the wallpaper has come free.

I try again: 'Darling, are you well?'

He shrugs his shoulders, mumbles, 'Fine,' and picks up another bit of shelf.

He inspects the tear in the wallpaper, smooths the bare patch over with his fingertips. He taps at the wall to see if it's plasterboard. It's made of solid brick.

He shakes his head. 'How did it happen?'

'I heard a crash. It just came down. So much is shoddy these days.'

Reuben sighs and pulls a screwdriver from his corduroy jacket. It is far too small for the task at hand, unlikely to be of any use. I look round for a toolbox but it seems he's only brought this one tool. He's never been a practical boy, he always preferred reading books.

He's holding that screwdriver as if it's a pen and he's working on some sort of technical drawing. I smile because it's clear as day that my son doesn't have a clue what he's doing. He'll be hopelessly slow. He'll be at it for hours. And he'll be here in my flat all that time.

I offer Reuben a whisky. It's after four, I'm going to have one. 'Darling?'

He doesn't answer. I'll fix us both a whisky with ice.

I wonder if I should have made sandwiches? Perhaps he'll stay for dinner. I think I'll put a little music on the gramophone. Maybe jazz, because that's what he likes.

I dig out *Ella and Louis* from the record box. It's been years since I've heard it – it was Leo's really, not mine. I slide the needle over and place it gently. Ella sings 'Can't we be Friends'.

I tap my foot and pour whisky into tumblers. I hum along with Ella as I drop in cubes of ice. I'm happy. Really happy. It feels like all is well in the world. I'm fixing my son a whisky. I pour in a little extra splash.

When I return to the living room the bookshelves have made a great leap forward. I smile to hide my disappointment; he's already halfway there.

'Reuben, I've fixed you a whisky,' I say. He looks at me oddly, like I've fixed him some arsenic. 'It's after four. I'm going to have one.'

He mumbles: 'You go right ahead.'

I hear the criticism but I drink my whisky. And after that I drink his as well.

The liquor warms me as I sit on the sofa and watch my son. I say nothing when he picks up the wrong bit of wood, though it's obviously too short and it obviously won't fit. I say nothing when he knocks into my lamp. Nothing when he scatters the screws.

It's wonderful just to sit here and watch him, he looks so handsome my heart swells up with pride. It's a good sign Reuben is helping his mother. He didn't once tell me to get a professional in. It shows that, underneath it all, part of him still cares about me. I feel like the luckiest mother on earth: my son has come to pay me a visit.

I can't wait to tell Margo he's been round. Perhaps this could become a regular fixture? I imagine Reuben calling his wife to warn her he'll be late home. *'I'm so sorry, Alice, we just got talking. I won't need supper. Mother made sandwiches.'*

I fix myself another whisky and relax into the sofa again. There's so much I want to ask him that I don't quite know where to begin. I mustn't criticise, that's important. That's where it's always gone wrong.

I light a cigarette. 'Your hair. Is that the style?'

He swears loudly as his screwdriver slips.

I go back to sipping my whisky and pretend I haven't asked. Reuben is focused on the task, I shouldn't have brought up his hair.

I watch him work for a few more minutes then I offer him the bowl of cashew nuts. 'They're your favourite,' I say, but he brushes them away and goes back to tightening a screw.

'Eat them, eat them, darling.' Why wouldn't he want his favourite nuts? He's too thin. 'Is Alice feeding you properly?' I remember the pans by the sink and the silly frilly apron in the kitchen. 'Tell her you need to eat proper meals. Meat and potatoes, something solid in your stomach.' I'm his mother. 'Is she looking after you, darling?' I want to know he's well, that he's happy.

Reuben starts piling my books back on the shelves. He throws them on willy-nilly, not bothering which way the spines face. When he turns round his expression is angry. I'm shocked. Have I said something wrong?

He grabs his jacket and heads for the door. 'Mother, I'm almost thirty years old. I don't need looking after any more, haven't done so since I was a child. But if you really want to know, she looks after me better than you ever did.'

Then he's gone and the room is quiet and I'm sitting on the sofa with an empty glass.

# 18

*She looks after me better than you ever did,* were the first words in my head when I woke up this morning. They hovered in the background all day like the smell of sour milk.

This evening they're all I can think about, though I've tried to drown them out. They stayed stubbornly there through supper and the seven-thirty news on TV.

*She looks after me better than you ever did.* I take off my clothes for my bedtime bath. *She looks after me better than you ever did.* I scrub at my face with the flannel.

Many bad things have been said to me in my life, but nothing that hurts me as much as this. It hurts because it wasn't my fault and it hurts because it's true. I never once cooked for him or sewed on a button, I never did his sums with him or helped him brush his teeth. I never did those things a parent does because I didn't know how to do them. No one ever showed me how to be a mother, so I simply let the nanny take over.

If I could go back I'd shake myself. *'Just be his mother!'* I'd say. I should have given it a chance. Who cares if the food gets burned or the button falls off?

I did other things for him, bigger things – made sacrifices that changed my life for ever. But they don't count because he'll never know about them. So it's the little things I didn't do that matter.

My arms are covered in goose-bumps, I always put too much cold in this bath. I turn on the hot tap with my toe: sometimes the boiler still works. The water comes out icy so I switch the tap straight off again.

*She looks after me better than you ever did.*

When Reuben was a newborn he'd snuggle up against my shoulder sometimes. I remember the baby smell of him, the weight of him, the shape of his head. I remember how he blinked his eyes as he fought to stay awake. He'd snuffle into me and fall asleep like I was the only safe place in the world. I remember how, just for a moment or two, I felt like a mother should feel.

The first time Reuben pushed me away I was sitting with Frank in the living room. The nanny brought him in to kiss me good-night before taking him up to his bed. I was still feeling anxious. My confidence had gone – it wasn't long after that terrible fever. I couldn't get over how close I'd come to losing him.

When the nanny handed him over to me his face screwed up and he howled.

She tried to reassure me. 'Baby's just tired, that's all.'

I stroked his cheek, tried jiggling him, but nothing would calm him down. My face flushed red, sweat prickled my forehead. 'Don't cry, darling. It's all right, I've got you. Mummy's here, darling. Please don't cry.'

The nanny reached over and took him from my arms. She held him on her hip and his tears stopped straight away. She smiled. 'There's a good boy. Say good night to Mummy.'

Frank said he was just being grumpy. He'd had a long day, missed out on his nap. He said it had nothing to do with me. But I could see it was his nanny he wanted.

*

The water's too cold just to lie here and wallow. I sit up and reach for my towel.

It's an old towel, grey and rough as sandpaper. I rub myself dry and enjoy its harshness: little needles scratching warmth into my flesh.

Perhaps it's just too late for me and Reuben, perhaps I should accept that. My son has someone else in his life who can sew on his buttons now.

Alice has never had to struggle – it's all been so easy for her. It's easy to be loving and caring if you've been loved and cared for too. I've met her parents, they're dull but nice. Just an ordinary couple doing what ordinary couples do. Her father wore grey slip-on shoes at the wedding but he couldn't stop smiling when he spoke about his daughter. His speech was short and simple, every word of it filled with pride.

Her mother wouldn't touch the champagne and drank the fruit cup all day instead. She toasted the happy couple with it, though a sip of fizz wouldn't have hurt her. I could tell she didn't feel comfortable, would much rather have been at home with her wireless. She was weeping when Alice made her vows, I saw her mopping her eyes.

She spoke to me while they were cutting the cake. 'They grow up so fast. We'll miss our little girl. I expect you feel the same about Reuben?'

I put on my nightgown and go and fix myself another whisky. Just a small one – just a finger or two – to quiet these jangling thoughts.

I am cheered by the smell of it and the feel of the glass in my hand. I sit and sip it quietly in the living room. There's no point in trying to sleep before you're ready. No point in trying to sleep with so much upset in your mind.

Sometimes when I think of Alice, I see a child too young to be

60

a wife: she still has that peachy bloom on her cheeks, she still has those innocent eyes. People, men in particular, want to protect her. People, my son in particular, want to keep her safe.

I was younger than her when I married Frank and no one protected me.

# 19

I learnt the name of my future spouse while I was sitting eating breakfast in the dining hall. I'd come to the end of my porridge when Matron handed me the letter. The address on the envelope was in Father's slanted handwriting. I held it for a minute and stared. Father never wrote letters to his daughters. Oatmeal churned in my stomach.

His words were confined to half a side of paper.

*Paris, June 1934.*
*Dear Gilda,*
*You'll be leaving school soon and your mother and I want to see you settled like your sister. Germany isn't safe now, we won't be going back.*
*I've discussed you with a business associate and I've made arrangements for you to meet him. His name is Frank Goodman, he's from Hamburg but now lives in London. He manufactures shipping crates and I want him to handle our exports in Europe.*
*How fortunate, Gilda, that England has become your home. You understand the language and customs – I think you'd make an excellent match for him. So, you see? Everything happens for*

*a reason. This could benefit all of us.*
*I'll telegram later to finalise the details.*
*Father*

At seventeen I still had long dark plaits that straggled down my back and got tangled in my school bag. I wore neat white socks that pulled up past my ankles and a knitted woollen vest that reached my knees.

I'd never seen a naked man, not even in a diagram. They taught us more about reptiles at school than they ever did human beings. Or at least, I was aware that there might be something else; something important I hadn't been told. I didn't find out what that was until my wedding night.

It's true, I sometimes thought about men, but not with any focus and certainly never below the waist. A character in a book perhaps, or an actor in a film. I imagined a sort of composite beau, whose form would shift with each romantic novel: dark hair (or blond), blue eyes (or green), square jaw (always), a good deal taller than me.

We had just one male teacher at school. He was thin, grey and married, lost an eye at Verdun. Most of our teachers were spinsters and we didn't want to end up like them. Marriage was the target, that's what we were told, and proposals were badges of honour. A life on the shelf was a fate worse than death. Anyone was better than no one.

Other girls had brothers with friends, or friends with brothers, or cousins with friends. They had gentle introductions to boys of their own age. They had high teas and dances and tennis doubles in the holidays. Some of them were debutants. That was never on the cards for me.

# 20

They're all over the news again – young girls crying and screaming at a concert. A frenzy of adolescent hormones in boots and
miniskirts. They're wailing and they're fainting and they're hurling
themselves against the stage and it's all for some boys in too-tight
trousers who don't even know their names.

I wonder where all of this high-pitched emotion comes from,
I wonder what all of this crying and screaming means. Pure in-
dulgence, that's what I think: they'll be out there screaming for
someone else next week. They've thrown off self-control like it's
yesterday's knickers.

It wasn't like that for us; we sat on our emotions. We kept them
locked away inside and hoped that they would fade. No one was
interested in what we thought. If we'd made a fuss, who would
have listened? Young girls were supposed to be silent and decora-
tive. Failing that, just silent.

The lens fixes on a girl in a white school shirt. She's holding a
home-made banner that says *Marry me Mick!* with a heart. Her
face is flushed and damp with sweat, her hair is plastered to her
teenage forehead. Her eyes roll back as she screams for the camera.
There's a prefect badge pinned to her collar.

A faceless male presenter tells us: '*This young lady's got stiff competition if she wants to get a Rolling Stone down the aisle, that must be the wish of every schoolgirl here! But the boys are off to America next week and they'll have no time for romance. After all, what is it they say? A Rolling Stone gathers no—*'

I flick the set off, my stomach clenched with irritation. I pour myself a whisky and swallow it down in one.

# 21

I was in a state of high anxiety as I changed for the journey into London. I tried to choose an outfit that this unknown man might like. I didn't have much: a flared navy skirt, a cardigan, a white shirt with a sailor collar. I had to wear my brown lace-up shoes because the black ones had gone at the heel.

I piled my hair up high on my head in a way I thought might be sophisticated and I stared into the speckled mirror by my bed. I tried to see myself as a stranger would, to see what was truly there.

I saw a large pale face with a solemn expression, a tight little mouth, wispy, dark hair. I was too tall and too clumsy and didn't know a single man in England. I should be grateful for whatever chance I got.

The chauffeur arrived promptly and ushered me to the car where Father was waiting. I hadn't seen him for more than two years. I was greeted with the words: 'Hurry up, girl.'

We neither of us had the skills to make small talk, so we sat in silence to begin with. Father sucked his pipe with a focus that ruled out chat. The vanilla smell of his tobacco took me straight back to Hamburg, straight back to his study. I was desperate to open a window but Father wanted it shut.

He seemed to relax a little once we reached the city so I asked him to tell me more about Mr Goodman. He shrugged. 'You'll meet him soon enough.'

Finally, through tight lips he told me the Goodmans were well thought of in Hamburg. He said Frank's business was very successful and he'd been in England 'for some time'. 'Mr Goodman is an important man. He moves in the right circles.'

I asked how old he was and Father said: 'I've no idea.'

Then I asked the question that had troubled me since I first got Father's letter. I toyed with a thread on the car-seat upholstery. 'Father, what will happen if I don't like Mr Goodman?'

He tutted at my foolishness. 'You'll like him very much. You've got no choice.'

We were to meet at a Lyons Corner House. I hadn't been to one before, though I'd heard the other girls talk of them. It was vast and bustling – a brightly lit emporium. I told myself I was shaking with excitement, that the tightness in my stomach wasn't fear.

I struggled to keep up as Father jostled through the crowded rooms. He strode quickly, dodging customers and waitresses, barging past tables and cane-backed chairs. He shouted 'it's this way' from time to time but didn't once look back to check on me.

My first sight of Frank was of an olive-skinned balding man. He was sitting with a book at a table in the corner of the room. He didn't see us until we were right there in front of him and he stood up very quickly, all five foot three of him. It flashed through my mind how queer we'd look if we ever embraced – a little monkey shinning up a tree.

He shook hands with Father and offered a shy nod in my direction, his brown eyes skimmed my face quickly as if afraid of getting caught. We sat down, Frank on one side, Father and I on the other. The two men lit their pipes and talked about shipping crates.

Father took a notebook out. 'Some of the art will need very careful handling.'

Frank nodded twice and pulled on his pipe. 'We're used to packing delicate items.'

Eventually one of the staff came over and asked us what we'd like to order. Father looked irritated at being disturbed and Frank ordered tea and cakes. By the time the drinks arrived the men were deep in conversation. I sat and watched them as I picked at the layers of a custard slice.

Frank was in his late thirties and seemed very old to me then. He had laughter lines around twinkling eyes. I was fascinated by his eyebrows, luxuriant beneath his hairless pate. He deferred to my father, which Father liked. And he didn't once speak to me.

After a further hour talking about shipping routes, Father seemed satisfied and paid the bill. Frank shook his hand again, and for me, that shy little nod.

Then we got in the car and we drove back to school in silence. When Father left he said, 'Right, then,' as if something had been settled.

He leant in and kissed me awkwardly on the cheek. Warm vanilla breath; the tickle of his moustache. It was the first time he'd touched me in years.

## 22

I'm sitting with Margo in the Peter Jones cafe while she gathers her strength for our shopping trip. I've come to buy Reuben a shirt for his birthday and she's tagged along for the ride. She's sipping her coffee with painful slowness and I'm anxious to get on with it.

'Hurry up,' I say. 'We haven't got all day.'

She dabs at the last of the cake crumbs with her index finger, then raises an eyebrow. 'Haven't we?'

I am doubtful about the menswear assistant as soon as I spot his sideburns. You expect a bit more from a place like Peter Jones. The boy lacks focus, he tells us about his mother's shingles but seems clueless when it comes to menswear, clueless when it comes to his stock. He points out shirts in yellows and browns when I've told him the colour I want. He asks me if I've thought about something in nylon.

'Nylon's all the rage,' Margo says.

I tell her: 'No, it has to be smart. His old shirts are terribly scruffy.'

He pulls out dozens of shirts in light greens and blues, though anyone can see they're wrong. He shows us pale green, apple green, emerald green and mossy green.

For the tenth time. 'It needs to be forest green.' Those sideburns must be blocking his ears.

He starts to huff and sigh as he unfolds each shirt. He takes out pins and cardboard stiffeners and tosses them aside. He waves the garments under my nose in a way I find most offensive. Nothing is quite the right colour of course, not a scrap of forest green in sight.

A laundry-load of discards later, we finally find it, the ideal shade. A button-down collar and a lovely fine cloth. It even has a pocket on the breast, which Reuben can use for his fountain pen.

Margo says: 'It's perfect. We don't need to see any more.'

The shop boy seems utterly thrilled with the shirt and I forgive him his many transgressions. He takes us straight to the front of the queue to pay, which I think is rather nice.

## 23

I met Frank twice more before the wedding and we spoke to each other hardly at all. Three meetings – I know the girl who treats my bunions better than that.

No one suggested I should slow things down. In fact they all seemed thrilled for me, patted my back and said well done. Girls who'd once bullied me now sought me out at mealtimes. They wanted to hear all about my fiancé, what he looked like, where he came from, what he did. And it felt good to be the focus of some positive attention. It felt like I'd achieved something in getting engaged so young.

I hid the fact that Frank was German, I said he was a London businessman. I gave them the impression he was very tall and had bright blue eyes like Gary Cooper.

Only Margo seemed a little unsure and I thought perhaps she was jealous. She spoke to me in our lunch break while we were taking a stroll through the grounds. I remember the crunch of teeth into apple as she worked her way round a Cox's Orange Pippin.

Her expression was serious. 'Have you thought about your exams?'

I shrugged. 'I don't suppose I'll need them.'

She went quiet again, which wasn't like her. Eventually she asked, 'Is he a kind man, d'you think?'

I considered it: his laughter lines, warm brown eyes, that shy little smile. I nodded. 'Yes. I think so.'

She linked her arm with mine and patted my hand. 'Well, then. I dare say he'll do.'

# 24

I feel excited as I wrap my gift carefully in strong brown paper, sealing wax and a length of parcel string. I imagine my Reuben's face as he opens it. How the dark green will bring out the hazel in his eyes.

He'll want to call me straight away. He'll be touched when I tell him how hard it was to find. I'll say: 'It was nothing, you're worth it, darling.' I'll describe that awful shop assistant and we'll share a little joke about his sideburns.

I've found the perfect card as well. It has a blue car on the front like the one he used to play with. That blue toy car was always his favourite. I bought that little car for him.

The card says *Happy Birthday, Son* in big gold letters right across the front. Inside I write: *Happy birthday, my darling. From your loving mother.*

# 25

The dress arrived with a knock from the postman – a chic black box with French stamps on the front. We were staying with Father's London cousin at the time, it was less than a week before the wedding.

I tore through layers of tissue paper to a pool of champagne satin. I pulled it out and held it up. Chiffon sleeves fluttered like butterfly wings and a trail of pearl buttons stretched right down the length of its back. The fabric reflected all the light in the room. I couldn't believe it was mine.

I twirled with it in front of the bedroom mirror, pressed the cloth against my cheek. I imagined dancing in it – how beautiful I'd look, how my sister would hate me.

Mother said she'd picked it out herself from an atelier off the Champs-Élysées. She told me it was exquisitely tailored. She put down her vodka to show me the price tag.

It was then I saw the label, sewn discreetly into the nape of the neck. Small black stitches. One treacherous word: *Petite.*

It would have looked exquisite on my mother; it would have looked stunning on my sister too. But I hadn't been petite since I was twelve years old, surely my mother knew that?

I whispered: 'It's tiny. I'll never get into it.'

She shook her head. 'Nonsense.' But a small crease of doubt appeared between her eyebrows. When was the last time she had looked at me?

She poured herself another drink and insisted I put the dress on, though by then I didn't want to. The champagne satin turned to sausage skin and the corset carved ridges on my hips.

'It fits you like a glove,' she said as she strained to do the buttons up. She smoothed my hair and smeared her lip tint on me. She pinched some colour into my cheeks and then she said: '*Sehr gut.*'

I'd imagined my wedding dress dozens of times, sitting beside Lena at Mother's dressing table. I'd sketched it out for Margo in the back of a textbook. I'd pictured myself as a fragile waif, trailing silk beside my towering husband.

What I saw in the mirror was trussed up and ridiculous. Chiffon wings fluttering from too-broad shoulders. It was hopeless, clearly. Nothing could be done. I looked like a giant moth.

My sister came over with Gustav for the ceremony. They'd been married three months by then, but it still seemed wrong to me. Lena appeared happy enough, had a new fur coat and mono-grammed suitcase. Gustav looked like an elderly uncle on a trip with his favourite young niece.

On the eve of my wedding she knocked on the door while I was reading. She opened it a crack and poked her head round. 'Gilda, has anyone told you what will happen on your wedding night?'

I squirmed and said: 'I think so.'

She came in and sat on the bed beside me. 'No. I mean, *really* told you.'

I wasn't completely in the dark by then, I'd gleaned this and that from the girls at school. But it was still a jigsaw puzzle and I hadn't put the pieces in place. I was anxious about how much it might hurt but more than that I was scared of looking foolish.

Puberty had been a series of awful surprises: the hair that grew in secret places, the budding breasts, the excess sweat. It was Lena, not mother, who calmed me down when I found a spot of blood in my pants. She said it was something that happened to girls. It was messy and unpleasant but wouldn't last more than a week. I was horrified the following month when the spot of blood appeared again.

This time my sister relished imparting her newfound knowledge. 'It's always painful the first time you do it. You'll bleed all over the sheets.'

I squeezed my eyes shut. 'How big is it, exactly?'

She thought for a few seconds. 'It's bigger than a fountain pen but smaller than a rolling pin.'

'And what does the woman have to do?'

'She lies there very still until he's finished.'

I could hardly believe it would happen to me but Lena's expression was deadly serious. 'It'll start straight away, as soon as you're married. And after that you do it once a week.'

I shook my head, dumbstruck.

'Gustav likes to nibble my ears.'

I glanced at them, expecting tooth marks.

That night I dreamt of fountain pens and rolling pins. I was alone, in my single bed, for the very last time.

# 26

I call my Reuben first thing in the morning to see if he's got his present and to see if he likes his card. I want to tell him about the shop assistant – my hunt for the perfect forest green. I need to say happy birthday and tell him he's a wonderful son. I am full to the brim with a mother's love. 'Happy Birthday, darling!' I say.

But he's in a rush for work this morning and he doesn't have time to chat. When I ask him about his shirt he says: 'Thank you, yes, it's nice.' Then he passes the telephone to his wife and I never get the chance to tell him about the shop assistant. He doesn't know I chose that shade of green to bring out the hazel in his eyes.

Alice says she's taking my son to Luigi's for his birthday. I'm pleased she's listened to her mother-in-law's advice. Reuben hasn't been before and I think he will like it. I can picture him there in his new green shirt, eating *zabaglione* from a glass.

It turns out she had a change of heart and gave him a jazz record as her gift. She tells me the name of it, but it's no one I've heard of. Some trumpeter they saw in a nightclub, she says. 'It's a miracle I managed to track it down.'

She is pleased as punch with herself, though frankly it's just a record. She tells me the whole story and I struggle not to yawn. Letters were exchanged. Someone sent it from New York. She was scared it wouldn't arrive but it turned up in the nick of time.

The upshot is that all of it was worth it. Reuben made her play it over and over. He hummed along while they ate their breakfast; tapped his feet under the table. 'Oh, Gilda, he was thrilled with it. We both had so much fun.'

'How lovely,' I say. Still, I think he'll like his shirt. I do hope he notices the blue car on the front of his card.

# 27

Father had arranged the invitations for the wedding and by far the largest name on those glossy cards was his: *Mr and Mrs Karl Meyer* in copperplate gothic at the top. Underneath in smaller type: *invite you to be present at the marriage of their daughter to Mr Frank Goodman.* The venue was a Hampstead synagogue, the date December 5, 1934. My name was nowhere to be seen on the card. It might as well have been Lena getting married.

We all know what should happen when your mother sees you on the morning of your wedding day – the gasp, the tear-filled eyes – we've seen it in the films. Well, my mother made a little tut of disappointment. She pulled at my skirt and ordered me to stand straight.

I cried that morning, but my mother's eyes stayed dry.

My sister said the dress was beautiful, and it would have been on her. But I would have liked to hear, just once, that I looked beautiful myself. On the morning of my wedding day it would have been nice to hear it.

I was focused again on the dress as the chauffeur drove us to the *shul*. I'd eaten nothing since the night before but the corset still dug into my hips. Mother sat beside me and stared out of the window while Father listed all the people he'd invited. The list was very long and Father seemed excited. I didn't recognise a single name.

I saw Frank waiting outside the synagogue, he was wearing a skullcap and a pair of gold-rimmed spectacles and for one queasy second I wasn't quite sure it was him. But then an older man came over and handed him a flower for his buttonhole. He smiled that shy, gentle smile and I knew it was Frank after all. And I felt a rush of gratitude because he could have married anyone, couldn't he? He might have changed his mind completely, decided he was better off alone. I'd have had to go back and face the girls at school. My father would never speak to me again. I wanted to be married – I needed to be married.

Once we'd signed the contract, Father walked me to the *chuppah*. We were arm in arm and he told me he was proud. I remember his words exactly. 'I'm proud of you, Gilda. You've done better than I thought you would.'

My voice shook with nerves as we stood in front of all those people. More scared of embarrassing myself than scared of the commitment ahead. I wondered what they all made of us: a music-hall punchline of a man and a woman. Frank small and neat in his little gold spectacles, while I towered in my too-tight dress. I tried to stay calm and breathe. I tried to stand up straight. Most of all, I tried to suck in my stomach.

And it doesn't take much to get married, you know: a few steps round your husband, a few sips of wine. At the end of the ceremony you stamp on a glass and that's it. *Mazel tov!* You're done.

Getting married is the easy part. It was staying married I found hard. Once you've made those vows no one helps you.

Margo was there at my wedding, but I didn't catch sight of her until after the ceremony. How I could have missed her pink hat will forever be a mystery to me. I saw her outside the synagogue, clutching confetti in her white-gloved hand. In the blur of strangers' faces, her hat stood out like a pimple.

I was so pleased to see her that I went up and hugged her. She was the only guest I'd invited myself amidst hundreds from who knows where.

She beamed at me and kissed my cheek. 'Gilda, you look truly beautiful.'

I blinked back tears and then I lied too. I told her I liked her hat and that cerise really suited her complexion.

The reception took place at the Connaught Hotel in Mayfair. Men packed the ballroom like a bank floor or a business convention and Father stood in the middle of it all, patting backs and shaking hands.

I didn't eat much, it was trout and it still had the bones in. It felt very queer to be sitting next to Frank. Impossible that I was his wife.

After the meal, the staff cleared the tables away. The band started up and the men began circling. They cheered and clapped in time to the music as they forced Frank and I out onto the dance floor. We were grabbed and gripped and jostled. Someone trod on my dress hem in the crush.

They whooped and laughed as they pushed us onto spindly chairs. We were hoisted high on strangers' shoulders and paraded round the room like coffins.

The rocky movement, the gassy champagne, all those people staring up at me and the dress cutting into my flesh. I looked over to Frank whose knuckles were white where he clung to his seat. He said something and smiled weakly, but I couldn't quite make it out.

It's hard to be sure, even now I'm not quite sure, but I think he said: 'Let's try and make the best of this.'

\*

Father was delighted with the ceremony and reception. It gave his business an enormous boost, I think. Money alone can't buy such good will, particularly when times are hard. It takes something really special and a wedding is just the thing.

# 28

I take my evening stroll past Luigi's for a change. They are three tables back from the window, on the left. I'm only passing briefly, I don't intend to linger, but it does seem like they're enjoying themselves, the two of them, which is nice.

Only Reuben is wearing a blue shirt, I notice. It's faded and scruffy; not fit for the occasion. His green shirt would have looked lovely with that jacket. His green shirt would have been just right.

My son and his wife are sat at a small square table. It's draughty, the spot they've chosen. The candle between them stutters in its Chianti bottle. They are sitting right next to the fish tank too: a dozen little eyes stare out at them.

I look for the round table where Leo and I used to sit and it's still there in the corner with a view of the whole room.

Leo and I went to Luigi's every Saturday when we were together. The special *saltimbocca* is what Leo always ate. He'd joke that it was kosher: 'Prosciutto isn't really pork, you know.' The tang of sage would be still on his tongue when he kissed me as we walked home.

We had some good times at Luigi's, Leo and I. We were happy, mostly. I sometimes forget that.

Alice is eating those little shrimp balls – Scrumpy or Scrampi, I'm never quite sure of the name. Reuben has his elbow on the table so it's hard to see – chicken perhaps? He's terribly fussy when it comes to food, his nanny used to complain of it.

Alice and Reuben hold hands as they eat. I wonder if they always do that or just on special occasions?

It's as if they're Siamese twins, these two, they cannot bear to be apart. Reuben doesn't let go of her hand to pick up the napkin he's dropped on the floor. Alice struggles to cut through her lettuce. She stabs it with the prongs on her fork. They look crippled and clumsy despite the soft glow of candlelight, as if they've chosen romance over table manners.

Leo and I had a terrible argument in Luigi's. We'd been drinking red wine – too much of it. Cheap wine, fighting fuel for a couple who were nearing the end. The restaurant was full to bursting, the tables packed in around us.

Leo was eating a lobster, cracking its claws and sucking out its flesh. Flecks of juice spattered his crisp white shirt. Fragments of shell on the tablecloth. He was drinking the wine like water, filling his own glass and leaving mine empty. A plate of cold chicken Milanese sat in front of me. I couldn't swallow a bite.

It started as a conversation but Leo's voice kept getting louder. I remember trying to shush him, trying to keep him calm. Everyone around us was shifting in their seats. Waiters and guests glanced anxiously our way.

'You killed him!' Leo spat the words at me.

None of us was sure if he dropped the glass or threw it. I remember the jangling crash as it hit the tiled floor. Red wine and shards of glass formed a puddle by my feet. The waiter rushed over and cleared the worst of it but the diners' shocked faces remained.

Leo said the worst thing he could think of – the thing he knew would hurt me the most. Then he walked out and left me sitting there, blotting my tears with a dark blue linen table napkin.

I could never go back to Luigi's after that.

# 29

There was an awkward hesitation in the doorway to our honeymoon suite when neither of us was sure if Frank would carry me over the threshold.

It was a queer little moment – a mutual sizing up – neither certain what the other would expect.

Frank looked me up and down with frowning concentration. It went on for just a fraction too long, he appeared to be searching for a handhold. His face was serious, I could see that he was calculating. Was I heavier or lighter than a shipping crate?

My feet stayed planted firmly on the ground, arms folded tight. I looked down at the top of Frank's bald head and I thought, *There's just no way.*

I nudged him aside, picked up my skirts and stepped over that threshold quick smart. He followed me in laughing, more relieved than disappointed, I think.

Bad luck to start a marriage by buckling under the weight of your bride.

And then there we were just the two of us, in a suite we'd been given by my father as a wedding gift. A couple who barely knew each other, expected to spend the night.

The double bed loomed large in the room – a monster draped in burgundy silk. Velvet cushions lay scattered at one end, lolling like thick, pink tongues.

Frank went up and stroked the slippery bedspread. He picked up one of the cushions to inspect. Turned it over and put it back down. I perched myself on the only chair and stared at the pattern on the carpet.

Frank said: 'Well, Mrs Goodman . . .' The tremor in his voice made things infinitely worse. I remember trying to smile and feeling a muscle flick in my cheek.

He lent forward and touched me very briefly on the top of my arm, as if he were tagging me 'It'. He asked me did I know about '. . . men-and-women'. He took my nod as his signal to begin.

Everything my sister had told me was true, and yet the experience was entirely different. I'd imagined it as orderly: crisp and certain, like a visit to the doctor. Instead it was messy and muddled and confused. His hands shook. He didn't speak. Occasionally he cleared his throat.

And, oh God, there were all those little buttons. Hundreds of tiny pearl buttons right down the back of my dress. He couldn't undo them and I couldn't help him. His panicked breath was hot against my neck. He fumbled and fussed while I sat there and endured it. He moved slowly, clumsily, button by button.

I didn't see him naked that night. Just a glimpse of dark chest hair and then I looked away. Dark, wiry hair against olive skin. An animal pelt I hadn't guessed at.

But the act itself really wasn't so dreadful. Some poking and prodding and then it was over and done. Frank pulled the sheet up, pecked me on the cheek and went to the bathroom to wash.

*

Did I feel like more of a woman afterwards? I thought about it later as I tried to get to sleep. It reminded me a bit of the time I stood on my head in gym class. Uncomfortable, yes, and a little undignified. But an achievement to have done it at all.

# 30

I'm standing in the queue for the 31 to Margo's when I spot Alice in the distance with another young woman. I watch them approach from the top of the street, they are pushing a large black pram.

Alice doesn't see me at first, but when she does she waves. Her eagerness cheers me, it's nice to have some company. I shove *A Caribbean Mystery* in my bag.

The pair pull up and Alice does the introductions. 'Gilda, this is an old school friend, Tamsin. Tamsin, meet my mother-in-law.'

Tamsin holds out a hand for me to shake. She's wearing some very short shorts. She's the same age as Alice with a boyish jet-black crop. But when she says 'pleased to meet you' her voice is so girlish it grates.

Alice pushes back the hood of the pram. 'And this,' she says, 'is Xanthe. She's exactly two months old.'

I look in the buggy to where Xanthe is asleep, her mouth slightly open in a tiny rosebud 'o'. Her arms are raised each side of her head, little fingers splayed in surrender. Tamsin says: 'She's been a horror all morning. Look at her now though, butter wouldn't melt!'

Alice smiles and bends into the pram. 'You haven't been a horror, have you, Xanthe?'

Tamsin gives me a knowing look. She raises an eyebrow at my-daughter-in-law. Alice catches her friend and frowns. 'One day, maybe, Tamsin. Not just yet.'

The 31 arrives so I say a quick goodbye, I wave at them both from the downstairs window. My jaw is tense as the bus moves off and I struggle to muster a smile.

*Not just yet*, that's what Alice said, as if it were solely her decision; as if she could simply snap her fingers and order a baby like a sofa from a catalogue. Has she even considered what Reuben wants? I bet he's anxious to get on with it. He's thirty now, not young any more. I know he'd make a wonderful father.

I suspect my daughter-in-law has other priorities: doesn't want to spoil her figure; doesn't want to be tied down. Perhaps she wants to keep her husband to herself – doesn't want to share him with a child.

But the fact is, I need to be a grandmother soon – I've thought about it, of course I have. A baby would bring us all closer. They'd need my help, they'd ask me to babysit. A baby would break down the walls of their fortress, they'd have to let others inside.

*One day, maybe,* that's what she said. Well, I'm not sure I can wait that long.

# 31

We returned from our night of honeymoon to our marital home in Guildford – a market town near London, not far from where Frank's factory was. It was a red-brick house large enough for a family of twelve to live in. It had wide bay windows, a grey slate roof and a mock-Tudor gable on the front.

In one sense I was lucky, I think: Frank was not a demanding husband. He was kind and gentle by nature and asked little of me in return. It wasn't the sort of romance I'd read about but I thought that might be due to his age. He was busy with the factory mostly and usually away on business at weekends. I saw him in the evenings when we often had guests. We spent our nights lying side by side. We rarely had cause to converse.

Everything was so new to me, I spent those first months with my head in a spin. I'd been plucked out of boarding school without preparation and dropped in an adult world. I was in charge of a cook, a maid, a gardener and a housekeeper. I'd never been in charge of anything before. I was eighteen, too young to be a wife.

I muddled through the days, unsure how much was required of me. No one had supplied a job description or a list of things to be done. The servants looked at me expectantly sometimes. They left pauses, which I struggled to fill. I suspected they were laughing at me but the meals still got served and the clothes still got washed. I thought it best to put up with it; to ignore it and let them get on.

I was afraid that I might be disappointing Frank, failing in all sorts of wifely duties. But if I was, he never said so.

I woke up late. I still wake up late. If you start the day too early then you've got too much day to get through. Hours drag by. You're ready for a whisky and it's only two o'clock. Starting the day too early can get you in trouble.

So in those first years of marriage I never got up before half past ten. Frank was already at work by then and the staff had all busied themselves. I took breakfast in bed, then slowly, slowly bathed and dressed myself. No point in hurrying. I made it last. I washed and cleansed my face. I brushed my teeth going one tooth at a time. I gave my hair a hundred swipes with a boar bristle brush that made my scalp itch. I put on my make-up slowly, carefully. If I made a mistake, I'd wipe it off and start again. I painted my lips into a deep red bow. I sculpted my eyebrows, plucked them out and then drew them back in. I powdered my face a smooth matt white. I coloured my cheeks in with rouge. I checked my reflection from every angle. And then it was time for lunch.

I ate lunch in the dining room, usually on my own. Just me and the silverware at one end of the table. The maid would set the food down with a 'here you are, madam'. I'd wait a few minutes before starting and then cut myself small mouthfuls, which I'd chew at least fifty times. I always had dessert and coffee; then fruit, which I peeled with a sharp little knife. I could pass a whole two hours that way.

Beyond lunch there was the long gap until evening drinks. I became an expert in wasting time, could spend an entire afternoon buying lipstick.

The fifteen minutes before five were the longest. I'd check my watch with foolish frequency. I counted down the seconds. At two minutes to five I made my way to the living room. When the drinks cabinet came open I'd be waiting.

Thank God for the whisky – whisky was my prop. I made sure I'd had at least three drinks by the time our guests arrived. During dinner I'd keep going. I handled it well and didn't mix it. I was always discreet. I never caused a scene; never slurred my words or fell off my chair.

The truth is I haven't had many friends in my life: one or two have passed through, and Margo, of course. But when I've been lonely, anxious or unsure there's always been the whisky there to warm me.

## 32

Margo is out the back when I arrive; it takes her an age to answer the door. She's wearing her father's old corduroy trousers and holding a large pair of garden shears.

'I'm right in the middle of sorting out the roses.' She licks a bead of sweat from her upper lip. 'Come through and we can talk while I'm pruning. I'd like to get it done, if you don't mind.'

Margo lives on her own like me, though she did have a housemate for several years. Joyce was a bus conductress, she moved in after the war. They seemed to get on very well – even went away on holiday together.

I'm not quite sure what went wrong with the arrangement, poor Margo was dreadfully upset. I suppose she'd got used to that bit of extra income. Still, she's rather old to be living with a housemate and it's nice to have the place to ourselves.

Margo's garden's smaller than my living room, plus it's hot and there isn't any shade. She carries out a kitchen chair and puts it on the edge of the patio for me. Then she fetches me a glass of lukewarm water and gets back to the job in hand.

She yells to me over her shoulder. 'I haven't seen you all week. How have you been? Tell me about Reuben's birthday!'

I have to compete with her neighbour's lawnmower, I lean

forward on my seat and shout. But once I've started, the lies come easily. 'He rang me as soon as he opened his present. He was full of excitement, couldn't wait to try it on. He said he'd been hoping for a nice smart shirt. Apparently that colour's just the thing!'

Margo turns and smiles: 'That's lovely, Gilda! What did you all get up to?'

'We went to Luigi's to celebrate. Alice arranged it but Reuben insisted I come. He wore his new green shirt for the occasion. It looked perfect, it could have been made for him!'

Margo smiles and nods. 'Oh good! How was the food?'

The sun is beating down and my neck is turning pink, I should really go inside to the shade. My voice is rather hoarse but the words keep coming. I can feel my confidence swell with each fiction.

'It was lovely, Margo. I had the duck, Alice had those little shrimp balls and Reuben had the same as me. I'd planned to treat everyone to dinner but Reuben insisted on paying! He said he wanted to spoil his favourite girls and who was I to stand in his way? At the end of the evening Alice got the bus back while Reuben escorted me home. I told him he was a very special son and he said he felt lucky—'

The lawnmower stops and the sudden quiet throws me.

Margo steps in. 'That's nice.'

But she doesn't turn to smile and she doesn't ask me any more questions.

# 33

I've lived in England now for thirty-seven years – that's more than twice as long as I ever lived in Germany. Yet people still see me as a foreigner, hear my accent and ask where I'm from.

I can't hear anything different myself, but Margo insists it's still there. She says I sound guttural, such an ugly word, like clogged up gutters. It's queer that my accent has stayed so strong when so much else has been lost along the way.

I can't remember the last conversation I had in German. I haven't spoken it since Father died. My vocabulary dates me, its pre-war sentences sound quaint and old-fashioned. I wouldn't fit in at all, I don't think, if I ever went back to Hamburg.

Frank and I always spoke English with one another; his grasp of the language was patchy, but we carried on just the same. It used to make us laugh when he mixed up his words or mangled a sentence. 'The instructions are on the backside,' or to a waiter: 'I become the chicken.' It was one of the things that amused us. It was one of the few things we shared.

I remember the time when Frank was given a bronze plaque of his factory by a business associate. He told me he'd been given a plague at work, when I knew that it was a plug. We squabbled all evening – plague, plug, plague, plug – both of us teasing the other one, both of us sure we were right.

Then Frank, in desperation, showed the silly thing to the house-keeper, this pompous bronze plate with his factory picked out in relief.

'Oh, you mean a plaque,' she said, and the three of us laughed until the tears rolled down. I bet she dined out for months on that: her foolish foreign boss who was given the plague at work.

We reached for German only in extremis. When all the other words failed us, our mother tongue came out. Later, near the end of our marriage, when we'd used up all our English politeness, we'd curse and shout and rant at each other in the language of our parents.

But I'm getting ahead of myself, because at the beginning we didn't argue. In those first few years my husband was courteous and polite. We rarely spent time alone together; our evenings were filled with guests. After a day in isolation, the contrast felt like a slap.

Frank called our set his friends, but they were business contacts really. They were only friends like Father had friends – every one of them with a reason to be there. They were buyers and bankers, industrialists and their wives. A different generation. Older, even, than Frank.

We saw them in groups of eight or more for cocktails or dinner. We'd drink with them or eat with them most nights of the week. Their conversation was loud and guttural, yes guttural, that is the word for the way we sound.

The talk round the table back then was always of Germany. Voices grew louder as the evening drew on. Each story was more shocking than the last. Businesses destroyed, stones thrown in the streets, friends who'd been spat at, colleagues barred from their jobs.

Five years had passed since I'd been in Hamburg and so much had changed in that time. Lena and Gustav had moved to New York and my parents were in Paris, planning to follow them. Germany seemed very distant to me. My ties with the country felt slight. I tried to make myself remember the others – the schoolmates and neighbours I once saw every day. But they were prosperous people, respected, well fed. Impossible to imagine them otherwise.

Everyone was worried, of course, many of our guests still had family in Germany. But 'Hitlers come and Hitlers go'. No one thought the Nazis would last.

I never joined the conversation, I sat quietly and listened. No one ever asked for my opinion, it was clear I was out of my depth.

After dinner there were coffees and brandies. It was always well past midnight by the time we all stood up. Frank would pat the men on the back, put his arm round their shoulders as he walked them to the door. There'd be whispered conversations, hearty handshakes and farewells.

With me, the guests would pause, as if wondering for a second who I was. Then they'd kiss me politely on the cheek and say: 'It's been lovely, Gilda. Thank you. Really lovely.' And I'd ask myself: *Has it really been lovely?*

When the last guests departed they took too much life with them. Frank and I would stand side by side and watch them disappear down the driveway.

Then Frank would walk back in on his own and I'd say nothing to keep him. He'd sit in the living room and pour himself a brandy: a little time for quiet contemplation before he turned in for the night.

If I'd been a different wife, if he'd been a different husband, I might have joined him there by the fire. We could have talked about our evening – swapped gossip, shared thoughts, laughed at the things his friends said. Perhaps we could have found some common ground. Perhaps that half-hour would have saved us.

But by the time my husband came up I was always fast asleep. Sometimes he'd lie up close to me and I'd be woken by his warmth.

He was tender with me, Frank. He never demanded too much of me. Our marriage went wrong but he wasn't a bad man. He doesn't deserve the things I've done.

# 34

She seems propelled by purposefulness, my daughter-in-law: arms swinging, back straight, those little heels hit the pavement with surprising force. We're going shopping, Alice and I. We're heading for the Finchley Road.

It's nice to have this outing together. Nice to spend some time with my daughter-in-law. We really should do it more often. Go out just the two of us like this.

Only she's moving far too quickly for me and I do wish she'd slow down a little. My blouse, fresh from the cleaners, is already limp with sweat. My face is turning red. I dread to think what's happened to my hair. Each bench we pass cries out for me to sit. I'm huffing and puffing like Margo.

I get a few seconds' pause, a blessed relief, while she stops to cross the Finchley Road. I hang back and watch her progress at the traffic lights.

She looks so small with the cars rushing past her; too young to be at such a busy junction by herself. It feels like someone bigger, older, should be with her to hold her hand. I ponder it for a moment or two – perhaps I could step up and join her? I shake my head, it's a silly idea. After a while the traffic lights change and she trots across the road without me.

It was pure coincidence I spotted her this afternoon. I was only just approaching their house when I saw her coming out. I almost called to her, but then she looked so determined and I didn't want to hold her up. It just seemed less intrusive to follow at a distance instead.

I watch her stride through the doors of John Barnes department store but by the time I've crossed the road she's nowhere to be seen. I have to ask a doorman for help and he points me down to the self-service supermarket.

When I get there I see goods piled high. Aisles stretch ahead of me. Shoppers push wire trollies and just take things off shelves without asking for permission. I can't get over how much there is to choose from. I've never been in a such a place before.

I walk up and down a bit and finally spot Alice by the vegetables. Her cotton skirt stretches tight across her rump as she bends to pick potatoes from a bucket. I find myself a place to stand tucked behind a stack of washing powder. I have a good view but she can't see me. I peer out past packets of Omo.

She's gathering tomatoes. She squeezes each one gently. Her expression is thoughtful, as if they have something to tell her. She is careful with them. Delicate. She cups the chosen fruit in her hand. She smells each one, eyes shut, before placing it in her basket.

Her movements make me think about her with my Reuben: the two of them alone, that same look of tenderness. I shake my head, the image disturbs me. And yet I can't look away.

She wanders over to the mushrooms and the slow selection process continues. Each little mushroom is dusted down and held up to the light. Each one is then rejected or selected and placed gently in a paper bag.

I'm struck by the care that Alice is taking. Such close inspection, each morsel considered. I look round the hall at the other women shopping and I don't see that thoughtfulness in them.

My daughter-in-law moves over to the meat counter. The woman in front of her interrogates the butcher. I twitch with impatience, but my daughter-in-law waits calmly. When it's her turn she buys a large leg of mutton. She puts it in her basket and steadies it.

I picture her in a few years' time, filling that same basket with a meal for her family. I picture myself at the table with them – chatting to the children as Reuben carves the roast. And the vision is so clear that I can almost smell the tender meat, I can hear my grandchildren's laughter, I can taste the spicy sweetness of the wine. For a moment it feels like I'm part of their lives.

Alice takes the whole lot over to the till and I stand at a distance and watch her pay. She chats to the cashier as she packs the goods. Then she leaves, lugging two heavy bags.

When I step outside I spot her by the Underground. She's standing with her shopping at her feet as if she's waiting for a bus. I hold back and watch her as she looks towards the station entrance. She scans the commuters, her brow slightly furrowed.

Finally I see Reuben emerge, he swings his briefcase as he strides towards his wife. He greets her with a kiss on the lips and he smiles like he's really pleased to see her. She says something I can't make out then hugs him and neatens his tie.

He looks relaxed and happy as he picks up her shopping bags. He holds them both in one hand and links Alice's arm with the other. She takes his briefcase and skips along beside him. I watch their backs as they head off down the street.

The walk seems longer as I trudge alone to my flat. I notice the potholes, the dog-muck on the pavement, the half-eaten sandwich in the gutter.

When I get in, I turn the wireless on for company. My empty glass is right where I left it.

## 35

It was only much later, after the war, that I found the stack of letters. I was going through Frank's bureau, looking for my birth certificate. The stamps alerted me, a falcon and a swastika. The postmarks said 1938.

My hands were clumsy as I slid the first one out of its envelope, it was from Frank's old professor. I remember the handwriting, jagged and urgent. The German words sliced across the page.

> *You are our last chance.*
> *I ask nothing for myself, I ask only on behalf of my daughter.*
> *Every day it is getting worse. They have taken over our home.*
> *Life is growing intolerable.*
> *I fear our time is running out.*

The second letter was from an elderly neighbour. The third a former colleague. They needed deposits, jobs and guarantors – they were pleading for their families and their lives.

I counted twenty-three letters in total. Different handwriting on different paper. A stack of little envelopes, too small for such frantic emotions.

*

What I know now, what I wish I'd known then, is that Frank replied to every one of those letters. He must have saved dozens of lives. Yes, he had his contacts, but, still, it can't have been easy.

I don't know why he didn't tell me at the time. He never spoke of it once. When I think of all those hours I wasted shopping for lipstick.

# 36

I know now that I should have tried harder in my marriage. Those evenings with Frank, I should have joined him by the fire. I should have been more of a wife to him, made an effort to play the hostess like my mother. I should have smiled more; laughed more. I should have loved my husband more.

It wouldn't have been hard to take an interest in Frank's life. I could have talked to his friends at dinner, learnt the names of their children and wives. I could have asked him about his day at work instead of always sitting at the table in silence. Touched him, just lightly, on the back when I passed him. Stroked his shoulder or straightened his tie.

I'm sure he would have liked it if I'd shown him more affection. It would have been so easy and yet I don't think I ever once tried it. Frank deserves affection — Berta's always at it. She's always holding his hand, touching his knee. She never leaves the poor man alone.

When I found out I was expecting Reuben I should have been happier, I'm certain of that. Frank was over the moon with happiness and I should have been happy too. Something was wrong with me, I wasn't like the other pregnant women. I should have been nesting, knitting, patting my stomach, trying out baby names, planning the nursery.

*

These are the things that have been keeping me awake at night. The could-haves and the should-haves and the why-didn't-I-do-thats? If I could go back I'd change it, but life doesn't give you that chance.

So instead I'm going to change myself – to become the sort of mother my son deserves. It won't be easy but I know I can do it. Alice is showing me how.

# 37

I didn't realise I was pregnant until I was already two months gone. I went to see the doctor because my back had started to hurt. He told me to take my girdle off, which I thought was rather queer but I did it anyway. He felt around a bit and prodded my stomach. 'You're pregnant, Mrs Goodman!' he said.

It should have been a happy surprise. The doctor thought it would be. I remember how his eyes blinked as he waited for me to respond. He was grinning, lips open, showing every one of his little yellow teeth. 'Mrs Goodman, you're going to be a mother!'

He had one long white hair in his left eyebrow, it dangled almost down to his cheek. I wondered why he didn't get rid of it. Take some scissors and snip it right off.

'Mrs Goodman, congratulations.'

The doctor raised his eyebrows and the white hair moved up too.

'Mrs Goodman, this is happy news! Mrs Goodman, are you all right?'

The receptionist put her hand on my arm to stop me leaving. She said something I didn't hear as I stumbled to the door. I walked out of the surgery and I kept on walking until I got home.

*You're pregnant, Mrs Goodman*, played over in my head.
*You're going to be a mother*, he'd said.

Even now, I find it hard to understand. I'd always wanted children, like every other girl at school. Getting married and having children is what makes you a woman, that's what we were taught. You'll get married and then you'll have children. It's the most important job in the world.

I'd expected to glow in early pregnancy, stroke my stomach with a secret smile. I'd imagined the excitement of telling my husband.

Instead I felt numb and like it didn't belong to me – as if I were wearing a girdle with a pregnant bump attached. When I looked at my growing waistline in the mirror I couldn't picture anything in there.

Maybe it was the shock of it, my body had rushed ahead of me. It hadn't bothered to warn me first, it hadn't asked my permission. We didn't use contraceptives, Frank hadn't mentioned them and I was barely aware of such things. But I knew I could get pregnant in theory, my sister had told me that.

Just somehow I didn't think it would happen so quickly (though goodness knows, five years isn't quickly). I thought Lena would be first, she was older, married longer.

I didn't tell Frank straight away, I kept it hidden from everyone. I'm not sure if I wanted to get used to it or hoped it would just disappear. For a few weeks life went on as before. I got up late, I drifted through the days and spent the evenings deep in war talk and whisky.

I must have looked different though, more tired, perhaps, a little fuller round the middle. Eventually Frank asked: 'Gilda dear, are you all right?'

His face was pinched and anxious; I was surprised to realise he cared. I smiled and pressed my hand to my stomach. 'I'm pregnant.'

'Oh, my darling, that's wonderful!' He tried to lift me but I pulled away. 'I can't believe how lucky we are.' For a second I thought he might cry. 'Gilda, my love,' he kissed my cheek. 'I was starting to think it might never happen. I was so afraid I wouldn't get to be a father. I can't tell you how happy you've made me.'

That evening he was quieter than usual – sat at the table just smiling to himself. He didn't take his brandy on his own and he came up to bed when I did. He kept a hand on my hip, just the lightest of touches, holding me there as he drifted off to sleep. I told myself to feel different: to feel safe and happy and loved.

He watched me closely in the months before the birth – made an effort to get home earlier from work. He went on fewer business trips, said he'd rather spend his weekends with me. He wouldn't let me lift a finger, not carry a bag, not open a door. He made sure I was eating properly and I cut down to just one little whisky with my last cigarette of the night.

I liked the way he looked after me, he'd run to fetch a cushion if I shifted in my chair. It made me feel treasured, as if I was something of value. I was weary towards the end of the pregnancy, far too tired to join the group at dinner. I enjoyed those peaceful evenings spent alone in the double bed. I read books I hadn't read since school and I felt I was myself in a way I hadn't since I got married.

Sometimes I'd reach down and touch my belly and the fullness I found there would surprise me.

# 38

Betty Grable in a little black mini-dress looks out from the pages of my morning paper. She's holding a cigarette, surrounded by the press. Her bare arms and legs are on display. I'm oddly pleased to see her there, it's like bumping into an old acquaintance. I remember the pin-up girl, coy in her swimsuit. It's her first trip to London, for a play.

I put on my reading glasses and scan the accompanying article. She's fifty-two years old, the same age as me. Her hair is bleached blonde and curves softly to her chin. I look once more at the contours of her face. There's a puffiness there that I recognise.

But the thing that strikes me most about the photograph is the crowd of journalists – men in the main – who gaze on her with rapt attention, transfixed by whatever she's saying. I can't recall the last time anyone looked at me that way. I can't recall the last time anyone looked at me and really saw me.

I take the newspaper with me to the bedroom. I pull the curtains closed, though I'm several storeys up. I switch on the light and step over to the mirror. A woman, neat and sensible, stares back.

I slowly lift the hem on my calf-length skirt. My heart beats faster, I'm pleased with what I see: two female legs in flesh-coloured nylon that don't look fifty-two unless you cast your eyes upwards. They are slim and shapely, not a varicose vein in sight.

# 39

Girls have special classes these days; lessons designed to prepare them. They have breathing and exercise and helpful advice and they're told about what to expect. It wasn't like that for us – too vulgar for those white-gloved times. My mother didn't talk to me once about giving birth. No one spoke about things like that.

I saw our doctor just twice before it happened. Once to confirm I was pregnant and again to learn when I was due. I should have asked questions, clearly I should have. But I was shy and afraid to look silly.

And there wasn't really anyone around I could talk to. Neither Margo nor my sister had children and Frank's friends were all so much older. My fears grew bigger as the baby grew bigger.

Instead of getting facts, I sought reassurance in novels and films. I created a comforting picture for myself and told myself that's how it would be. There would be some pain (but not too much, surely). I imagined I'd whimper slightly as the midwife wiped my brow. I thought the doctor would hand me my infant, all new and pink and parcelled up in wool. I'd be sitting up prettily in a freshly made bed and I'd take my child – surprised to be a mother.

*

It took sixteen hours to push my Reuben out. The contractions were brutal. They reached inside me and twisted. I didn't know people could make such sounds; that those noises could come from me.

The midwife told me to be quiet. She wrinkled her nose in distaste. 'Perhaps it's different where you come from, but English ladies don't make a fuss.'

I wished I'd accepted Margo's offer to be there. I'd been prudish and embarrassed – squeamish about her seeing me. She told me I'd need to have someone who cared but I thought I'd be all right on my own.

My mother didn't even cross my mind because, really, she wouldn't have helped. She'd have poured herself a stiff vodka tonic, struck up a Gauloises cigarette; she'd have said it was all taking far too long and wandered off in search of entertainment.

Still, I should have had someone with me. Down the hall in one of the guest rooms, Frank was fast asleep.

Reuben was finally born at lunchtime. I could hardly speak or hold up my head, could barely take in what I'd been through. But then they handed me my scrunched-up little son and I saw how utterly perfect he was. I couldn't believe he'd come from me; that Frank and I had made him.

I experienced a rush of such powerful love; I didn't even know such a feeling existed. I remember, just for a moment, thinking – I remember it so clearly – that maybe, it would be all right. For a second I thought I could do it.

And then the midwife took Reuben off to weigh him. And Frank came in and started weeping with happiness. And then Reuben started howling and I was so exhausted and so overwhelmed that I just wanted them all to go away.

# 40

My stomach flutters as I arrive at Hair by Raymond. The salon air is greenhouse hot and it smells of burning hair. They're playing some dreadful music, but I won't let that put me off. I go up to the desk and I ask for Mandy. I am strong and confident. In charge.

I've had enough of this tight little helmet. I've had enough of these corrugated curls. I want to see some other me in the mirror.

The receptionist glances up from her magazine and yells: 'Mand, it's your two o'clock.'

When Mandy comes out, she's a blank-faced teenager; eyes glazed as if she's just woken up. The receptionist points at me. 'This is your lady.' Mandy's mouth is hanging open. I'm surprised she can be trusted with the scissors.

The receptionist hands me an orange gown. I struggle into it without any help and it covers up my outfit entirely.

Mandy leads me over to the back of the salon where the music is louder still. The walls are a riot of DayGlo measles and a spotlight flickers near our heads. She sits me down on a moulded plastic chair, which I know will be uncomfortable in seconds. She stands behind me and looks at her fingernails: 'What d'you want doing?'

I dig in my handbag and pull out the newspaper clipping which is folded up right at the bottom. I feel rather foolish as I show it to Mandy.

She looks at the picture, then at me. She picks up a bit of my limp brown hair. She is rolling her eyes – I can see her in the mirror. She's sighing and puffing out her cheeks. And I think she's going to say it's impossible. I think she's going to tell me no way. But she doesn't, she says: 'Right then. You going to have the colour done too?'

And I nod my head yes. Why not do the colour? I'm here because I want to change.

An hour later I'm still sitting in the corner and my hair is poking out of a hedgehog highlight cap. I was right about these chairs – the seat has stuck to the back of my legs. When I try to separate flesh from plastic it's painful, like ripping off a plaster.

For twenty years Freda's been setting my hair. Twice a week, like clockwork, I go to her salon. The setting lotion she uses now is the same one she used on my very first visit. You couldn't ask for anything else. She wouldn't know what to do. And if I'm going to change, it needs to be a real change. I want a revolution, not just a polite little trim. So I know I'm right to be trying somewhere new.

But Mandy hasn't been over to check on my progress once since we started. She put on the colour ages ago and my back can't stand much more. Nobody has offered me tea or coffee. Even a glass of water would be nice. The light in here makes my skin look grey. When I catch myself in the mirror I am old.

It feels like several days have passed when Mandy finally returns to take the colour off. She leads me over to a row of basins and orders me to sit at the end.

She tips me until my head's in the bowl and my back is in agony – fiery pokers jab my spine. The water is at first too hot, then icy cold, then hot again. The girl scrubs away like she's scouring a saucepan.

Just when I think it's over, Mandy dollops on more shampoo. I have to endure another round of scrubbing before she jerks my head up and wraps it in a towel. There are soap suds in my ears, there's a stream of water trickling down my neck. I do my best to mop it with my collar as she leads me back over to the chair.

Once I'm seated, Mandy whips the towel away. And, even damp like this, my hair's much lighter. Its fairness makes my eyes look black and my skin look even paler than before. I can't stop staring, I'm hypnotised. For the first time, I resemble my sister.

Mandy doesn't talk as the cutting begins. She doesn't say a word and I'm grateful. She is focused and fast. I'm glad of it. It's what I want. I need this change over and done with.

She combs my hair out straight and then slices into it with confident snips. The ends are neat and sharp as a razor blade.

When she's finished, she leads me over to the row of driers and sits me down underneath one. The leatherette is luxury after the plastic chair. I close my eyes and think about my son.

In my daydream I'm sitting alone in a cafe. I look up from my coffee as Reuben walks in. He stands in the doorway and stares at my new hair. For a second I'm afraid he doesn't like it. Then he smiles at me, really smiles at me. It's the same warmth I see when he looks at Alice.

I jump as Mandy taps me on the shoulder. She says: 'All done. Are you all right?'

I feel a little unstable as I stand and Mandy takes my arm like I'm an elderly aunt. When she shows me the mirror I am startled by my hair. She says: 'It's much more with-it, isn't it? That colour really flatters your face.'

It is blonde and sleek and belongs to someone else. Underneath it my mascara-smudged eyes look like two lumps of coal on a snowman.

# 41

It was shortly before I gave birth to Reuben that Hitler invaded Poland. I found the pairing unsettling, I couldn't keep the two things apart. So much pain and violence and bloodshed and fear, it was difficult to separate their pain from my pain. I read the newspapers, I heard Frank talking – somehow it all got mixed up.

I let the nanny do everything in those first few weeks while I was confined to my bed. She fed my son, she washed him, changed him and tucked him up. I told myself I'd take over soon, when I was feeling stronger, I would.

She was a young woman, younger than me, and she didn't yet have any children of her own. Still, she knew how to rock my son, to calm him and comfort him. She used some special magic when he cried. I tried to copy exactly what she did but the magic never worked for me and the crying just got worse. Fear fizzed in my stomach; I'd start to panic. Surely I was doing it all wrong. I wished I could ask if my anxieties were normal but that wasn't how one spoke to the staff.

I looked at my son in those early days and was terrified by how fragile he was. The world was such a hostile place – really, what chance did he have? The nearby park had been dug into trenches, air raid shelters sprang up like mushrooms. We were called to the

117

town hall to be fitted for gas masks. Reuben's seemed to swallow him entirely.

I watched him sleep and was afraid he'd stop breathing. When I gave him his bottle I felt sure that he'd choke. I was scared I couldn't do it, didn't have the strength to do it – I was sure that something terrible would happen to him.

Frank tried to tell me I was just being silly. 'He's a happy, healthy baby. Why torture yourself?' He'd give Reuben's knee a squeeze and joke about how chubby he was. 'He's going to be a heavy-weight wrestler when he grows up.'

Perhaps I was too sensitive, perhaps my husband was right. Perhaps I got it out of proportion, this feeling that Reuben was at risk. Anxiety is a wearing thing. It's always there, it seeps into everything. I loved my son from the very first second but those fears for his safety never left me.

## 42

Alice scans the faces outside Finchley Road station. Her expression is anxious – she's meeting someone. Her hair is neatly brushed and she's wearing lipstick. It's clear she's made an effort with her dress.

I find a spot just opposite, where I can see her through the gaps in the cars. She seems a bit impatient, keeps checking her watch. I check mine and it's quarter to eleven.

Eventually she sees someone in the station entrance and waves both hands. She calls out a name. It's hard to hear with the passing traffic. She waves again. 'Over here!'

The figure that emerges is a tiny woman – Alice's mother – who's wrestling with the catch on her handbag. She's dressed for the city in a long grey swing coat. Her face lights up when she sees her daughter. They hug each other: long-lost comrades. Then Alice's mother, Pauline is her name, holds her daughter at arm's length and inspects her. She smiles approval. Nods her head. Alice pats her sleek bobbed hair.

I notice how alike they are. Peas in a pod, the two of them. They both have the same clear English-rose skin. They both have the same tidy frames.

When they move off, they are arm in arm. They are deep in

conversation at once. Their strides are in step, perfectly attuned. Their hips sway in rhythm, side to side.

I watch their backs as they walk away and I envy them their easy closeness. When Alice leans her head on Pauline's shoulder I feel a tug in my gut.

What was it Pauline said at the wedding? '*They grow up so fast. We'll miss our little girl.*' She looked at me with tears in her eyes. '*We're lucky to have them,*' she said.

I turn and walk slowly back to my flat and I think about my own mother. I want to find a moment of warmth. A moment when things were good.

I remember the last time I flew out to New York. I went straight from the airport to the hospital ward. I was shocked by how old she looked: a shrunken version of the woman from my childhood. She was propped up on pillows, too weak to sit.

I hadn't seen her for several years, we fell out of touch after I left Frank. Father had been furious with me and naturally she took his side. Now here I was by her hospital bed and she'd never met my son, knew nothing of my life. But somehow she was still my mother and I was still terrified to lose her.

I managed a smile and told her she looked well. I could see she was happy to hear it. I sat with her for a little while and she let me hold her hand. Her skin was paper dry. I took some Ponds Cold Cream out of my bag. She studied my face as I smoothed it in. Her fingernails were manicured red.

It was quiet in the room, just the murmur of voices in the corridor. She didn't have the strength to ask questions so I started to talk about her grandson.

I told her how proud I was when he collected his degree from Cambridge I told her about his summer trip to Paris; that he'd found himself some work on a newspaper. It was peaceful really. Her jaundiced eyes fixed on me. It felt like she was really listening.

Then I dug in my bag for the photograph I'd brought. It was Reuben in his long black gown on graduation day. The lacquer frame had a small crack on one side; damage done during the long flight over. I told her I'd replace it. 'I'll buy you a new one tomorrow.' She smiled and nodded her head.

She waved for her spectacles as I handed her the frame. She held it up close and studied the picture intently. She ran a finger over the crack. Then she laid it down flat on the bed.

She gestured for me to come closer. 'You were never any good at looking after things.' The strain of talking made her cough and she pressed a tissue to her lips. When she spoke again, her voice was a whisper. 'You weren't the only one. I don't suppose it matters now.'

Then she closed her eyes and turned away and I could tell my visit was over.

As I walked back to my hotel room, I thought about what she'd said. Her words felt like a verdict on my life – a final summing up of how she saw me. After all those years, I was still a clumsy child. '*You were never any good at looking after things.*' Even now I can't be quite sure if she was talking about my son or the picture frame.

I've been over that visit many times in my head but this afternoon I somehow see it differently. It's as if I'm looking from another perspective. As if I hear my mother's words afresh.

It's the second part of her sentence that strikes me as I make my way up in the lift. '*You weren't the only one. I don't suppose it matters now.*' I was too upset to hear it back then.

I open the door to my silent flat. I walk over to my armchair and sit down in it. I feel a sort of hollowing-out. I am dizzy and shut my eyes.

'*You were never any good – you weren't the only one.*'

It is there, isn't it? A note of regret? An acknowledgement, at least, of her own parental flaws. Perhaps not an apology, but it's something – isn't it?

I think of Alice arm-in-arm with Pauline and the onrush of grief takes my breath away.

# 43

My parents sent me flowers when Reuben was born, but nothing for their grandson. It was Mother's handwriting inside the card, she said they'd been terribly busy. Things were going well, New York was swell, they were building up their business on the other side of the ocean. Lena and Gustav had been to the World's Fair. The weather was colder than expected.

Lena sent a postcard with King Kong on the front. She wrote: *Say hello to little Robin.*

Their lack of interest upset me greatly, though I'd heard very little since my wedding day. A first grandchild should be something to celebrate – they didn't even ask me for a photograph.

Now that I was a parent myself, I wanted so much to talk to my mother. All the troubling feelings, the doubts and the fears – I thought she might help me understand them. I begged her to get in touch. I sent her a telegram. I asked what time I might call her. She said phone calls were tricky: the time zones, too costly. She seemed blithely unconcerned about the war.

Margo, on the other hand, could not get enough of my son. She started coming to see me more often and sometimes she'd stay for the night. She played with Reuben for hours on end, tickled his feet and talked nonsense to him. She brought him some orange mittens that she'd knitted herself for my son. When I put them on Reuben, his hands became a pair of lobster's claws. It was sweet of her to do that. I still have those little mittens somewhere. Teeny tiny mittens with giant orange thumbs.

I loved it when Margo was with us, it made me feel like a real mother. We even took Reuben out together, just the three of us, to the park. I felt safe with Margo, she knew what to do: when Reuben started crying, she knew how to stop him; when Reuben was hungry she gave him his bottle; when Reuben needed changing, she changed him.

It was nice for us to walk together, we found ourselves back in the rhythms of our school days. Margo chatted about the gossip in her village and I just let her rattle on. Was there a man? There might have been at one point. I remember a bit of excitement, but whoever he was was short-lived. The stories were about the old folk, her parents and the flowers in the church, the land girls who'd come to live on a nearby farm.

She held Reuben like she'd done it all her life. She tried to show me how once, told me I should be calmer. She taught me a soothing song to sing when Reuben was ready for sleep. She should have had her own children really. Margo would have made a wonderful mother. Of the two of us, it should have been her.

It was Margo's idea to take Reuben to the swimming pool. I hadn't been swimming since Hamburg and was terrified and thrilled in equal measure. She made him a special little suit to wear in a shade she said was Sherwood Forest Green.

We took him to Guildford Lido, which was not too far from the house. The sun shone brightly and the place was packed full. Hard to believe there was a war on.

I got changed beneath a towel while Margo played with Reuben and then we padded down to the shallow end. The water was icy,

124

too cold, I thought, for a baby. But Margo insisted he'd be fine.

'Come on, Gilda. Dunk him under. He might be a bit unsure at first, but he'll love it!'

I held him to my chest and ducked down so both of us were under. When I came up Reuben's face was a picture of shock. Margo said: 'Smile at him, Gilda. Show him it's all right.'

So I smiled at my son and ducked under the water again. When we came up my Reuben was laughing.

'Again!' said Margo.

I ducked him again.

Cool, clear water and the sound of my Reuben laughing.

My son was almost one and a half when Margo got her job at the War Office. He was starting to take an interest in the world, he'd only just learnt to walk. She wrote that she was going to be typing up papers. I didn't even know she'd applied for the role. I was surprised to learn she had such ambition, I'd thought she was content down in Dorset.

She'd been warned the work would keep her very busy and she was afraid she wouldn't be able to visit quite so often. She'd miss us, she said, she'd miss my little son. She asked me to write soon and send a photograph.

She wrote that she was worried about me. She hated it that I was so alone. I was confused by that because I wasn't alone – I had Frank and Reuben. Margo had no one.

I was cheery when I read the letter. I thought: *Good for Margo. Perhaps she'll meet a soldier.* I didn't think I needed her at all. I didn't think I'd miss her too much.

But after I'd read it, I remember feeling terribly tired. I thought perhaps I wouldn't bother with lunch. Instead I'd go upstairs and lie down.

# 44

Alice is pleased as punch with herself and I'm finding it all a bit wearing. She's landed herself a part-time job and she seems to think I approve. I don't know how she's got that idea because I don't approve at all and I've made that clear. I haven't uttered a word on the subject. I haven't once said 'well done'.

I actually telephoned to speak to my son and this morning it feels like Alice is an obstacle. I can hear him moving about in the background but she just keeps chattering on. He's going to leave for work in a minute and I'll miss him altogether if she doesn't stop talking.

It's maddening, she's got herself a part-time job at Harrods. You'd think she had a place on the board.

'It's perfect,' she says. 'I can't quite believe it. Three days a week on the Estée Lauder stand.'

She's going to work on a beauty counter selling over-priced perfumes and creams.

'They'll show me how to demonstrate all their products. I'm really looking forward to learning something new again.'

A shop girl is a shop girl, if you ask me.

Neither of my husbands wanted me to do paid work. They were the providers and I understood that. Sometimes the days felt long but I soon found ways to keep myself busy: I did my hair, I shopped. I never poured a whisky before four.

And oh, this is tedious, she's going to tell me all the details. All about the hours she'll work, the people she'll work with, the perks. 'I'll get a staff discount, Gilda, that means Christmas presents from Harrods this year!' As if I care about Christmas presents. As if I've ever cared about Christmas.

She forgets that I'm Jewish, you know. That her husband is Jewish. Brushes over it like it's nothing, as if none of it matters at all. It's like the ham in the canapés at their wedding – she ignores his background like it's just a bit of history. Frank was right, those canapés were disrespectful. I wish I hadn't eaten quite so many.

Besides, make-up girls are dreadfully cheap. I can't imagine Reuben will like it when she comes home looking like a dolly bird. I can't imagine he'll like it when she's pestered by strange men on the train.

So I tell her – because someone has to – that I'm worried my son will feel neglected.

She says: 'Oh, Gilda, I love looking after him but he's a grown-up. Don't worry, he'll be fine.'

And it's all far too much at this time in the morning, when I haven't had my coffee yet, haven't brushed my teeth. I didn't even call to speak to Alice. I just want to speak to my son.

I say: 'Is he there?' and she tells me I've just missed him.

'He left a couple of minutes ago. I'm so sorry, you should have stopped me.'

She says she'll ask him to ring me tonight and I say 'please do' and put the phone down. But there's a scrunched-up fist of irritation in my stomach and I know that Reuben won't call.

In fact I know exactly what will happen: they'll eat their supper and they'll drink their red wine. They'll talk about everything under the sun but Alice won't mention I rang.

Then afterwards, when they've cleared away the dishes, they'll put on some music and relax. They'll sit side by side on their orange sofa and they'll laugh and play gin rummy until they're tired.

Then one of them will yawn and they'll go on up to bed together. And they'll brush their teeth. And they'll turn out the light. And they won't think once about me.

# 45

There was a dark time when it all seemed empty and black. A time when I couldn't get up. It happened just after Margo left, as if she'd gone and turned all the lights out. And it's strange because the room was white, the bedclothes were white, my nightgown was white. For all that time I was surrounded by white. And yet everything felt so black.

It started very simply one morning; I decided not to get up. I thought I'd stay in bed and rest for a while, but the next day I felt just the same. I didn't feel unwell exactly, but I really couldn't see the point any more. My husband would go on working, my son would go on growing, soldiers on both sides would go on fighting. None of them needed me.

Was it an illness? I'm still not sure. There was an ache, a dull ache, but I couldn't pin down the source. My limbs hurt, my joints hurt, my skin hurt, my bones. Small noises made me flinch – the tick of the clock; Reuben's laughter.

I did see doctors, Frank brought them in. They examined me from top to toe but they couldn't find anything wrong. They thought I was a fraud – I could tell by the sideways looks they gave me. I could tell by the way they shrugged their shoulders and the vitamin tonics they prescribed.

And I wondered if they were right because I didn't feel ill exactly. It's just that I wanted to sleep. It's just that it all felt black.

It was hard on my husband, he couldn't understand it. He saw it as a weakness, a flaw he hadn't been warned of, like finding a moth-hole in a still new cashmere jumper. He must have felt cheated, poor Frank.

At first he did his best to jolly me out of it. He'd stride into the room and open the curtains. 'Come on, Gilda, it's Saturday. Reuben and I need your help to dig for victory!'

But after a while his cheerfulness frayed. 'Gilda, won't you come downstairs? Come on, darling. What's all this about?'

And I couldn't explain because I didn't understand it myself, the tiniest of tasks overwhelmed me. I was worthless, pathetic, not good enough to be Reuben's mother. I'd do the wrong thing, let everyone down: his fever, the time I – no, best not to remember that. I loved my son with all of my heart but I thought he was better off without me.

Frank moved into the spare room. I was glad of it, as I recall. I didn't miss his throaty snores or the sleep-sweaty heft of him beside me. We were never a couple who fitted together naturally. Looking back I think both of us knew it.

I was selfish, I can see that now. The outside world didn't exist. It took everything I had just to wash myself or brush my teeth. My only real interest was sleep.

It was 1941, the height of the Blitz and London wasn't so far away – yet food appeared on a tray every day, my sheets were laundered, Nanny took Reuben out. The household continued much as before. Nothing broke through my cocoon.

I didn't listen when the servants spoke of war; turned the radio off when the news came on. One of the maids heard her brother had been shot down and I felt numb as I offered my condolences.

I refused to leave the house at all, even when the sirens wailed. Frank carried Reuben down to the shelter. It was Frank who kept him safe. I lay there in my room and tried to block out the noise with a pillow.

Reuben suffered most in all of this, though Nanny brought him in to see me every day. She'd knock on the door to my bedroom and I'd try to force a smile.

He was Nanny's little darling by then and I lay there and watched that girl get closer to my son. He clung on to her hand, sought her face for reassurance. Hid behind her legs until she pushed him forward.

And it hurt me, of course it did, but I watched him, unmoving. I didn't try to touch him. I just lay there in my bed and let it happen.

Reuben changed a lot in those months. He grew slimmer and his face less babyish. He had his first haircut. He had his second birthday. His first word was 'nanny' not 'mummy'.

Perhaps he can't remember any of it. But I think these things stay with you. When he struggled to make friends at school, when he wet the bed for longer than he should, I thought about those missing months and I wondered if I was to blame.

# 46

I happen to be passing their house, that's all. I haven't gone out of my way. And since I'm passing in their direction it's natural I should pay them a visit. I've been thinking about the two of them, wondering how they're getting along. I'm curious, that's all, like any mother would be, to know how they're settling in.

It's a Thursday afternoon and they're both of them out, which is a shame but it can't be helped. I'll just take a peek through their downstairs windows, there's no need for them to be home.

This time I don't have to trample through the flowerbeds. I go straight to the passageway, through the side door and into the rear.

The lawn's deserted again this afternoon, it's veiled in smoke from a neighbouring bonfire. If I strain, I can just hear the road nearby. A small dog yaps at an aeroplane.

I go right up to their patio doors. The lights are off inside and it's hard to see though the gloom. Even pressed against the glass, I can only see a little way in.

I try the handle just in case – they aren't exactly security conscious. It turns and the door slides open. The easy glide of it throws me.

*

The living room walls look very different up close. What seemed like a dreary beige outside is actually a lovely golden cream. The paintwork itself is less impressive, that skirting board is a disgrace. Reuben is a clever boy, but he isn't any good with his hands. Just look at the mess he made of my bookshelves.

Still, it's good that they've settled in a bit more. It's good to see some knick-knacks on the shelves. They've framed a couple of pictures from the wedding. There's one of Alice's parents, I notice. I can't see any of me.

I feel a bit uneasy about going upstairs without them here, but I'm not going up to pry. I just want to make sure it's all as it should be. I tread softly, hold the banister, take each step as quietly as I can. Most mothers would have had a full guided tour. Reuben tells me nothing.

I push open the door to what I guess is their bedroom but it turns out to be a bathroom. Their suite is turquoise blue. There's a damp towel lying in a heap on the floor. I pick it up and hang it out to dry.

There's a box of medicine on the shelf. I take a closer look, just to check my son's not ill. I'm relieved to see Alice's name on the prescription label. The pretty pink packet says *Gynovlar*. I can't see any sign of what it's for.

Inside the box I find three strips of pills, each one labelled with a day of the week. I count them – twenty-one on each strip. I'm shocked, she's left her private pills where anyone could see them. I tidy them discreetly out of sight.

I walk back out to the corridor and try the next door, which turns out to be a giant fitted wardrobe. Most of it is taken up with Alice's clothes, just a few hangers there for my son. She has a lot of dresses, my daughter-in-law, and very few extend below the knee. I take one out and I'm surprised by how light it is. It's raspberry

133

red, quite pretty. It has big white plastic buttons down the front.

I turn round to look at the other dresses and that's when I spot Reuben's forest green shirt. I take it out to see how it's wearing and at first I'm really pleased it's good as new. But then I notice the Peter Jones tag, still firmly attached to its cuff. It's been more than a fortnight since Reuben's birthday and he hasn't worn his green shirt once.

The bedroom door must be the one at the end of the corridor. It's ajar already, so it's fine to go inside. When I enter I'm struck by how small it is. There's hardly any space to stand. There's a slightly musty, tea-leaf smell which I can't quite put my finger on. One wall is painted Colman's Mustard yellow and the curtains are patterned with brown and white zigzags. But what shocks me most is the sight of their unmade bed. The blankets are in a tangle with the sheets. The pillows are scattered willy-nilly. Alice's nightdress is scrunched down at the far end. It's mauve and looks like it's nylon.

I can see which side Reuben sleeps on – there's a science fiction book on his bedside table. She has a women's magazine on her side. There's a picture of a blender on the front.

I walk over to my Reuben's side. I plump up the pillows and place them nicely in a stack. I pull the blanket back and smooth out the creases from his sheet. I straighten the covers he'll lie beneath and I tuck them in neatly at one end.

There. Much better. I smile at the thought of him sleeping soundly. It feels good to look after my son.

As I approach the patio doors to leave, I spot a pair of keys on the inside of the lock. There's a spare hanging down on a narrow wire loop. Somehow its smallness makes it OK to take it. I ease it off the loop and slip it into my jacket pocket. It's so light I can hardly tell it's in there.

# 47

Margo wrote often during my illness, though I rarely read her letters to the end. The details of her life seemed too vivid. I didn't want to hear about the war.

When she finally got a few days' leave she telegrammed to say she was coming to visit us. I washed my hair, tried to make myself presentable. I'd thought I might get dressed, but in the end that proved too much.

If Margo was shocked by my appearance she didn't show it. She brought me a bunch of flowers she'd picked and put them in a vase by my bed.

I felt awkward with her. She seemed different, more capable. I thought she was a little bit slimmer. She was wearing a rather smart skirt.

She told me she'd taken a flat in Pimlico with an air raid shelter in the boiler room. She shared it with Diana, a girl our age. 'She's marvellous, Gilda, we're the best of chums. She's mad about the movies too. She does her hair like Rita Hayworth's. I'm sure you'd love her just as much as I do.'

She couldn't get over how much Reuben had changed, her mouth fell open when the nanny brought him in. She picked him up and swung him around and said, 'What a big boy you are!'

I was struck by how happy he seemed. How he ran into her arms when she held them out.

'He's huge,' she said. 'What have you been feeding him?'

I tried to smile but I couldn't manage it because I didn't know the answer to her question.

# 48

Margo doesn't like my new hair. She says it reminds her of Myra Hindley. It's too blonde for someone with my dark features – too far from my natural look.

She's eating British Rail fruitcake as she offers this wisdom, stuffing great chunks of it into her mouth. I can see the fat schoolgirl in her again. 'Should you really eat that?' I say.

And yes, her comments on my hairstyle are fair. But I've found the change liberating so it's going to stay put. Yesterday at the doctor's, the receptionist didn't recognise me; she asked for my name like she'd never seen me before. Acquaintances walk straight past me in the street. Even Margo had to look twice.

It was her foolish fancy to come to Brighton for the day. The seaside in late September would never be my idea of fun. I was about to tell her no, but then she looked so very hopeful. She doesn't get out that often, poor Margo, and I could see how much she wanted to come.

The rain is lashing down when we arrive, just as I knew it would be. I asked Margo to check the forecast but she clearly didn't bother to do so. It hits us as soon as we get off the train. The wind blows straight through me and my headscarf won't stay put.

I want to turn back but Margo says I'm being a spoilsport. 'We're going to the beach if I have to carry you there myself. Come on, Gilda, it'll be fun!'

I don't like Brighton much, if I'm honest, even in the summer it lacks charm. The lanes are full of cheap and tacky baubles, displayed in shop windows like they're diamonds.

Margo tells me: 'Smell the sea air.' But all I can smell is car fumes and chip fat. She's pulling at my mackintosh sleeve: 'Look, there's a seagull!' We're by the sea, what did she expect?

I remember the last time I did this walk down from the station. It was Leo and me, we were arm in arm. My heart was beating fast, fear and anticipation all jumbled into one. We stopped in one of the pubs along the way. I gulped down three whiskies in a row.

Margo wants to buy some postcards but she doesn't have anyone to send them to. I'm her only friend and I'm here with her. She insists on buying three just the same.

When we get to the beach, I'm cold and wet. The sky is dark grey and there's no one else about. The shoreline is littered with soot-black seaweed.

Margo shouts: 'It's beautiful! Take off your stockings and shoes!' She wants us to go for a paddle, I think she might have gone mad.

There's absolutely no way on earth that a single item of my clothing is coming off, but Margo's already kicked off her shoes and has one stocking down round her ankle. I stand and watch her, she's just like a child sometimes. 'Five minutes,' I say, 'then we're going somewhere warm.' Margo nods and trots off to the sea.

She looks quite a sight as she hobbles into the water. Her bare feet negotiate the pebbles with an astounding lack of grace. It's obviously freezing but she's screaming and laughing as the waves crash in. Margo's fifty-three, that's older than me. Sometimes I wish she'd remember that.

Her feet are bright pink when she finally emerges, she's panting and grinning and looks very pleased with herself. 'Gilda, it was wonderful! You should have come in!'

'Yes, well someone had to stand here and look after your handbag and shoes.'

I pass her her stockings and she uses them to dry her feet.

Margo wants fish and chips for lunch. She says that's what you do when you're on a seaside trip. But I'm cold and wet and I'm blowed if I'm going to eat lunch from a newspaper. We're going to a decent restaurant and I'll pay for us both if I must.

We walk away from the beach and head for The Lanes. The drizzle is constant, just a few more people around. Margo keeps spotting restaurants she likes but none of them is quite what I'm after.

Eventually we come to an Edwardian building, it's a proper fish restaurant with white linen table cloths. Margo is worried it will be too expensive but I head on inside.

The maître d' is charm itself and doesn't flinch at Margo with her stockings in her hand. He apologises for the dreadful weather and shows us to a table by the fire. I send Margo off to make herself presentable. I can still see a tidemark on the hem of her brown skirt.

The waiter brings us both a dry sherry.

'Well, this is nice,' I say.

Margo doesn't seem happy at all, she doesn't take a sip of her sherry. She looks at the menu with a worried frown. She whispers: 'I'll just have the soup.'

I tell her lunch will be my treat as it was my choice to come to this restaurant.

She says, on reflection, perhaps she'll try the Dover sole. Perhaps she'll have some petit pois. And a glass of white wine would be nice. I don't bat an eyelid. I order the trout meunière for myself.

And we'll share a bottle of wine. Why not? And perhaps another glass of that sherry.

When the food arrives it's delicious and really piping hot. I tell Margo the news about Alice's job. She says she's pleased, which surprises me.

'She sounds like a clever girl, Gilda. I'm glad she's not stuck at home. A lot of them work now and I think it's a good thing. It's 1969 – a different world from when we were young. We need to try and keep up with the times.'

'Yes, that's all very well. But who's going to look after Reuben?'

She picks at her fish bone with greasy fingers. 'He'll be out at work himself all day. It's not going to kill him to cook his own dinner once in a while.'

She's not his mother, she doesn't understand. He's already lost too much weight.

It's still raining when we leave and I'm tired and full and ready to go home. Margo wants to look round the antique shops though I tell her they're all full of tat. We go in four or five and she comes out disappointed. Most of the items belong in a junkyard, even Margo can see that.

Eventually she finds a painting of a stormy sea with dark skies and waves crashing onto a beach. It looks very amateur if you ask me, but she says she has to have it. The perspective is all wrong and I've never seen a sea that shade of green. She pays two pounds, six shillings for it. Money she could have put towards lunch.

I can't see why anyone would want such a picture, but Margo says: 'It will remind me of our lovely day out in Brighton.'

I know we're going to pass the guest house long before we do. It's the obvious way to go and by far the quickest route. I could have taken us up a back street I suppose, but something stopped me. I realise I want to see it. Remember what Leo and I did there.

It looks exactly the same: the same seedy frontage, the same tatty sign. The paint is still peeling like a nasty skin disease. The windows are still caked in grime.

It's been more than twenty years and nothing's changed. The Bellevue Guest House, well, that name's a lie. I can see the room we stayed in on the third floor, the window that looked onto the car park. Stale sweat, mildew and an ashtray that hadn't been emptied.

I quicken our pace, worried the owner might come out. She was a vile creature, that one – wheezed as if she had consumption. She tutted as we paid the bill and made us feel like criminals; as if we were the dirty ones while she and her fleapit were clean.

Margo doesn't know about this place. I've never told her how or where it happened. She's going on about her blessed painting. You'd think she had the ceiling of the Sistine Chapel tucked under her arm.

# 49

Margo is a good person, I've never doubted that. But the fact is I'd still be married to Frank if she hadn't gone and written that letter. After the split she was very judgmental; kept reminding me of my marriage vows and my duty towards my husband. But she was the one who got me the job in London. She's not as blameless as she thinks.

I can picture it now so vividly: Margo in her Pimlico flat. All rosy cheeks and bright, clear eyes and doing her bit for Blighty. She'd have sat there in that messy little room with jumble all over her bed, thinking: *What can I do to help poor dear Gilda? How can I perk her up?*

And then it would have come to her, the perfect solution. She'd find me a volunteer job. Show me people worse off than myself. I needed saving and Margo would save me. She would tell her friends what a hole I was in and together they'd pull me out.

The maid brought the letter into my bedroom and I recognised the handwriting straight away. Unsophisticated. Round like her face. It's still unsophisticated now.

*London, October 1941.*

*Dearest Gilda,*

*I've been speaking to a friend who works with Jewish refugees. She's looking for people to teach English to German-speakers and I thought you'd be ideal! She says it doesn't matter if you don't have experience. She just wants a teacher for a few hours a week.*

*London has been quieter these past few months. There is still the occasional air raid but nothing compared to what we've been through. Old Hitler seems more interested in Russia now. We're all doing our best to get back to business as usual and that is where you come in! Imagine how much fun you could have! You'd meet people from all over the world. You really would make an excellent teacher. I couldn't think of anyone better.*

*Darling, I know you've been unwell, but this is a chance for you to really make a difference. Gilda, people need you.*

*All my love,*

*Margo*

I read the letter twice and I thought it was ridiculous. I was lying in an unmade bed in a crumpled greying nightdress and with hair that hadn't been washed. Whatever else was going on in the world, nobody needed me.

I woke to find Frank standing over me. 'Gilda, I have to talk to you.'

It had been a few days since I'd seen him and I realised he looked older. His face was thinner – dark shadows under his eyes.

'Margo says she's found you some volunteer work. I've written back to tell her you'll take it.'

I was upset by that. I felt they were plotting against me. I said I couldn't do it. I didn't have the strength to do it.

He shook his head. 'Gilda, please, this has to stop. You and I have so much to be grateful for.'

# 50

It just so happens that I'm running out of face cream, and if I'm going to buy some more, I might as well buy it from Harrods. Estée Lauder has an offer on, I saw it in *The Times*. If I'm going to splash out on a brand new jar, I'd be foolish not to buy it from there.

So what if it's Alice's first day on the job? It's nice that I'm going to support her. It's not as if I plan to make a nuisance of myself, I'll just buy my jar of face cream and then go. I haven't told her I'm coming, of course. I thought that was only considerate. She'll be nervous, I'm sure, about getting things right and I really wouldn't want to make things worse.

The sky is dark when I open the curtains and the windows are streaked with rain. It's not what I'd hoped for when I made this plan. I'd imagined my trip to Knightsbridge in clear crisp sunlight. I'll have to rethink the outfit I put out. More ironing, such a pain.

I look through my collection of dark navy slacks and sigh at the dullness of them all. Then I remember, tucked away at the back of my wardrobe is a pair of white capris pants. My sister made me buy them last time I was over there. I haven't worn them once since then, not even to try them on.

I pull them out; they still have their New York tags on. She told me they were slimming, though it's hard to imagine it. The white glows pristine in the gloom of my bedroom.

I have to really pull at them to get the fabric over my thighs. I battle with the zip, which catches at the flesh on my hip. I have to suck my stomach in, but they're supposed to be tight-fitting. Once they're on they're as snug as a long-line girdle. I put a nice warm twinset on top and slip on a pair of kitten heels.

I brush my hair with extra care because Alice hasn't seen my new style. I apply mascara, rouge and lipstick. I want to look my very best.

When I look at myself in the hallway mirror, my reflection makes me smile. My sister was right, these trousers do make me look slim. It's modern – the outfit goes well with my hairdo – but it's modest, not too mutton dressed as lamb.

I take the lift down to the lobby and peer out through the glass to the street. It's black as night; the pavement is awash with puddles.

The concierge looks me up and down. He puffs his cheeks and tuts. 'It's Noah's ark out there this morning.'

He looks at my capris pants and grins.

It's only a very short walk to the Tube but the rain finds its way through my mackintosh in seconds. It trickles down through the buttonholes and my capris pants soak it up like a sponge. The wind is so strong that my umbrella's useless. My fingers are freezing. My headscarf has slipped.

By the time I get to the station I'm soaked right through to the skin. There are muddy spatters up the backs of my legs and my hair hangs in straggles round my chin.

And I wonder for a second what on earth it is I'm doing here. Why I felt I had to make this trip with the weather as bad as it is. But the thought of going back out in the deluge is worse than the thought of pushing on. So I buy myself a Tube ticket and I put myself on the escalator and I let myself be carried down and down.

## 51

Frank came upstairs to wish me good luck as I got ready to go to London to meet Margo's refugee friend. I was sitting at the dressing table, putting on my make-up – drawing on my eyebrows with a pencil.

He kissed me softly on the top of the head, the contact surprised me and made me jump. The hand that was holding the pencil jolted and my left eyebrow went on crooked.

He looked better and happier than he had done in weeks and I realised how worried he'd been. I smiled at his reflection in the mirror. My drawn-on crooked eyebrow made a question of it.

I had to stop to catch my breath on the short walk to the station. It had been almost a year since I'd left the house and I felt like a child dressed in someone else's clothes. Everything was too big for me. My shoes were too heavy and I toppled on my heels. The street felt too wide. The few cars on the road moved too fast. Even the sky seemed dirty and grey. I wanted to turn and go home.

The train to Waterloo was crowded – soldiers and civilians all jostled in together. More people and noise and smells and smoke in that one carriage than I'd seen in a year.

The contrast with my bedroom was almost too much. I was

dislocated, none of it seemed real. When a woman accidentally knocked me with her handbag, I was surprised that I actually felt it. When a soldier offered me his window seat, I was astonished he'd noticed me there.

I wiped the condensation from the glass and looked out at a landscape I no longer recognised. We crawled past nameless stations and I felt myself utterly lost. It was only when Battersea Power Station loomed that I realised, with relief, we were almost at our destination. Its familiar chimneys soothed me.

Waterloo Station was bustling with men in khaki. I took the Underground to Euston and I walked the rest of the way.

I'd tried to hide from the war since I got ill, but I hadn't been able to avoid it altogether. I'd seen the city glow from my bedroom window, heard the bombers flying overhead. Now I strode past streets of buildings dissected like dolls' houses, trees stripped bare as if winter had come early. I smelt the open drains and powdered brick, I felt the crunch of glass beneath my feet.

But when I turned the corner into Bloomsbury Square, people were sitting on benches smoking just as if there were no war at all. I wondered how they did it, those people. How they coped with it every night. How they got up in the morning and dusted themselves off and then turned up for jobs on time.

## 52

The Harrods doorman tilts his cap as I enter but I know I look a mess and head straight to the ladies' room. The toilet attendant turns the other way as I blot at my capris pants with the hand towel.

My nose is red, my mascara has run and my eyes look bright and fevered in their sockets. I comb my fingers through my ratty hair and try to lift it where it's plastered to my scalp. I powder my nose but the red shows through it. I smear on some lipstick but it clashes with my wind-blown cheeks.

I had thought I might say hello to my daughter-in-law, show her my new hairstyle, buy a jar of face cream. I take a last look at my ravaged reflection and decide that's out of the question.

The cosmetics hall is neon lit and bustling. It takes me a minute to get my bearings and to see my way down through the throng. I spot the Estée Lauder counter on the other side of the room. The customers are several-deep around it, all of them pushing to be served.

I find a quiet place where I can observe. It's next to a giant column, tucked nicely out of sight.

There are four assistants at the Estée Lauder stand and they're not what I expected at all. Their faces are soft and subtly made-up. They are all wearing neat navy suits.

I almost miss Alice because she looks so very different. Her hair is scraped back into a high, sleek ponytail. She is smiling brightly as she serves a woman who's dithering over her change. My daughter-in-law waits patiently, though the customers behind are jostling for attention. When the woman finally puts her purse away, Alice moves straight on to the next.

She gets no time to catch her breath but it doesn't seem to unnerve her. She looks thoughtful and engaged, her pace doesn't falter. No one would ever guess this is her first day on the job. No one would ever guess that her mascara is usually smudged.

I'm rather impressed, despite myself, though a shop girl is a shop girl and there's no escaping that. If she's not going to stay at home and take care of my son, at least she's doing something she excels at.

And a strange thing happens while I'm watching Alice: it's like I step back into my younger self. I forget I'm a divorcee in damp capris pants. For a moment, I'm the same age as she is.

I remember how good it felt to be engaged like she is now. I remember how it felt to be needed. Sometimes I got so busy that I didn't even notice the time. Sometimes I got so busy that hours passed like minutes.

I envy my daughter-in-law that confidence, that absorption. I had that once.

# 53

Bloomsbury House was a grand old building near Holborn station. It rose proudly above its neighbours like the tallest boy in the school. Men in shabby overcoats leant against the sandbags and smoked. I felt their eyes on me.

Doubts crowded in. I shouldn't have come; I had nothing to offer. I wished I had eaten some breakfast that morning. I wished I'd worn a different coat.

I almost turned round, but something kept me there on the doorstep. I reached for the bell and I pressed it.

Zelda Ward, the organiser, was not what I'd imagined. She was young for a start and she didn't look terribly Jewish. She had a froth of orange curls on her head.

She said: 'Welcome, Mrs Goodman. I'm delighted to meet you.' And she pumped my hand heartily as I stood there on the threshold. Then she gave me a look of such kindness and sympathy that I wondered if she'd got me mixed up. I was about to explain that I wasn't a refugee when she stopped me with a hand on my shoulder. 'Margo's told me so much about you. I'm so very glad you're here.'

I wondered what I'd done to deserve her sympathy. I was anxious about what Margo had told her.

She led me into the entrance hall, which felt like a faded stately home. A spiral staircase swirled up from a fine mosaic floor. One of the walls was covered with notices: rules and instructions, situations vacant and rooms to rent, efforts to find lost family and friends; all of them written in German.

We went through a passageway into a vast and crowded reception hall. Older men and women sat reading in their overcoats while younger ones stood in line to discuss their cases. The room was cold and smelled of damp. A sense of tired endurance prevailed.

It was queer to hear so much German being spoken – to be truly surrounded by it, as if I were back there. I heard a Hamburg accent and turned round to see who it was. But I didn't once think: *These are my people*. I didn't once think: *This could be me*.

Miss Ward stopped and looked round at the room. 'These people have given up so much. They've lost their homes, their possessions, their families. They've been through unimaginable hardships. They desperately need our help. What we try to do is to offer them some hope of a new life here. All our money comes from donations and all our workers are volunteers too. Sometimes it feels like we barely touch the surface but everything we do will make a difference to someone. We mustn't lose sight of that.'

She took me into an office and asked a girl to bring us tea. We sat together and there was a pause in which that sympathetic look appeared again.

I was afraid Miss Ward was going to ask too much of me. I couldn't help those people fix their lives; I couldn't cope with too much rawness. I'd been ill. I hadn't left the house for a year. There were others who were stronger, could do more.

When the tea arrived, Miss Ward poured it. It was weak as water and there wasn't any sugar. 'So what I hope, Mrs Goodman, is that you can teach a few classes. The more English they can learn the easier it will be for them. It's dangerous to speak German here these days. The sooner they can get by without it, the better.'

I looked down at my lap. 'Yes. I see.'

'Margo was right, your English is flawless. We could really use you. Do you think you could spare a few hours out of your week?'

Later that evening, I thought about Miss Ward's question. I thought about how the days dragged, how Frank only kissed me on the top of my head, how much my son seemed to love his nanny and how timid he was now with me.

I rang Miss Ward the following morning and said yes.

# 54

Margo wants me to go with her to the doctor's surgery this afternoon. It's just an ingrown toenail, but she wants to have somebody there. Friendships can get terribly mundane, and the longer you have them, the more mundane they get. There was a time when a phone call meant an invitation to a dinner party. Now it's doctor's surgeries, dental appointments and shopping for support tights.

'Do come, Gilda,' her voice is plaintive. 'It'll be nice. We can go and have a cup of tea later.'

I'd like to go with her, of course I would. Who wouldn't want to see a toenail operation? I live for outings like that. But unfortunately, I have plans already. I can't just rearrange my day.

She is upset. 'Come with me, Gilda. It's good for you to get out. They're going to take my toenail off. I might need your help to get home.'

She's fifty-three, for goodness' sake, she can sit in a taxi on her own.

The Harrods doorman smiles as I enter and says: 'Madam. Nice to see you.'

I head straight for the cosmetics hall and my pillar near the Estée Lauder stand. It isn't too crowded so I can get a really good

154

view. I've remembered to wear my comfortable shoes so I can stay here all day if I like.

It calms me to watch Alice at work. I like the way she interacts with customers. She never frowns or argues back, takes even the worst ones in her stride.

I find this version of my daughter-in-law fascinating, I stand and watch and the afternoon flies by. I like the way she helps people with their choices, stops and considers before choosing them a lipstick. I like the way she wraps up purchases, so quick and decisive and neat.

## 55

The first time I met Alice, my son took us for lunch at The Cosmo on the Finchley Road. They'd been together six months by then and Reuben was very excited.

The Cosmo used to be Leo's favourite place. It was full of refugees, people he knew from his past. He'd spend his afternoons there, playing chess and eating squares of sweet *szarlotka*. He said it reminded him of the cafes of his youth. It was crowded and always dense with smoke.

I hadn't been since Leo left and I felt nervous as I walked through the door. Reuben was already there, sitting at a table in the middle. My son with a blonde girl. The only blonde head in the room.

They didn't see me, they were locked in conversation. His hand was on the back of her chair and he leant his head towards her. I noticed his eyes were soft and full of love. I was shocked. I didn't realise he could do that.

And it wasn't just that I was seeing another side to him, it felt like I was meeting a stranger; as if I didn't know my son at all. And it felt like they were already a unit and I was left out on my own.

She stood up to greet me and I saw straight away how small she was. She went up on tiptoes to kiss me on the cheek, ignoring my outstretched hand.

'Mother, this is Alice.' My Reuben beamed with pride. I noticed her nose was too small for her face. Tiny. No bigger than a toddler's.

Alice was friendly and charming and kind, and right from that first minute I could tell I'd struggle to like her. My Reuben looked at her as if she were perfect, as if she were a goddess at his side.

The waiter brought the menu over and Alice almost vanished behind it. She asked me what a *Schnitzel* was and I realised she didn't have a clue. She said she'd never had *Sauerkraut* before. When I told her it was pickled cabbage she wrinkled her nose. She made me feel more foreign. She said: 'Gilda, this all looks so interesting.' Then she went and ordered chicken, so bland she could have eaten it anywhere.

After the meal they brought over coffees and Alice went to the ladies' room. Reuben watched her as she crossed the floor. Finally it was just me and my son.

He said: 'I'm going to ask her to marry me.' His eyes shone bright and his smile was very wide. I thought how rarely I'd seen him that happy and I knew I should be happy too.

And I said: 'Gosh. That's really wonderful, darling.' Though I didn't think it was wonderful and I wasn't quite sure why. I asked him: 'Do you think she'll say yes?' And I hoped beyond hope she'd say no.

Then Alice came back and she sat down at the table and Reuben didn't look at me once after that. And I knew that he would propose very soon, perhaps even ask her that night. And I knew that she would say yes, of course. How could any girl refuse my son?

Later that evening I telephoned Frank to tell him I'd met Alice too. I convinced him the whole thing was Reuben's idea – that he'd wanted his mother's approval.

Frank said he was pleased for me, happy I'd met her at last. 'Did Reuben tell you he's planning to propose? Berta and I think it's smashing news.'

I said: 'Yes, of course.' Though I didn't give a damn what Berta thought. 'I expect she'll start to feel part of the family now she's finally met her future mother-in-law.'

# 56

I was more nervous than I'd been on my wedding day as I walked into the classroom that first time. There were sixteen of them there waiting for me. Sixteen faces watched me falter in the doorway.

I'd chosen my outfit carefully, a tweed skirt and jacket and some sensible brown shoes. I thought they looked like teachers' clothes, I thought at least I'd look like a teacher.

And it must have worked because they all stood up as if I was the person they were waiting for. I wanted to tell them they'd made a mistake and hide away at the back of the room. But I managed 'good afternoon' in a quavering voice and they all said 'good afternoon' back. I hit my hip hard on the corner of the table. It was painful and I wanted to rub it.

I'd planned to write my name on the blackboard but my hand shook so much I couldn't get the chalk to work. Instead I had to say it: 'My name is Gilda Goodman.' The room was silent. I looked round at all the faces. They thought I knew what to do.

Flustered, I turned to the pale young woman on my right. 'What is your name?'

She looked even more scared than I was. She cleared her throat and said 'My?'

I asked her again.

159

She pointed to herself. 'My name Esther Levy.'

I corrected her. 'My name *is* Esther Levy.'

I turned to the older man sitting next to her. 'What is your name?'

'My name *is* Joseph Beckman.'

And that was it. I'd made a start.

It was an unconventional classroom. There were no desks just one large rectangular table. Never quite enough chairs despite my pleadings, one or two of the younger students always went without. They'd spend the whole two hours standing against the cold back wall and never complained of it once.

There was a small blackboard and some cheap white chalk, which crumbled into dust no matter how lightly I pressed. I finished every lesson with white smudges on my skirt and sweater.

My pupils that first year were a mix of ages and backgrounds. There was a baker from Prague, a young housewife from Berlin, lawyers from Budapest and Krakow. All of them had made it to England in the final wave of refugees. They'd come over with nothing and were struggling, still, to find work.

But in the lessons we never talked about the lives they'd left behind. Questions about families and homes were often too distressing to answer. Instead we focused on the words they needed to get through the challenges ahead of them. I learnt as much as any of my students did. They wanted words for things I'd never done before: queuing for coupons, pawning a watch or finding directions to the nearest air raid shelter.

I started to see how very fortunate I was. When they asked about my life I felt embarrassed to answer them. My family was healthy, we lived far enough from London to feel safe. We still had staff, a car, a house with spare bedrooms. I'd never cooked a meal for myself.

My students worked hard; they wrote down everything I said in notebooks or on little scraps of paper. The young ones learnt quickly, they heard something once and they knew it. The others – the lawyer, the baker – found it all more of a strain. It made my heart ache to watch those older men stumbling.

The class was just a few hours three times a week. I came home tired yet full of excitement. I found myself with things to say: I had opinions and stories to tell over dinner. I regained my appetite, took an interest in the world again. I felt I had something to contribute.

Those teaching afternoons became the high point of my week and the other days arranged themselves around them. I spent my free time planning lessons, looking up grammar points and marking homework.

Margo was thrilled. 'Zelda tells me your students adore you. She says they're practically fluent already. I knew you'd be a hit.'

We'd get together before class sometimes to eat lunch in a cafe near Russell Square. She couldn't stay long, just half an hour and then she'd walk back to Whitehall. It was nice for us to have that regular connection again. We were two working women together.

And somehow during that first year I started to believe that I was a decent teacher. Not the best there is, not inspirational, but I did have something to offer. It was wonderful to watch my students improve and to know I'd given them the words they were using. I was proud of them. I was proud of myself. I think Frank was proud of me too.

# 57

It's Wednesday morning and I'm at a loose end, I'd planned to go with Margo to a flower show today but her toe is still painful and she says she needs to rest it. I should be kind and offer to sit with her. I'm filled with claustrophobia at the thought of it.

Instead I think I'll drop in on Alice at work. It's something I've been doing quite often of late. It's nice to get dressed up for these outings – it adds a sense of purpose to my day. It's a little queer, I suppose, but I'm getting to know my daughter-in-law. It's good to have this window onto her life. It makes me feel closer to my son.

I normally get to Harrods after lunch but today I get there just before noon. I stand in my usual spot by the pillar and watch her, quite happily, for an hour. Her hair is pulled back neatly in a tortoiseshell headband. She's learnt how to use the little till. The other girls seem to like her, I can tell by the way they nod their approval. Alice has become part of their team.

At one o'clock it's time to get a sandwich – the cafe down the road does a nice egg and cress. I pick up my handbag and turn towards the exit. My mouth floods with saliva at the thought of it.

There is something about the dark-haired man that stops me in my tracks. He strolls across the hall like it's his harem. He nods to a perfume girl, who titters into her hand. He smiles at the middle-aged woman on Chanel, who blushes but doesn't smile back.

He is tall and lean yet solidly built with the chiselled jaw and cheekbones of a matinee idol. His teeth are as white as his freshly starched shirt. His suit is expensively cut. There's a baize-green badge on his left lapel, which tells me he's a member of staff. A purple silk cravat adds a touch of the playboy.

I monitor my response as he passes me and am pleased to notice the lack of one. These days my heart no longer flutters for a handsome face, my pulse no longer races, my stomach has ceased to contract. I'm well aware of his masculine beauty, but I can make a cool assessment, unclouded by matters of desire. There's a certain sort of symmetry to him, a hunger, an animal strength. Once it would have drawn me like a moth to a flame; now I see the danger behind it.

His path takes him near the Estée Lauder counter and I notice my daughter-in-law stand a little straighter. She pulls her shoulders back and lifts her chin, to emphasise her minimal bust. She raises one hand and touches the side of her neck. She looks at the man and then looks away quickly. A moment later, she looks at him again.

At first I'm unsettled by this sign of disloyalty, I worry what it means for my son. But I tell myself her reaction is a reflex: she's a human adult in her reproductive prime. It's over within seconds and she's focused on her work again. There's nothing there for anyone to mind.

## 58

Reuben was still very shy with me. He was two years old, just starting to speak. My illness had created a distance between us and I struggled to bridge the gap.

I'd stand on the train on my way back from work and rack my brain for things to say to him. *I just met a big orange cat in the driveway. Don't you look smart in your new pyjamas?*

I remember the flutter of nerves I felt as I heard his slippered feet on the stairs. I smiled at the door as the nanny led him in.

His hair was always neatly combed. His scalp showed white beneath his knife-sharp parting. I breathed in his smell of toothpaste and soap, tried not to see the tension in his face.

'I – I just met a big orange cat – in the – driveway.'

He turned to watch his nanny as she made her way back to the nursery.

'I – don't you look smart . . .'

He stood stiff as a board.

'Come in properly, darling. It's lovely to see you.'

He shuffled in slowly to the seat that was furthest away from me.

'Did you see the soldiers in the park today?'

A slight nod of the head as he looked at his lap.

'Did Nanny play a game with you?'

Shrug.

'Did – did you have toast and jam for tea?'

I told myself it would get easier: once he knew more words, once he'd learnt to read. I'd never spent that sort of time with my own parents, I didn't know what to expect. I told myself he was a quiet, shy boy, just not the sort of child to show too much affection. Next time, perhaps, I'd ask him about his train set. I'd find the perfect thing to say next time.

And little by little it did get easier. Slowly I felt it change. One day Reuben didn't look back for his nanny. One day he sat a fraction closer to me.

The summer he turned three he asked me to read him a story. We went up and chose the book together: *Pets and Playmates*. He wanted to see the pictures of Topsy so he climbed up and sat on my knee.

My whole body tensed as he leant his weight against me. I felt the solid warmth of him as he sank down into my lap. His hair smelt of carbolic soap and the mince he'd had for tea. Every time he wriggled I held my breath, terrified he'd want to get back down.

He studied each picture as if it were a map. He wouldn't let me turn the pages, he had to do that. He followed my finger as I scanned the simple sentences, made sure I didn't skip a single word.

When we finished he asked me for another book. We went back upstairs and chose *The Bee Who Would not Work*. I did a special voice for lazy old Fumble Bee and Reuben giggled with delight.

When Nanny finally came to take him he asked me for one last tale. I told him it was bedtime though I wanted him to stay.

She said: 'Come on Reuben. Mummy has things she needs to do.'

He took her hand as they left the room, but in the doorway he looked back and he smiled at me.

## 59

I am keeping an eye on the dark-haired man. Someone has to, it's only sensible. Alice is so young and pretty – vulnerable, I think. It's just a little thing I'm doing for my son.

I've learnt his routine off by heart: he walks through the hall on his way to his lunch break. As my watch strikes one he steps over the threshold like the little wooden cuckoo on a cuckoo clock.

He grooms his hair as he crosses the room: pats it with both hands, one to front and one to back. It's a practised gesture, precise in its configuration. It makes me suspect a hidden bald patch.

He passes my pillar as he walks towards the Estée Lauder counter. He nods at the perfume girl, smiles at the woman on Chanel. Increasingly, these days, he stops for a chat with Alice.

Today my daughter-in-law is serving a customer so he tries to look casual as he waits for her to finish. He makes a comment to her horsey colleague who giggles like a love-struck teen. When the customer leaves, my daughter-in-law looks over. The dark man moves closer like he's drawn on a string.

Their chemistry is visible, even from here. The man strokes the counter top as if he's preparing to mount it. Alice tucks a strand of hair behind her ear. She looks up at him through her lashes. He is doing most of the talking. My daughter-in-law nods along.

Finally he moves to leave and I realise I've been holding my breath. He leans a little further over the counter and offers a parting remark. Alice throws her head back and laughs, eyes shut, exposing the flesh of her neck. It takes her several seconds to compose herself. My heart beats violent in my chest.

# 60

Leo Zubek had been a teacher back in Poland. He'd been a husband and a father and taught English in a school. By the time I met him he was none of those things, though he didn't yet know it and he wouldn't have believed it. He still thought his wife and son were somewhere in Europe. Both of them together, alive.

I'd been working at Bloomsbury House for almost two years when he sat in on one of my lessons. I didn't want him there at all but Zelda had asked me to allow it. I'd never had an observer in my class. I thought he was there to spy. I felt put upon. Resentful. Defensive on behalf of my students. If I could have called it off, I would have.

Leo stood at the back of the classroom. He was tall and dark. He chewed his pencil and took notes on my performance. I was painfully aware of his every movement. Each time he wrote a word it distracted me.

I was so flustered I got my grammar wrong and my students had to correct me. Then I asked the Hungarian the same question twice. I dropped the chalk and whacked my elbow against the blackboard. Leo just smiled and made another note in his little grey pad. I almost asked him to leave.

After the lesson he stayed behind and told me he'd enjoyed the class. He suggested we go for tea and talk about it, he thought we could swap ideas. I didn't want to go with him. I wanted to get back and read to Reuben before bedtime. But Zelda had asked me to help this young man so, reluctantly, that's what I did.

We went to the cafe near Russell Square where Margo and I had our lunches. It was bright and light and crowded and I felt we'd be safe sitting there. Leo ordered our watery tea and he drank his black with three sugars. He stirred the cup long after it was necessary. The sound set my teeth on edge.

When he was happy with his tea, he brought out his grey notebook and without any preamble he tore my lesson apart. He took me through every slip-up I'd made. He teased me about the chalk marks on my skirt. He said I'd got one of my tenses muddled. I should be speaking less German; get the students to speak more English. By the time he'd reached the end of his notes I was ready to lean over and slap him.

And I was about to tell him how I'd never been trained and was doing my best in difficult circumstances. And I was about to say that if he was such an expert perhaps he'd like to teach the class himself. And I was about to say that I was sorry, but actually my students liked how I taught. I was about to say all those things, but he got in there first.

'These mistakes are small, Mrs Goodman, you really are a wonderful teacher. Your students adore you and they seem to be learning fast. You're very natural in the classroom. Not everyone has that gift.'

I think it was then I noticed his eyes were really more green than brown and he had tiny flecks of grey hair at his temples, at odds with his youthful face. He smiled at me again and my stomach flipped.

When he put his grey notepad away, I noticed he had beautiful hands.

# 61

It's the end of the day and Harrods is closing, I decide to wait for Alice by the Basil Street exit. It's still nice and light and the weather's unseasonably warm. The clocks go back in a fortnight so I'm right to make the most of it.

Basil Street is narrow and the Harrods staff exit is halfway down. I stick to the shadows on the other side of the road. I find a recessed doorway with a large metal bin from the next door café in it. Damp cardboard on the floor suggests I'm not the first to stop here. The stench of urine catches at my throat. I take my scented hand cream from my bag and dab a little dot beneath each nostril.

I am shielded by the dustbin as I scan the faces emerging from the building. I feel like an anxious mother at the school gates. The youngsters call down the street to one another. 'You going to the Ad Lib later?' 'See you at the Stockpot!' The air is charged with Friday night excitement.

I spot a couple of Alice's colleagues: the curly haired one and the tall one with the equine features. They skip out onto the pavement, their cigarettes already lit. The horsey one pulls a compact from her bag and blots at her forehead with a powder puff.

I study the pair for a couple of minutes, both clearly single and hunting for husbands. The curly one rolls up the waistband of her skirt. It's already inches shorter than it should be.

I sense Alice's presence before I see her. There's a tingle at the back of my skull, a prickle, almost like pins and needles. I fix my eyes on the Harrods doorway and slowly count to ten beneath my breath. When I get to nine, I force myself to turn away. When I turn back to the doorway, there she is.

I look round, exhilarated, for a witness to this bit of magic. There's no one there, of course. There never is.

I focus again on my daughter-in-law. She seems a little weary. Her make-up has worn off and her shoulders are hunched. She looks like she's ready for home.

The curly girl calls over: 'Alice, we're off to the pub. You'll come with us for a quick one, won't you? Barbara says there's going to be a band on.'

My daughter-in-law shakes her head. 'I can't tonight. My husband's expecting me.'

The horsey girl pipes up. 'But you have to, it's Friday night! One drink won't hurt, will it?'

'Come on,' shouts the curly one. 'I'll buy you a Babycham!'

I can see the indecision in Alice's eyes. These are still new colleagues and she wants to be part of their gang. She bites her bottom lip. Reuben, surely, won't mind. He sometimes has a drink himself on a Friday. She won't be more than half an hour late.

She walks towards the girls, smiling and shaking her head. *Go on then, but just the one. I shouldn't really, but go on.*

Just when I think that everything's settled, the dark man emerges from the Harrods building. The girls turn towards him as if in response to a signal.

His smile seems, to me, to be directed at Alice. He exposes every one of his Dulux-gloss teeth. He's got a friend with him, a greasy Teddy Boy. Cocksure is the word that springs to mind.

The curly girl calls: 'Hiya, lads. We're just off to The Grenadier. There's going to be a band tonight. D'you fancy it?'

172

The Teddy Boy winks at the dark-haired man. 'What d'you reckon, Terry? Shall we risk it?'

Alice stares at her hands. She doesn't acknowledge the dark-haired man. She doesn't smile and giggle like the other two girls. She doesn't encourage him to join them.

The dark man shrugs. 'I don't see why not. I think this lot'll be gentle with us. Won't you?'

I pretend to tighten the strap of my handbag as I follow the group down the street. The dark man slows his pace so he's next to Alice. She doesn't react to his presence. He turns to talk to her but she avoids his gaze. She looks at shop windows, the pavement, the cars. She calls: 'Is it far?' to the girls in front. They tell her it's just round the corner.

I remember how it was that first time with Leo, how I tried my best to ignore him while my heart hammered hard inside my chest; the sickening clench of excitement in my stomach; the mix of confusion and fear; how aware I was of every movement, every sound. I couldn't turn it off, even when I wanted to.

That's what Alice is feeling now – her lack of response to him gives her away. It's not her fault, when it happens you can't control it.

I picture my Reuben's worried expression as he waits for his wife to come home.

The Grenadier turns out to be a narrow white building and I watch the Harrods group walk up to the doorway. They are all crammed together, jostled by the drinkers each side.

The dark man lets Alice go ahead of him. His eyes don't leave her for a second. And it's only very brief – so quick I can't be totally sure – but I think I see his hand dart out and pat her on the bottom as she passes.

I tell myself I must have got it wrong. Alice walks on as if nothing has happened. Perhaps he stopped short, didn't quite make contact? Perhaps she didn't feel it through her skirt?

Then I see the smirk on the dark man's face. I taste acid at the back of my throat.

When I get back home, I pour myself a whisky. I drink it straight down and pick up the telephone. I dial Reuben's number with an unsteady hand. It rings several times before he answers.

'Hello, darling, it's your mother. Is Alice home?'

I can hear the television on in the background.

'No.'

'Oh, I thought she'd be back by now. Doesn't she leave a bit early on Fridays?'

'Does she?' There's an edge of doubt in his voice.

'Perhaps she's gone for a drink with her work friends.'

He is silent for a second. When he speaks again his voice is tense. 'Right, well. I'll tell her you rang.'

# 62

Leo didn't sit in any more of my lessons but our teas became a regular fixture: every week after class at the cafe near Russell Square.

He'd set up his own class, for pupils more advanced than mine. He was full of ideas and had boundless enthusiasm. We talked about our teaching and our favourite students, it felt like we were colleagues together.

He could stretch the smallest anecdote into a saga: a lost pen, a student's runny nose, the spam and cabbage fritters he'd eaten for lunch. Truth was no barrier and the taller the tale, the more I adored it.

'Klara Levin used to dance with the Kirov ballet. It's only since she's come to England she's put on all that weight.'

Or: 'Samuel keeps a rat in his satchel. It came all the way from Warsaw with him. He says it's lucky, protects him in the raids. He won't let it out of his sight.'

And I thought it was perfectly natural that we should have these meetings, just the two of us. Work colleagues sit in cafes and discuss their jobs all the time. If we were in a proper school, we'd have met in the staffroom. We were two diligent teachers who liked to talk about teaching. Nothing there for anyone to mind.

Only, he never asked me about my husband and I never asked

about his wife. And I found myself running to the ladies' room after class to brush my hair and put on lipstick.

It also seemed strange, though I didn't think too much about it, that I never told Margo or Frank about those meetings.

Still, it was nice to have a colleague like Leo. My classes went from strength to strength.

# 63

They're not holding hands this evening. There's a distance between them I haven't seen before. Reuben walks quickly and Alice trails behind. She's rooting around in her handbag. My son looks handsome in a dark red velvet jacket, he's clutching a bottle of wine. Alice is frumpy in a funnel-neck tunic. Her bare legs are mottled with cold.

She frowns: 'No, it's not in here. Bugger. I must have left it on the kitchen table.'

Reuben smiles. 'It's OK. I'll run back and get it. We'll only be a few minutes late.'

'That's not the point, I was sure I had it. My head's all over the place. I don't even want to go this evening. I'm so tired I can hardly think straight.'

He shrugs. 'So, you forgot the address – it's hardly the end of the world. What's wrong? Are you still upset about Friday?'

'Yes. You need to trust me.'

'I explained. I thought you understood.'

'That doesn't mean I want to live with it, Reuben. It isn't fair. I'm not your mother.'

He laughs. 'Thank God! Give me the key. I'll be back in a minute.'

She hands him the door key and he runs past me up the hundred yards to the house. I listen to the slap of his smart leather shoes recede up the tarmac path.

It was a spur-of-the-moment decision to come here. I had thought perhaps I'd try and talk to Alice. I was partway up the path when I saw them both come out. I panicked and stepped off into the shrubbery.

I turn back to the road and study my daughter-in-law, her jaw is clenched tight and she stares into the gutter. She doesn't step away as a lorry speeds by inches from her. She doesn't turn to watch her husband as he runs back down the path towards her.

'Got it.' He waves a scrap of paper, his cheeks are flushed and he's grinning. 'On the table, just like you thought it was.'

He moves to touch his wife on the shoulder. She shakes her head and shrugs him off.

I feel the rejection along with my son. I'm struck by the petty meanness of it. Reuben puts his hand in his pocket and trudges off down the street without her. Alice bites her lip and hurries after him. She says: 'I'm sorry, darling. I'm just tired, that's all.' She says: 'Slow down, I can't keep up.'

# 64

Strange that it was something as dreary as a bit of rain on a Thursday afternoon. That something of such everyday dullness was the trigger. Frank, Leo, Reuben and I – we'd all be living different lives if it hadn't rained that Thursday. And if I could go back and stop that rain from falling, would I?

It wasn't such a downpour but it was cold and windy with it. The benches on Russell Square were empty and the grass was empty too. Everyone had gone inside, it felt like winter though it wasn't yet September. Leo tried his best to shelter me but the wind blew his brolly inside out.

In the end we ran to the cafe. I went splashing through puddles in my best suede shoes. We arrived to find it full to bursting point. Every table already taken.

Two old women were occupying our seats; the ones we always sat in near the window on the right. They were deep in conversation and they looked like they'd be there for some time. I hovered, prepared to wait them out. But Leo had already moved on.

'Over here!' He waved me to a table at the rear of the room. There were three men sitting there in khaki uniforms. There was a little slice of tablecloth free and a wooden bench just big enough for two.

Leo asked the soldiers if we could join them. I could see they didn't want us there but they grudgingly said: 'I suppose so.'

The two of us squeezed together on the bench with our backs to the rest of the room.

It was that squeezing together that did it, I think. We were sitting so much closer than we'd ever sat before. Our thighs and arms kept touching, I could feel his heat through his clothes. At first we tried to keep our limbs apart, but then we just let them rest there. The windows were steamy and the room was warm, but it was the squeezing together that changed things.

The soldiers assumed we were a couple. One of them winked at Leo with an 'I know what you're up to' leer. And rather than think what a cheek it was, I remember how I wished it were true.

Everything was different between us, the way we sat, the words we used. We didn't talk about teaching or students, we talked about ourselves and our lives.

And it didn't feel wrong, though really it should have. I told Leo all of it: the separate bedrooms, the distance between me and Frank. And Leo sat there and nodded quietly and he didn't stop me and he didn't judge.

I said: 'I don't think it's ever been right. Frank is a good man but there's always been something missing.'

It was such a relief to say it. It was such a relief to let it all out.

When he started talking about his family in Gdańsk I felt honoured that he'd chosen to confide in me. He spoke quickly, quietly, rattling through the words in his Polish accent. 'I was the only one to get a visa, I didn't want to take it but Katya was determined. I felt like I was abandoning them, I begged her to let me stay. She told me I had to leave for the sake of our son, that I was their only hope. She convinced me it was for the best.'

The soldiers stopped all pretence of conversation. They leant forwards, arms folded, hanging on his every word.

'I was so sure that once I got here, I'd be able to bring them over too. I imagined I'd find a job for Katya and meet them from the boat when they arrived. But I've tried and tried to get them here and no one wants to listen. No one seems able to help. I've heard nothing from my wife for two whole years now. I won't give up. I've written hundreds of letters and I'll keep on writing. I can never stop trying, just in case.'

There were tears in his eyes and I hoped he wouldn't cry because the soldiers wouldn't like it. And I remember how much I wanted to make it better – would do anything to take that pain away.

People talk about love as hearts and flowers. It's bolts of lightning and 'suddenly I knew'. But when I fell in love with Leo it was a feeling of being understood.

I should have felt guilty: I was a mother and a married woman and I'd made those vows to my husband. But I knew what I wanted that afternoon. And I knew it wasn't going away.

We stayed in the cafe until it closed – far longer than our usual hour. I looked at my watch and saw it was late but it didn't seem to matter that much. I knew I'd miss reading a story to my son and the nanny would be resentful and Frank would be worried. But though all those things registered with me, they didn't seem important somehow.

When we left the cafe the rain had eased and Leo walked me to the station. He looked into my eyes and smiled. He lent in and gently kissed me on the lips. I knew he felt the same way I did.

# 65

That's three times I've had the same dream now. I wake up from it, heart racing, and I can't get back to sleep. It's painful and it's ugly and I don't know what it says about me. I don't want to dream it again.

It starts off well: Reuben rings me up. He chats away, like he never does in real life, and he tells me they're going to have a baby. I'm thrilled, at last I'm going to be a grandmother. My Reuben's going to have a little son. I feel hopeful. This will be a chance for us to mend things. Really, it couldn't be better.

The dream turns sour when the child is born because nobody rings to tell me. I'm the grandmother – I should be the first to hear – but no one thinks to call and let me know.

I go round to their house to meet my grandson. I knock on their blue front door. The lights are on, I can hear a baby crying, but no one comes to let me in.

My knocking gets louder. I knock with all my might. I shout and smash my fists against the door.

Eventually Alice comes out. She's ghostly white and she will not let me in. She says: 'Gilda, go away. There isn't any baby.' But I can hear a newborn crying behind her.

I push past her and run through their monochrome hall. The

house is in chaos, there are packing cases everywhere. I charge from room to room trying to find my grandson. His cries are very loud but I can't see him.

Alice tries to block me. She shouts: 'Stop it, Gilda. Stop!'

I open drawers; I look in cupboards; I rifle through boxes; I look under beds. I go into every part of that house, but I can't find where he is.

Finally I see a giant fitted wardrobe and somehow I know he's inside. I open it up. It's packed full to bursting. But my grandson is in there. I'm sure of it.

I dig through piles of clothes and shoes – layer upon layer – to reach him. There are coats and jackets and jumpers and skirts. I throw them all onto the floor. Eventually I get to him. He is deep, deep down at the bottom. I peer at him and his face is very red. His eyes are glassy marbles and I'm scared.

I reach down and pick him up. I hold him in my arms and cup his head in my palm. He looks up and sees me smiling and his crying stops straight away.

He grins at me exactly like my Reuben used to. And my heart is full to the brim.

I turn round to my daughter-in-law and I say: 'Here he is, look. He's fine.'

Then somehow I – he slips from my arms. Before I know it he's falling and falling. And she was right not to trust me, my daughter-in-law.

# 66

It was almost nine by the time I got back and the nanny had gone home hours ago. Frank came to meet me at the door and asked me where I'd been.

I could have simply lied to him, it wouldn't have been hard. I could have come up with an excuse about an air raid, the weather, the trains. But I knew what I wanted with Leo so clearly – I was a naive child in love for the first time. So I told Frank before I'd even taken off my coat, while the two of us were standing in the hallway. I stared at the fawn gabardine of my coat-sleeve. 'I'm late because I've been with someone else.'

Frank gave a little half-smile and I realised he didn't believe me.

I said: 'He's a teacher at the centre.'

My husband walked away. He said nothing, just turned and walked off.

I finished removing my coat and went to pour myself a whisky. And then I sat on my own and sipped it. I couldn't think what else to do.

What did I expect? A fight perhaps? An ultimatum? Honestly, when I look back on it, I didn't think he'd mind that much. We were already more or less living apart, hadn't shared a bed for several years.

I spent the next hour dreaming of a new life. I'd finally met a man I could love and felt sure we would make it work. Even Reuben's future seemed clear, he'd simply come and live with Leo and me. A nanny, food, furniture, somewhere to stay – well, we'd have to work those things out later.

Frank came and found me that evening in my room. I was already in bed and just about to turn the light out. He stood between me and the doorway, close enough that I could smell the brandy on his breath.

When he spoke his voice was cool and calm. 'Your actions have shocked me deeply, Gilda, and I'm not going to pretend I'm happy with the situation. But I'm also a realist, I know these things happen in a marriage. We're grown-ups. We have a child together. We have responsibilities. I believe we can come to some sort of arrangement. It doesn't mean the marriage is over. I won't stop you seeing this teacher as long as you're careful and no one else gets to know about it. My business would suffer if there was a scandal and there are too many people depending on me.'

Nothing needed to change, he said. We'd carry on in our separate bedrooms, keep living our separate lives. Only I mustn't talk about Leo to anyone, mustn't flaunt him in public or introduce him to our son. Frank wouldn't stand for it if any of his friends found out. Leo's name couldn't be mentioned.

I nodded my head, though it wasn't what I wanted. Frank was a decent man and I could see the sense in what he said. He seemed so very practical, barely raised a single objection. If anything, my pride was hurt – shouldn't he protest just a little bit?

But then I was so ignorant about these things. Perhaps it was perfectly normal for a spouse to turn a blind eye. It would be simpler, certainly, to hide it from our friends. Better for Frank's business and better for Reuben. My parents seemed to have a similar arrangement. Perhaps that was just how marriage worked.

He spoke once more before he left the room and I remember his words exactly. He was standing in the doorway. His face was bloodless. 'We have a son together, Gilda. We have a comfortable life. Don't do anything to put those things at risk.'

# 67

The cosmetics hall is busy, there must be another promotion on. There are three heads behind the Estée Lauder counter: a curly one, a dark one and a blonde I think is my daughter-in-law. The room is so crowded, I keep losing sight of her. It's like trying to find the hostess at a cocktail party.

I leave the safety of my spot behind the column to see if I can get just a little bit closer. I think if I can make it to the Lancôme display my view will be uninterrupted.

Alice is rather flustered today. Half of her hair has come loose from her chignon. Her cheeks appear flushed, though she might have overdone it with the rouge. She's serving a woman with a silver bun and a dancer's posture. The customer is being difficult, keeps shrugging her slender shoulders.

Alice pulls out jar after jar, bends beneath the counter like she's bobbing for apples. The woman is still unhappy. Nothing is quite the right thing.

My daughter-in-law turns and scans the shelves behind her. She fetches the little wooden ladder and slides it into place. She climbs until she's up near the top then reaches to her left and picks out two jars. She clutches them to her chest with one hand and guides her way back down with the other.

She is halfway down when she loses her grip on the jars, I hear them land with a thunk on the marble. Alice yelps and jumps the last rungs to the floor. She picks the jars up – unbroken – and puts them on the counter. The other girls shoot her a 'no harm done' smile. My daughter-in-law appears stricken.

She manages to finish serving the customer but her face is white and she fumbles with the money. She shoves the jars in a bag without wrapping them. She looks like she needs to sit down.

Just when I think she's pulled herself together, she turns to the curly haired girl and whispers something in her ear. The girl nods and Alice looks relieved. She walks quickly out of the room.

I wait for my daughter-in-law in my spot by the Basil Street exit. She's usually so proficient at work. I just want to check she's OK.

The staff door opens and she emerges looking tired and tearful. Her coat is buttoned up to the neck and her handbag's slung across her chest. She steps out into the street and I ready myself to follow, but then she stops and turns her head back in response to a voice from inside. She pauses, hands in pockets. She turns back to the street again. She shuts her eyes and heaves her shoulders. I'm not sure if it's a shrug or a sigh.

The dark man appears in the doorway seconds later. He walks up to Alice with a grin that says he thinks he's worth waiting for. She keeps her head bowed but my fingers tingle with anxiety for her. And even from the other side of the road, I'm dazzled by the whiteness of his teeth.

As they set off down the pavement, the man offers Alice a cigarette. She shakes her head no and he pulls one out for himself. He stops to light it, but she keeps walking. He shouts: 'Hold up. What's the rush?'

They are side by side, less than half a yard apart. It's colder than it has been and Alice pulls her coat a little tighter. His right hand hovers near the curve of her back. I can see he wants to touch her but he doesn't.

When they get to Knightsbridge station, Alice peels off. The dark man says something in an effort to make her linger. As she walks further into the station his comments get louder. 'Don't run off, we're just getting to know each other! Come and join me for a glass of wine. Go on, Alice, don't be like that. You look like you could do with a drink.'

Alice turns briefly. She doesn't smile. She lifts a single hand, palm held towards him. I can't tell if it's a stop sign or a wave.

# 68

I don't think it was ever equal. But perhaps love can't be equal. I think I always loved Leo rather more than Leo loved me.

He was my first love – the only man I've ever loved apart from Reuben. I threw myself into it without hesitation, but it wasn't the same for him.

He warned me at the beginning though he tried to put it gently. He said he'd always love his wife and son, no matter what happened with us. And even in those first few months – when I wanted to spend every second with him – he was writing, visiting, pleading with anyone he thought might be able to help them.

And for all that time when he heard nothing, when no one had seen them or could tell him where they were, he never stopped hoping and he never stopped loving them. He never stopped trying to get them out.

So I think that even if things had gone differently – if I'd given him what he wanted, done everything he asked – he would have still loved them most, the wife and son he left in Poland.

It's natural. He loved them first.

# 69

I bump into Lizzie next-door more often these days, just as I feared I would do. This afternoon she comes up in the lift as I'm about to head down.

Her grin is broad and unavoidable. She is wearing some sort of kaftan.

'Gilda, just the woman. Will you come in and have a coffee with me?'

'I'm on my way to the library, sorry.' I hold up my book as proof.

'Do come in. I've had some good news and I'm dying to share it.' There's a swish of manmade fabric as she crosses the corridor. She shakes out her keys and inserts them in the lock. 'Just for a minute, won't you?'

She enters her flat and goes straight to put the kettle on. I sigh and follow behind. I sit down gingerly on her cat-hair covered sofa.

She comes back in and puts a plate of chocolate Bourbons on the coffee table. 'Biscuits, seeing as we're celebrating.' She hands me a mug. 'A gallery's taken one of my paintings.'

'Oh, how nice for you.' That explains the dreadful abstracts on the wall.

'It's only a small gallery, but still, it's a start. I haven't been paint-ing that long.'

I bite into a biscuit to avoid the need for comment. I brush the crumbs from my chest.

Lizzie sips her coffee. 'I took it up after my husband left. I was thinking just the other day, it's been almost five years now.'

Her openness embarrasses me. I sip my coffee a little more quickly.

'And you, Gilda? What do you do with yourself?'

'This and that. I like to read. Neither of my husbands wanted me to do paid work.'

'But you're not married now, are you? How do you fill your days?'

I pick up my book and ease off the sofa.

'Oh, I keep myself busy.'

# 70

It must have been very hard for Frank, I didn't try to hide my happiness. The spring in my step, the satisfied glow – he had to see that every day. Love had transformed me. I had a joy and a confidence I'd never known before. I'd go into London most afternoons and come home smelling of Leo.

It's strange, but I didn't feel even slightly guilty. Frank pretended he didn't notice as I went up to straighten my clothes. It was like I was immune to it all – the filth, the five-inch baths, the terrible trains. Even the air raids did nothing to shake it. I couldn't keep the smile from my face.

When I look back I think how extraordinary it was – Frank poured me my evening whisky and didn't ask a single question. We had dinner with his friends, just as before, and he'd act as if nothing were amiss.

He never asked where I went in the afternoons or what I got up to on the weekends when he was away. We'd say goodnight and we'd go off to our separate bedrooms, then we'd get up in the morning and we'd do it all again.

Just occasionally I'd catch him staring at me without any hint of warmth in his eyes. Occasionally, I'd see a flicker of impatience if I stumbled home after the blackout. I wondered, then, what was going on inside. What it cost him to keep up his pretence. But then my thoughts turned back to Leo again.

## 71

Harrods men's grooming department has oak-panelled walls and an air of the clubhouse. There's an olive leather armchair by a potted fern and a copy of *The Times* on a coffee table.

The dark man, Terry, stands by a desk with a bottle of Old Spice cologne in his hand. He takes a step forward as I approach and asks if I'd like to sample it. He spritzes his wrist and holds it out for me. My senses spring to life as I lean in.

He isn't quite as young as I'd thought, perhaps pushing forty now I see him up close. There's something oddly static about his mane of blue-black hair. The pores on the tip of his nose are enlarged and deep lines bracket his mouth. Two whiskers protrude from one of his nostrils.

I smell cinnamon and vanilla plus the musky undertone of his own aroma. Pilchards for lunch and a cigarette, I'd guess. When he smiles I'm transfixed by his teeth again.

I shake my head. 'No. It's far too sweet.'

He laughs and sniffs his wrist himself. 'That's prob'ly why I like it.'

His laugh is a little too coarse for my taste, it belongs in a pool hall or at a football match. He's not as refined as he tries to make out: he dropped the second syllable in 'probably'.

195

He asks if I want to sample something else. He reaches for another bottle and pulls out the stopper. His yellowed fingers taper towards the tip. His nails are in need of a trim.

I say: 'No. I'm in a bit of a rush. Perhaps I'll come back another time.'

He asks: 'Who are you shopping for? Is it a gift?'

I nod and tell him yes it's for my son.

# 72

It was difficult to juggle so many lives: a teacher, a lover, a mother, a wife. But whatever hurtful things Frank said to me later, I never forgot about Reuben.

I tried to make it home in time to read his stories. I was thwarted by the wartime trains, which were delayed, diverted or cancelled at short notice. Even when I managed to fight my way on board, they moved so slowly it was simply unbearable. I'd be shoved up against a soldier's armpit, swallowing tears of tiredness and frustration. I tried to imagine I was already at home with Reuben. Thought of all the things I had to say to him.

When I got back so late I was always exhausted, but I still had to eat with Frank and his friends. I still had to play the dutiful wife, make small talk as they smoked their cigars.

I went to see my son as soon as I could, while my husband was drinking his brandy. I'd sit in his nursery for an hour or more and listen to his breath as he slept.

I'd tell him the little details about my day. The sandwich I ate for lunch or the broken piano I saw on a bombsite. Sometimes I told him Leo's stories: the student who kept a pet rat in his satchel, the fat girl who danced with the Kirov ballet.

I made sure not to disturb him. I was always careful not to wake him. I pointed my little flashlight at the floor and I whispered my words into the darkness.

When Nanny told me Reuben had been asking for me, I was pleased at first. The trains had been dire since the tracks were bombed near Vauxhall and I'd been getting home later than ever.

He was sitting on the floor of his nursery with a jigsaw puzzle. The pieces were scattered all around him. When he saw me, he reached up. 'Mummy!'

I didn't hesitate. 'Hello, my darling!' I swept him up in a hug. And he hugged me back, pressed his cheek against my shoulder. He didn't speak again but he clung to me. I told him I was sorry there hadn't been time for our stories lately. I told him I'd bought him *The Runaway Bunny*. I told him I thought of him every day. I promised we'd go to the park together very soon. I told him just how much I'd missed him.

After a while Nanny came back in. She said: 'That's better, Reuben, isn't it? I told you Mummy would come when she could. Are you going to be a good boy and eat your supper now?'

I tried to put him down but he wouldn't let go. Nanny had to prise him off me. He was sobbing. 'Stay! Please Mummy, stay!' He batted his nanny away.

And though it upset me to see him so unhappy, I thought it proved how close we were; how tightly bonded we'd become.

## 73

Harrods is about to close and I wait in my doorway near the Basil Street exit. He comes out at six and flicks up his collar, he lights a cigarette with a flourish. He's unencumbered, neither briefcase nor umbrella. No hat, lest it flatten his hair.

I study his stride as he walks down the street. He bounds like a younger man, legs slightly bowed. He doesn't look at the shops he passes, though he turns his head once as a girl goes by in hotpants. He moves quickly and I struggle to keep up with him.

I'm out of breath by the time we get to Knightsbridge station. I pause for a minute at the top of the stairs. I let several commuters pass before I make my way down. Then I scan the concourse for his quiff.

He's standing, smoking, perilously close to the platform edge. He turns to look as a Piccadilly line train approaches. His hair holds stiff in the gust of warm air that precedes it.

I watch him make his way onto the carriage. I clamber into the adjoining one just as its doors are closing. A schoolgirl asks if I'd like her seat. I shake my head, no, and go and stand at the end. I can look through the window, past the coupling, into the next-door carriage. I am ten yards away from him, maybe less.

I study him – Terry – the man who's set his sights on my

daughter-in-law. So far I've thought of him as rather a dandy. As I look at him in the confined space I'm aware of his physical strength. He dwarfs the long-haired youth sitting next to him. His thighs look thick inside those worsted-wool slacks. His hand is broad where it rests on his inside leg and black hairs creep up from his wrist.

I wonder for the first time if I'm putting myself in danger. He glances in my direction and my heart is in my throat. But he looks away, he hasn't seen me, and his gaze rests on the younger woman next to me. I'm fifty-two, a middle-aged housewife, what interest could I possibly hold for him?

I count five stops before the dark man gets up. I look out of the window. Hammersmith station. I stay in my carriage until the very last minute and then dart through the door as it closes.

# 74

I've only known the bodies of two men in my life – it's strange the things that stay with you. I could draw you a picture of Frank's upper back, showing every single hair on his shoulders; the precise position of the mole on his left shoulder blade; the plump pad where his skull meets his spine.

With Leo it's his torso I remember – long, lean and smooth beneath my fingertips. It's the velvet-soft shadows in the dips above his clavicle; the salt-soap taste of his skin.

I'd been in love with Leo for almost a year before we managed to spend a whole night together. Up until then our romance had been piecemeal – an hour in a cafe, an afternoon in Leo's friend's car. It was never enough, we always left unsatisfied. We were young and we snatched at every chance.

That night, Frank was away on business in Manchester. Leo had left his shared digs in Shepherd's Bush and we finally had a room of our own.

I had thought I'd get a cab from Waterloo but the queue was full of GIs and I was too impatient to wait. I decided to make my way on foot, clutching my small overnight case. As I walked through grimy streets I imagined how it would feel, the two of us waking up side-by-side. I pictured sunshine through an attic window, our bodies under clean, white sheets.

It took me a while to find Leo's bedsit, above a grotty pub near Vauxhall station. I followed him up sticky lino stairs accompanied by the cloying scent of tomcat.

He opened the door to a space only slightly bigger than my wardrobe. There was a smell of stewed cabbage from a gas ring in the corner. I could see he'd tried – there was a wilting daffodil in an empty milk bottle – but I was shocked at how little he had. All his clothes were piled on a chair: two shirts and one pair of trousers, with a threadbare jacket on the chair-back.

I'd never been to a bachelor's flat before and I worried that his sheets weren't clean. There was a long-dead housefly on the windowsill and an overflowing ashtray on his nightstand. I'd never had to live without a maid or a cook. I'd never had to stick to a budget.

Leo led me over to his single mattress. 'I've wanted this for so long.' He took me in his arms and it felt right and natural like it never had with Frank.

I tried not to notice the cracks in the ceiling. I tried not to notice how the bed creaked.

# 75

I keep my distance from Terry as we leave the station – never closer than ten yards behind him, never further than twenty away. I almost lose him in the crowd outside Hammersmith Palais. Joe Loss and his Orchestra are playing. The kiosk queue is long and untidy.

Once we're back on track, I try to appear busy: check my watch, my handbag, glance in shop windows. Every few seconds I look up and search for his quiff. I am cool and casual. A woman on an afternoon stroll.

After half a mile or so he turns off into a side street. I lean against the corner wall and allow my breath to settle. I wipe my clammy hands against the front of my skirt. I slowly count to twenty then I follow him.

The street is lined with shabby terraced houses. It's quiet and I'm conscious of my footfall on the pavement. I walk past a mattress propped up against a garden fence. Two children play a listless game of conkers.

I can tell when we get to Terry's house because he takes out his key as he approaches. It's small, in yellow brick, at the far end of the row. There's a brown Ford Zephyr parked outside it.

I don't slow my pace, but I watch him enter. As I pass I see the outline of a pushchair in the hallway.

I walk the short distance up to the end of the street, then I turn and walk back past his house again. I glimpse a dark-haired woman in an upstairs window. There are nappies on the clothesline in the yard.

I feel rather pleased with myself as I head back to Swiss Cottage. He's married and a father, of course he is. This is useful information. Someone ought to teach him a lesson. If you break your marriage vows you have to pay the price.

I did.

# 76

My students gave me the vodka as a thank-you gift. Black market, no doubt, but it was generous and I didn't ask questions. The papers had told us the war was over in Europe and we were waiting for Churchill's announcement. I took the bottle to Leo's flat. I wanted us to hear it together.

At three o'clock we switched on the radio.

'*Yesterday morning at 2.41 a.m. at Headquarters, General Jodl, the representative of the German High Command, and Grand Admiral Doenitz, the designated head of the German State, signed the act of unconditional surrender . . .*'

There were cheers outside and church bells rang. I thought: *It's over. It's over.*

Leo lifted his glass. 'To a brief period of rejoicing, my darling.'

We downed our drinks and refilled them.

There was a freedom to our lovemaking that afternoon and I felt closer to Leo than I ever had before. Afterwards, I lay beside him as he dozed and thought of the times we had ahead of us. I imagined a life where we could live together as husband and wife, where I could run my bath as deep as I liked, where Reuben could have all the stories he wanted.

When Leo woke I topped up our glasses and he put Nat King

Cole on the gramophone. The two of us held each other and looked out past the tape on his one small window. Our neighbours were dancing round a bonfire they'd built right there in the street.

'*It is only a paper moon hanging over a cardboard sea, but it wouldn't be make believe if you believed in me.*'

Leo said: 'Everything's changed now, hasn't it? It will all be different from now on.'

I said: 'Yes, isn't it wonderful? We can start to think about our future.'

He turned to me and took both my hands in his. He looked in my eyes, then back towards the window. He was quiet for a fraction too long and I sensed that something was wrong. I was scared and I pulled my hands away.

When he spoke his voice was hoarse. I fought a childish impulse to cover my ears.

He said: 'Katya and Isaac – I'll have to go back and find them. You understand. Don't you, Gilda? If there's a chance my son's alive, I have to know.'

I nodded, filled my glass and drank it down. Then I ran out to the toilet and vomited.

I don't know how I made it back to Guildford. Leo asked me to stay with him but I insisted on leaving. The station was packed with revellers – a soldier gave me a swig from his hip flask. He said: 'Are you all right, duck?' He couldn't tell if I was crying or laughing.

The train carriage was gay with drunken chatter. Two girls in sailor hats sang 'Roll Out the Barrel'. A young man offered me a seat and I took it without saying thank you. I sat there with my head in my hands.

I arrived home just as everyone was sitting down to dinner.

Frank was exuberant: 'Gilda, you're back, come and join us!'

There were twelve of them wearing paper hats. The air was thick with cigar smoke.

'Sorry to disturb you all.' I shrugged off my coat and dropped it on the floor. I held onto the back of a chair for support. 'I'm afraid I've had a rather trying day. Will one of you pour me a whisky?'

Frank stood up and moved to put his hand on my shoulder. 'Darling, you don't look well. Perhaps you should go and lie down.'

I shook him off. 'No, Frank, we're celebrating. We have to put on a show for our guests. We have to keep up appearances, don't we? God forbid we should tell them what's really going on.'

Frank said: 'Go upstairs.'

# 77

It is different, this time, as I walk up the path to Reuben's house. I am certain, determined, sure of every step. I grip the little silver key in my pocket. It feels like I'm meant to be here.

I go straight down the passageway, through the side gate and into the rear. I unlock the patio door with ease; I feel a little glow of pride at the achievement.

I don't waste any time downstairs, I make my way up to the bedroom. The air is still and smells of dust, it's so quiet I can hear my heartbeat.

Alice has made the bed today, though she's done it in a rush and it's rather sloppy. She hasn't fluffed the pillows, I can see the dent from Reuben's head. There's a half-drunk glass of squash on his bedside table and a crusty cotton handkerchief on her side.

I walk over to the dressing table tucked in the corner. It's placed at an awkward angle so it gets a little light from the window. There are three faded stickers on the left side of the mirror: a peace sign, a love-heart and a grainy circle that says *Bunty*. The table is cluttered with grubby cosmetics. Blonde hair clings to a plastic hairbrush.

I pull out the stool, which is velvet-topped and fringed with pink. As I sit on it, I remember Mother's dressing room: the secret thrill of excitement as we stole our way into her world. I spritz on a bit of Alice's perfume. I reach for her block of mascara. I peer at my reflection as I blacken my lashes. It's like Lena is sitting here beside me.

I pick up a lipstick – *Soho peach* – in a pink and orange striped tube. I can tell it's too bright, but I try it on anyway. When I lick my lips, they taste of rose.

I go through four more shades before I find what I'm looking for: the frosted pink colour she wears for work. The scratched gold case says *Pinkberry Meringue*. I know I've got it right because the bullet is worn to a nub.

## 78

I became aware of something tugging at my foot. I was lying, curled up, on my side. My right cheek and ear were crushed against a rough, hard surface and my shoulder ached where my weight had been resting on it. It was very clear something bad had happened. *Oh God, have I done something bad?*

I moved my hand slowly up to my face. I rubbed at the patch of dried spit on my chin. The movement sent a shot of pain through my skull. I lay still and waited for it to pass.

I could sense that someone else was in the room with me. There was that pull on my foot again, a muffled whimper. I opened one eye – the pain was intense – and saw Reuben crouching by my leg.

I tried to say his name but my mouth was very dry. He was over near the door by the time I'd got my tongue to work. He called out for his father. His voice was high and scared. I tried to say his name again. The door slammed shut.

I lay still for a minute and took in my surroundings, I was inches away from an iron bed leg. Black springs stretched beneath a sagging mattress. The edge of a pale blue quilt hovered just above my head.

There was a queasy anxious pulsing in the centre of my chest. I felt sick and closed my eyes again.

I tried to order the fragments of memory. Leo by the window; the soldier at the station; all those grinning faces round the dining-room table. Frank had been so angry with me. I'd poured myself a drink from the living room cabinet. I'd felt so alone. I'd needed some comfort. I'd wanted to see my little son.

'Get up!' Frank grabbed me by the shoulders. 'For God's sake, Gilda, get up!'

I pushed him away. Acid stung my throat. I rolled onto all fours and heaved. He stood over me, unmoving.

'Reuben found you when he woke up. He thought you were dead. He's downstairs now and won't stop crying. He's only five years old! I don't care what happened yesterday, Gilda, this is not the way a mother behaves. I don't want my son anywhere near you when you're like this. Get up now, get dressed and get yourself downstairs with a smile on your face. You need to show him you're all right.'

I nodded my head and the nausea started again. I closed my eyes and breathed through my nose.

Frank said: 'I'm going down to comfort my son.'

# 79

Alice's sunglasses sit heavy on the bridge of my nose and leave patches of sweat where frame meets flesh. Her raspberry-red dress is too tight across my bust and the skirt rides up, so I have to keep tugging it down.

I'm aware of people looking at me – not so much admiring as curious. At first I was self-conscious but if I'm honest, I'm starting to enjoy it. I try to picture how Alice walks, the click of her heels, the sway of her hips. I add an extra spring in my step as I make my way down to the Tube.

A grey-haired gentleman tips his bowler hat and murmurs a quick 'good afternoon'.

I can't remember the last time anyone looked at me like this. I can't remember the last time anyone looked at me and really saw me.

It is almost three o'clock when I get to Hammersmith. There's a thick layer of cloud but I won't remove my sunglasses. I practise my lines as I walk the short distance to Terry's house.

The street is deserted and I pray his wife's at home. I don't know what I'll do if she's out.

I get to the end of the terrace and stop in front of their gate. I stand for a few seconds to steady my heartbeat. I breathe in deep. I reapply Alice's pale pink lipstick. I tug down the skirt of her raspberry dress. I stride up to the door and ring the bell.

The woman who answers is in her early thirties, pretty in a careworn way. She is holding an infant balanced on one hip. He is tired and nuzzling into her shoulder.

As she looks at me, her expression is kind. I notice dark circles under her eyes. She brushes back a strand of hair that's escaped from a messy topknot. She blushes. 'You'll have to excuse me. Sorry. I wasn't expecting company.'

Her shyness unnerves me, it's not what I expected. I'd pictured her as brassy and defensive; prepared myself for a fight.

For a moment I think I won't go through with it, she's probably suffered enough. But then I picture Terry's hand, the look on his face as he touched my daughter-in-law. I tell myself what I'm doing is right. More importantly, I'm doing it for my son.

I start to say the lines I've practised. I am careful to stifle any trace of accent. 'My name is Alice Goodman, I work with your husband at Harrods. I'm afraid he hasn't been behaving himself. I need you to tell him his advances are unwelcome. If he comes near me again it'll cost him his job.'

The woman's face appears frozen for a second, her eyes are glassy with tears. The small child wriggles and she shifts it on her hip. Finally she whispers: 'Alice, did you say?'

I nod.

# 80

Leo found out the truth about his family in the spring of 1946. He shut himself away and wouldn't even come to the telephone. For a whole week I heard nothing from him. I convinced myself he'd chosen to end our relationship. I tore myself apart with anger and blame. I turned up at his flat and demanded to be let in.

When he opened the door I was shocked by how gaunt he was. He ushered me into the room without a word. He didn't meet my eye; avoided my touch.

A chair lay on its side in the corner near the bed, legs in the air like a wounded animal. He'd smashed his favourite mug – I recognised the pattern on the fragments I stepped over. Only the handle was intact.

He didn't talk – just handed me the Red Cross letter.

The page was titled: *Whereabouts of Katya and Isaac Zubek*. Just a few lines printed on a little sheet of paper.

He stared at me as I read it. *Following your inquiries . . . our painful duty to inform you . . . Our deepest condolences*. I could feel his eyes burning into my face, watching to see my reaction.

I went to him and held him – I didn't hesitate. I rocked him like he was a little child and both of us cried that night. Leo was desperate, shaking with grief. I let him talk and I did my best to soothe him. I made myself imagine it was Reuben's name instead on that letter; I knew I couldn't have survived it.

Leo drank a great deal during that period. When I talked to him about it his intensity scared me. 'I feel like I'm coming loose,' he said. 'Without you I've got no one.'

He told me he needed something to hold on to – something in his life that was his. He said: 'I can't share you any more.' I could hear in his voice that he meant it.

For a while he was obsessed with Frank. He made me go through every conversation. He told me I had to leave – if I loved him that's what I'd do. And I understood. Of course I understood. And I was pleased that he needed me, pleased to be wanted. But I couldn't do what he asked of me. I had to look after my son.

Late one night after yet another drunken row, Leo held on to my arm and tried to stop me going home. I pulled away but his grip was too tight and my silk blouse ripped at the shoulder seam.

He said: 'Don't leave me alone, Gilda. I'm frightened of what I might do.'

And I looked in his eyes and I felt afraid too.

# 81

I'm almost at the dry cleaners when the boy and his mother walk towards me. It's Friday afternoon and the shops will be closed soon. They must be on their way home from school.

The little boy pauses and turns to his mother. 'Watch me. See how fast I can run!' He tugs at her coat sleeve. 'Mummy? Are you watching?'

The mother nods wearily. 'OK. I'm watching.'

He passes her his school cap and satchel, then adopts a sprinter's stance, hands to the leaf-covered pavement. He looks up through his fringe and scans the route ahead. His blazer stretches tight across his back.

He says: 'On your marks. Get set. Go!'

He hurtles towards me, a stone released from a catapult, scabby knees pumping in his grey school shorts. His face is alive with the sheer joy of movement: bright eyes, chin thrust forward, tongue a glimpse of pink through gappy teeth.

I stand aside and he passes with a whoop. He stumbles on a tree-root but carries on regardless. When he gets to the end of the road he stops at the curb and raises his arms in a victory salute. I want to cheer, but shyness prevents me. He looks straight past me to the woman behind.

'Did you see that, Mummy? Did you see me?'

His mother plods with heavy footsteps. 'Yes, darling, I saw you.'

# 82

Six is very young to be sent away to boarding school. My Reuben couldn't do up the buttons on his shirt cuffs. He couldn't tie up his own shoes.

It was Frank's decision to send him away and he didn't seem to care what I thought. He said we must plan for our son's future. 'The sooner the better,' Frank said.

I pleaded with my husband. Begged him to change his mind. 'He's just a little boy. He needs his parents. You're angry with me, I understand, but please don't take it out on our son.'

Frank wouldn't listen. He said I was just being selfish: 'Your life is chaotic, there's no place for a child. Reuben needs discipline. He needs more structure.'

He said it was best that he went.

We both took him to school that first time. One of the last things we did together. The long drive down seemed to go on for ever, just the three of us and the chauffeur.

My husband hadn't said a civil word to me in months. He barely even looked at me, spoke only to our son.

I sat next to Reuben who was tight-lipped with misery. I reached over and put my arm round him. 'Reuben darling, this is going to be an adventure, but Daddy and I – we're going to miss you terribly.' I struggled to control the crack in my voice. 'If I could, I'd keep you with me.'

My son pulled away as if I hadn't spoken. He turned and stared out of the window. Eventually, with his back to me, I heard him say he wanted his nanny.

When we arrived at the school gates there was a horrible tussle. Reuben wouldn't leave the car and tried to hold on to the door. Eventually Frank dragged him out. My son went limp in his father's arms. Frank said: 'Come on, brave soldier. It's not so bad. Chin up.'

We didn't linger. The headmaster said best not to. I kissed my son on the cheek and Frank shook him firmly by the hand.

I should have told Reuben I loved him – I wanted to tell him, so much – but I couldn't because people were watching us. So instead I said: 'Be a good boy.' Instead I said: 'See you soon.'

The journey home without him felt like driving away from a funeral. My husband sat in stony silence, I wept in the back seat, alone. It was my fault, I knew Frank was right. If I were a different woman, a better wife and mother, then my son would still be at home.

I kept seeing Reuben's face – dull-eyed with shock that his parents were leaving. I remembered the day my father sent me away.

We'd been driving for an hour when I asked the chauffeur to turn round. Frank was stiff with anger. He told the driver: 'Keep going.'

I pleaded with him to let me go back. 'This is wrong, can't you see? He's only small!'

Frank said: 'Gilda. Be quiet now.'

I wish I'd made more of a scene. I wish I'd screamed blue murder and forced them to turn. But instead I just sat there and wept as the car took me further from my son.

# 83

It's Friday afternoon and Harrods is closing as I make my way round to the Basil Street exit. I want to see if Alice is going to the pub with her colleagues again. I need to find out if my warning has worked: if Terry will dare to go with them.

I go straight to my spot in the recessed doorway and position myself beside the bin. The smell is especially bad this evening and my lavender hand cream fails to mask it. I breathe through my mouth but I taste it instead. I rifle through my handbag for a Polo mint.

I check my watch. It's half past five. Alice won't be out for another ten minutes. I look at the young people starting to gather, ready for a night on the town.

The weather is on the turn, I think. Not so warm now that you can do without a jacket. The girls are wearing boots and tights. The boys are in pea-coats and corduroys.

A city gent turns the corner into Basil Street. I look at him for a good few seconds before I realise he's my son. The shock drains all the blood from my limbs. He's twenty yards away, on my side of the road. I shrink back further behind the bin. *He didn't see me. I'm sure he didn't see me.* He must have come to meet Alice from work. He must have left his own office early.

Just when I think he's about to walk past me, he stops and cross-es over the road. He marches straight up to the Harrods doorway. He stands there with his briefcase – a sentry without a sentry box. He is stern and unsmiling, such a contrast to the other young people. He glowers at every man passing by.

A few minutes later Alice comes out. She kisses her husband on the cheek. His face lightens briefly as he takes her arm. She turns and waves her colleagues goodbye, but Reuben is already walking.

They are halfway down the street when Terry emerges from Harrods. His whole body tenses as he spots my daughter-in-law. 'Oy! Alice! Stop, I need to talk to you!' He pounds down the pavement towards them.

My son turns first, more startled, I think, than scared. Terry jabs the air in Alice's direction.

Reuben steps in front of his wife. He holds his briefcase as if it's a shield. Terry ignores him, yells past him to where Alice is stand-ing. His voice is rough but I can't make out the words. There's a burst of laughter from some nearby youngsters.

Alice is pale. She says something to Reuben. She pulls at his arm but he shakes her off.

Terry shouts over to Alice again. My daughter-in-law looks upset.

Reuben's face is a deep shade of red, his anger is about to boil over. Fear pricks at the back of my neck. A taxi passes.

My son lurches forward and pushes at Terry. Terry stays solid, doesn't move an inch. Reuben tries to push him again – he looks too slight in his smart tweed jacket. Alice covers her face with her hands. The two men are eyeball to eyeball.

Terry shifts his weight. He looks my son up and down. For a sickening moment I think he's going to punch him. Instead he shouts to Alice: 'Stay away from my house!'

Then he turns and strolls back in the direction of Harrods.

Reuben watches Terry retreat. Alice tries to take his hand. Her expression is pleading. *Let's go. Please. There's been a mistake. I want to go home. Can we go now?*

Terry is fifty yards away when he turns as if remembering something. He shouts it down the street, loud enough for everyone to hear. 'By the way, your wife's a little slut!'

Reuben charges at him, briefcase in hand. Terry ducks down, he smiles at first like it's a joke. My son slams the case into his head. Once, twice, three times. Terry falls to his knees. My son raises his case to bring it down a fourth time. Alice screams: 'Stop it! Reuben, stop it!'

My son straightens up. He's panting for breath. He doesn't look down to see the damage he's inflicted. He turns and heads back to his wife.

I stay still for a while, my eyes pinned to Terry. Two younger men pause to help him to his feet. His nose is bloodied, but he's able to stand. He waves the men off and lights a cigarette.

I feel a bit unsteady as I walk to the Tube. My ears still ring with the anger in their voices; with the sudden jolt of fear from the way that case slammed down.

*Did I do that? Did I cause that to happen?* My legs are weak like I've just stepped off a fairground ride. I need to go home. I need a stiff drink. I wish there was someone I could talk to.

# 84

Life at home was intolerable without our son. The fights exploded
once we had no one to rein them in for. We couldn't be in the
same room together. We stopped pretending in front of the staff.
We'd tear at each other no matter who saw it – with a look or a
cutting remark.

It would start as soon as I got home, I was a filthy drunk, unfit
to be a mother. The voice he used was different those nights. It was
harsher, tougher, often in German. *Schlampe. Luder.* His words
belonged to someone else. For the first time he reminded me of
my father.

We tried to keep to our separate corners but no house is big
enough for so much hatred. The misery seeped into everything
like a cloud of toxic gas.

The evening he tried to hit me I thought I deserved it. I'd said
the worst things I could think of, done my best to push him over
the edge. I told him he was inadequate in bed. I compared him to
Leo and said he wasn't good enough. I could see his temper building as I spoke. I could see the slap was coming and I welcomed it.

He pulled back just before his hand connected with my cheek.
His face bleached white and he ran from the room. Frank isn't
perfect but he's never been a violent man.

Later that night he sat down with me at the dining room table. He told me things had gone too far. 'This marriage has brought out the very worst in both of us. I can see it has to come to an end now.'

He said he'd grant me a divorce but only if I agreed to his conditions. 'I want us to do it right,' he said. 'This way we can minimise the damage.'

He handed me his three demands written in neat little letters on a sheet of headed paper. He'd signed it at the bottom with a jab of blue ink.

1) Your name will go forward as the guilty party in the divorce proceedings.
2) You will provide my lawyer with evidence of your adultery.
3) You will give up all rights to the custody of Reuben.

I didn't break down until I was with Leo, but then I cried so much I could hardly get the words out. I hadn't realised Frank could be so cruel. Whichever way I turned I'd lose. I felt tricked. Stupid. Backed into a corner. I remember thinking: *That's it then, I could never give up on my son.*

But Leo hugged me and stroked my hair. His voice was soft – such a contrast to Frank's harsh tones.

He said things weren't as bad as I thought. 'The boarding school has custody of Reuben most of the time. It won't change that much. You can visit him and see him in the holidays. He'll still write you letters. You can call him on the telephone. Really, it won't be that different.'

I would still be his mother, and that was the important thing. Whatever happened I'd always be his mother.

And I let Leo persuade me. I wanted to believe he was right. I knew how much he'd lost and I wanted to fix his hurt. He told me that he loved me and he needed me to be free. He's the only man who's ever said he loved me.

# 85

My neighbour's door slams and I sit bolt upright – Lizzie back from her gallery launch. I was just drifting off and now I'm wide awake again. I thump my pillow at her thoughtlessness.

I look at the clock. It's not even midnight. I get up and head for the loo. I feel a little tearful, like something has been stolen from me. The day was almost over, now it's not.

It's been a very long week, that's the truth of it. I haven't seen Alice or Reuben since what happened on Friday. Margo's gone to stay with a cousin in Gloucester. I haven't had a postcard or a phone call.

I've tried to ring my daughter-in-law, but no one answers. I've been to Harrods twice but she hasn't been in. I almost spoke to her horse-faced colleague but I lost my nerve and came home. I haven't seen hide nor hair of my son. When I went over there this evening the house was in darkness. His car wasn't parked in its usual space. I walked the whole length of the road.

I flush the loo and wash my hands. I fill my tooth-mug with tepid water. It tastes of soap but I drink it anyway. I turn off the light and shut the door.

*

I climb back into bed between still-warm sheets. I close my eyes and try to calm my thoughts.

I'm sure it's nothing to worry about, though it's natural I'm still a little bit jumpy. They've probably gone off to stay with their friends. Some sort of last-minute arrangement.

I can't go back to the way things were. I've started to rely on my Alice encounters. I got used to the quiet after Leo left, but now I see it's not enough.

I can't go back to the daily drag of it – the crossword, the Post Office, coffee for one at the Regency; the slow, silent hours until bath time and bed; the hopeless wait for visits that don't happen, the empty letterbox, the unanswered phone calls.

# 86

I handed control to Leo straight away. It felt like a relief. I let him make the arrangements. I let him book the guest house.

All I had to do was pack a small suitcase – my plainest clothes, my full-length nightdress. Things gained their own momentum and I was swept along. Everything had happened so quickly. Soon there'd be no turning back.

He seemed happy on the way to the coast. He'd never been to Brighton before and pointed things out from the train. I tried to read but kept losing my place on the page. My heart was beating out of my chest.

The weather was dreadful that time too, and Leo took my arm as we walked down from the station. We stepped into a pub for a drink en route and the whisky helped settle my nerves.

He was talking nineteen to the dozen about the beaches on the Baltic and how much he missed the sea. All I could think of was what lay ahead of us. I drank my whisky and I drank down another two and then I wanted it over and done with.

I knew The Bellevue wasn't going to be grand, but I couldn't have imagined how squalid it was – the skin-diseased paint, the stench of stale tobacco, the windows layered with grime. The landlady fawned all over us at first. 'Mr and Mrs Zubek, how charming.' You could hear the cigarette tar coating her voicebox. 'Welcome to the Bellevue,' she said.

She took us up a long narrow staircase, the carpet worn through on each step. We walked up three flights and she was wheezing and coughing. By the time we reached our room she couldn't speak.

Her hand was shaking as she unlocked the door and she went in and sat on the bed. She was gasping for air. Unable to form a sentence. Leo lit her a Capstan and she sucked on it.

When she'd caught her breath, she said: 'Toilet's down the hall.' Then she stubbed the cigarette out in our ashtray and left.

Leo walked over to the big bay window. We'd been promised a room with a sea view but the car park filled the frame. The ceiling was a map of dark brown water stains. The rosebud walls were damp to the touch.

It was only early evening but I didn't feel like dinner. I couldn't settle to anything. I didn't want to stay in that room.

Leo said we had to eat and so we changed out of our travelling clothes and went back into Brighton. We passed restaurant after restaurant but they were all too cheerful and bright. I didn't want to be near children or families. I ruled out anywhere with crowds.

I knew I was making things difficult and Leo began to lose patience with me. He said: 'I've had enough of this now.' We trudged back to the pub by the station.

Leo tucked into some pickled eggs and I drank four more whiskies. We didn't talk much but I felt a little stronger. All too soon it was time to go back.

*

The bed sheet was a weak-tea beige – coloured by age and in-adequate washing. There was a hole up near the pillow where it looked like the cotton had worn through. I pulled back the covers to see the rest of it and I gasped when I saw the stain. An ugly blot as big as my hand. The purple-brown of over-cooked liver.

Perhaps it was just a red wine stain – I told myself it was a red wine stain. I showed the sheet to Leo and he yanked it off the bed. He went straight down to change it and I got into my nightdress and sat in the only chair. It felt like he was gone for hours. I was stiff and shivery when he returned.

The sheet he carried was the same weak-tea beige. He told me he'd had to fight for it. The landlady had accused us of making the stain ourselves. She'd said she expected no better from foreigners. She said worse, but Leo wouldn't tell me.

I stayed in the chair, tired and tearful while Leo stripped the bed and remade it.

I had known the man was coming first thing but the knocking was needlessly loud. Leo got up and put on his dressing gown. When he answered the door the private detective was there, with the land-lady wheezing behind him. 'Good morning, sir. I represent Frank Goodman. I have reason to believe you are here with his wife.'

He was polite as he confirmed our names; asked nicely if he could come in. Kind eyes. He sought my permission before he took the photograph. He even suggested I cover up my nightdress. I was blinking as the flash went off.

Then he got out the confession papers and showed Leo and me where to sign. He said: 'I think we've got everything we need. With any luck it should go smoothly now.'

And all the while the landlady hovered in the corridor.

Afterwards, when we checked out, she raised her eyebrows and tutted at Leo. 'Mr and Mrs Zubek? And I'm the queen of Sheba.'

Leo wanted breakfast before we caught the train back to London. He said he was ravenous. He seemed to feel elated.

I told him I needed to get some air. That I needed just five minutes to settle things in my head. He said he'd meet me in the cafe by the station. He'd order me a coffee. 'Don't be long or it will get cold.'

As I walked I went over and over what I'd done. It had taken just a second to sign that piece of paper. I'd sat there in my nightdress and I'd signed away my son.

I thought about Reuben and the look on his face when we left him at school. I thought about how often I'd failed him, right from the start I hadn't been good enough.

I ducked into a telephone box because I didn't want to cry in the street. Before I knew it, I'd picked up the handset. I trembled as I dialled the number. Even though it was still so early, Frank answered the call straight away.

His voice was kind and gentle and concerned. I pressed Button A, though I was sobbing so much I couldn't get the words out. He said: 'Gilda, is that you? Are you all right? Gilda?'

And I managed to say: 'Yes. It's me.'

I tried to tell him what had happened at The Bellevue. I said I'd made a terrible mistake. It was all too sordid. I couldn't go through with it. I wanted to come back home.

But he said: 'No. I'm sorry. It's gone too far now. It's for the best – for Reuben, for all of us.'

I sobbed. 'We can just go back to how it was.'

But he said: 'We can't. It's too late.'

I heard another voice in the background. The maid coming in with his breakfast. Frank told her: 'Wait. I won't be a second.' And then to me: 'I have to go.'

I wanted to keep him talking, was desperate to keep the connection. 'Frank, please. For Reuben.'

He said, 'I've got to go,' and put the phone down.

I slowly put the handset back in its cradle. I blew my nose and blotted my eyes. I powdered my face and smoothed on some lipstick.

Then I walked up the hill to the cafe by Brighton station and I sat down at the table where Leo had my coffee waiting.

# 87

There's just one envelope in my pigeonhole this morning. One look at the handwriting and I know just who it's from. The letters are almost as rounded as the woman behind them and it's written in bright purple ink.

I tear it open on the way back up to my flat. There's a sunflower on the front of the card, which is pretty though it's part of a set.

*Happy birthday, darling!* The fat loops take up most of the page. *Fifty-three at last!*

Fifty-three is not a special age.

I've got the key in the door when I hear the telephone. I struggle with the lock and I get there just in time.

I snatch up the handset but it's Margo again. She's checking to see I got her card. 'I wanted to wish you happy birthday in person. Happy birthday, Gilda!' she says.

And this really is ridiculous because I'm seeing her at lunchtime. And she's tying up the telephone, which means no one else can call. So perhaps I'm a little more brisk than I should be. I bristle with impatience to get her off the line. She starts to chat and I cut her short. 'I'll talk to you later,' I say.

I wait and I wait. But the phone doesn't ring again.

*

It's Saturday, which means Margo and I are going to the cinema. I meet her in our usual cafe and she buys me a slice of cake. She insists on lighting a candle on the top, which is embarrassing but at least she isn't singing. It's a buttercream cake, her favourite not mine, but still, I suppose it's nice that she bought it.

She asks me if I got a card from Reuben and I tell her he sent me a big bouquet of lilies.

'Lilies,' she smiles. 'How lovely.'

I nod. 'I'm lucky to have him.'

After the film, we take a final cup of tea. Margo brings out a large flat parcel she's had hiding in her bag all this time. It's nicely wrapped in glossy purple paper and she's tied it up tightly with a strip of pink ribbon. I untie the ribbon carefully because I know she'll want to use it again and I peel back the paper to peek at what's inside.

And instantly my heart drops because what I glimpse is familiar. It's dark and solid, the corner of a picture frame. I know exactly where I've seen it before and I don't want to see it again.

I pull back the paper further, there's the heavy sky and the stormy sea. And the perspective is even worse than I remembered, that seagull looks big as a vulture. I never liked this ugly painting and now I'll have to hang it in my flat.

I smile and kiss her cheek. 'Thank you, darling. It's terribly generous.'

I kiss her cheek again and she beams.

I'm settling down with my evening whisky when the telephone rings and makes me jump. I grab the handset. It's Alice.

'Thank goodness we caught you, I was scared you might have gone to bed. Happy birthday, Gilda!' she says.

She asks me if I've had a good day and if I did anything nice. I tell her birthdays don't mean much now. Fifty-three is not a special age.

She says: 'But Gilda, fifty-three is a marvellous age. It's really something to celebrate. You've still got so much life ahead of you.'

I want to ask her where she's been all week but I stop myself.

Eventually Alice says she thinks Reuben would like to speak to me. She puts down the telephone in order to get him and she's gone for quite some time. I stand there with the receiver to my ear and I listen to the silence and I wonder if she's forgotten. Did she tell me to put the phone down too? Did she say he'd call me back?

And then suddenly my son is there and he says 'happy birthday' in his big booming voice. And it's as if all the lights have come on in the room and my heart feels like it will explode.

My Reuben's had a very long day and he says he's exhausted and cannot talk for long. He says 'I'm fine' when I ask him how he is and he adds 'it's getting terribly late'.

He doesn't ask me what I did to celebrate and he doesn't tell me where they've been. I'm just about to mention Margo's painting when he says he really must go.

So I say: 'It's been lovely to speak to you, darling.'

And I'm right in the middle of saying goodbye when he hangs up as if I wasn't there.

# 88

My father was furious about the divorce, though he didn't write to me, he wrote to Frank. He said he was ashamed of his youngest daughter. He hoped their shared business wouldn't suffer.

My mother refused to speak to me at all. Lena sent me fifty dollars in cash with a terse note telling me to save it. But Margo was the most upset, as if it was her family splitting up, not mine. I was surprised to find she cared so much. She took it as a personal betrayal.

She was shocked of course, I understood that. I hadn't told her about Leo so it seemed to come out of the blue. She was disapproving too, she said marriage vows were sacred. Mostly, she was worried for Reuben.

She came over to see me at the house before I moved out. She said Frank was a decent man. She thought it very wrong of me to leave him. She begged me to change my mind, though I told her it was too late.

She said: 'It's not just your life – what about your son?' As if I hadn't even considered him.

I told her that it wouldn't be so different. The school had custody most of the time and I'd still see Reuben in the holidays. I could talk to him on the telephone. I was still his mother, that was the important thing. Whatever happened I'd always be his mother.

She looked at me as if I were an imbecile. 'But he won't come and live with you, Gilda! His home will be here with Frank.'

I couldn't hear her. I didn't want to hear her.

I hoped she might meet Leo, but she wouldn't to begin with. I thought that if she saw us together she'd start to understand. I was desperate for her to like him. I needed to know she was on my side. I could be judged by my parents, by Frank's family and friends, but I couldn't cope if Margo turned against me.

Those months while we waited for the divorce to finalise were the worst for me. A period of limbo in Leo's tiny flat. It felt like we were in hiding. We saw no one but each other. It was suddenly just the two of us and I struggled.

I'd been used to having space and staff: a maid, a cook and a driver. I'd been used to seeing guests most nights, making small talk over whisky at dinner. I missed being a teacher. I missed my students. I missed the sense of purpose they gave me. Now my whole life was reduced to one small room.

Neither of us really cooked or cleaned. We didn't have much money or the skill to stretch our ration books so we survived on The National Loaf and tinned sardines. I missed seeing Margo, I needed someone to talk to. I argued a great deal with Leo and wondered if I'd done the right thing. It wasn't straightforward. There were times when I was thrilled to be free. There were times when I woke up beside him and thought: *At least I've got one thing right.* Then there were the other times, the times I couldn't speak. The times I didn't dress for days. The times when it all felt black again.

I yearned to see my son but I was also full of anxiety. I wasn't sure how we'd cope without a nanny in that dirty little flat where he didn't even have his own room. As the summer holidays grew closer I was frantic with the worry of it. I tried to talk to Leo but he just said Reuben was spoilt. He said there was nothing wrong with the flat, told me we were lucky to have it.

Eventually I called Margo. An act of desperation. It had been weeks since we'd last spoken and our friendship was strained to its limits. I was scared as I dialled her number. I thought she might hang up on me. But when she came to the phone her voice was kind.

'Gilda, darling, I've missed you.'

Margo knew just what to do about Reuben. 'Let's take him on holiday. We can stay with my parents in Dorset for the week. Reuben will love the beach. There's plenty for him to do.'

I can't describe the relief I felt. Just me, Reuben and Margo. It would be fun and bright and the sun would shine. And Margo could talk to my son.

# 89

Reuben has invited me round to his house for Sunday lunch. Well, Alice made the invitation, but Reuben will be there.

'Nothing grand,' she says. 'Just a nice simple roast. It's been far too long since we all got together.'

'Thank you, Alice. Yes, it has been rather long.' Excitement flutters in my stomach.

The first thing I do when I put down the telephone is go into my bedroom to decide on an outfit. I flick through all the hangers, but none of it seems quite right. A rail full of navies and burgundies and beiges: conservative dresses and sensible skirts. They're beautifully cut and were stylish in their time but there's not a single thing that lifts my spirits.

Kensington High Street is not my usual place to shop. This is not the sort of shop I'd usually choose to enter. I peer in the window past thick black swirls of paint. Do I really have the nerve to go in?

From the street, the interior looks gloomy and cluttered, more like a junk store than a fashion boutique. It's packed with shoppers but I don't see anyone my age. I clutch my handbag close to my hip. I should stick with Peter Jones where I belong.

I am just about to turn on my heel when three young girls

239

approach. They are Alice's age, I'd guess, all with the same smooth skin. They don't notice me, I'm older than their parents. They brush straight past and into the shop. I follow on behind, as if I'm their chaperone. 'Rita, you'll love it,' one says.

Once my eyes have adjusted to the dark inside I see clothes and hats on hat stands. The floor is checkerboard black and white and the walls are gaudy gold. I can smell something musky – slightly rotten, not quite clean. The place is a mess with clothes piled high. Everywhere you look girls are trying on outfits. A singer drones on about honky-tonk women. Modesty has gone with the wind.

I stand by the door. I'm a wallflower on the edge of the dance floor. All around me is noise and bustle. I can't see where to begin.

Eventually a shop girl comes over. 'Hello, madam, how can I help you?' She's drawn lashes on her eyes like spiders' legs.

I feel a little shy at first because it's clear as day I don't belong. I tell her I want to buy myself an outfit. 'Sensible. Not too outlandish.'

She smiles. 'I'm sure we can find you something.' She goes to one of the rails and comes back with a little pink skirt. She holds it up for my inspection. 'This is our most popular style.'

I tell her it's rather short for someone my age and she looks me up and down. She says: 'You're nice and tall, I think you've got the legs to carry it off. Why don't you go and try it on?'

Ridiculous flattery, I see straight through it. I take a look at the price tag – this tiny skirt costs more than my coat. But I will try it on because I do like the colour. It's a vibrant pink, which I'd call cerise but the shop assistant tells me is called 'bubblegum'.

The changing cubicle is minuscule and the pink skirt feels minuscule too. Once it's on, there's no weight to it. All I can see is leg.

When I come out the shop assistant beams. 'Goodness, you look fabulous!'

I try on the blouse she suggests, though it's rather sheer. I can see that the purple goes well with the bubblegum. That the loose sleeves flatter my shape.

240

'How about this?' The shop assistant hands me a maxi-dress – a parachute of peach polyester. It's not at all what I had in mind but she seems to think it will suit me.

When I look in the mirror I see someone else. Not younger exactly, but somehow more awake. And I think of all the dreary burgundies and navies in my wardrobe.

## 90

Reuben had changed a lot since I'd seen him. He'd be turning eight at the end of the summer and he wasn't a little boy any more.

He was quiet when we arrived to collect him from school. He didn't smile but said a weak hello. He wouldn't let me help with his bag and he dragged it all the way to the taxi.

He perked up slightly at the station and Margo managed to get him excited about the train. We had the whole carriage entirely to ourselves. 'It's just like being royalty,' she said.

Reuben seemed more relaxed with Margo. As we trundled along the south coast the two of them chatted away. Their talk was of beaches, the boats and the sea. Nothing I couldn't have managed. Yet whenever I tried to join in, the conversation seemed to fall flat.

It didn't matter, I was happy enough. I just sat there and stared at my son. Every time I looked at him I noticed small changes. His face was slimmer. His limbs were longer. He'd lost his chubby knees. Sometimes he caught me looking and frowned. It worried him, such close inspection. I tried to stop myself, but I couldn't look away for long. I had to take all of him in.

Margo's parents were warm and welcoming. Margo didn't tell

them about my divorce. They let us have the run of their ram-shackle house and their garden that went down to the sea.

It was wonderful to have all that space and light after months cooped up in Leo's tiny flat. It was good to be away from him too. Good to have a break from his intensity.

I felt happier and stronger as the days went on and Reuben seemed to as well. By the end of the week he was running around and playing with Margo. Sometimes he even left his book behind.

On the last day of the holiday Margo went swimming and I sat beside my son on the beach to watch her. He had a bit of colour in his cheeks and he'd taken his socks and shoes off.

I knew I should talk to him about the divorce, but I didn't want to spoil this moment together. I was scared to bring the subject up. I didn't know what Frank had told him. So instead we sat quietly side by side. We didn't say a word until Margo came out. She pulled a strand of seaweed from her costume and Reuben collapsed into giggles. I watched him laugh and then I laughed too and I felt a jolt of joy at the connection. There'd be plenty of time to discuss things later. No need to spoil a lovely day.

Afterwards we took him to the toy shop in the village. Margo said he should choose a souvenir so he'd have something to show his friends at school. I thought perhaps he'd choose a painted shell or a magnet in the shape of a seahorse. But Reuben fell in love with a blue toy car and he couldn't see anything else.

Margo said: 'No dear, it's far too expensive.' She tried to get him interested in an ammonite fossil.

But I saw my Reuben's face when he looked at the car and I needed to see that face again. I said: 'We'll get the car if that's what you want.'

Margo raised an eyebrow but she didn't try to stop me.

243

He hugged me. Properly hugged me. His arms reached round my middle and his smile stretched from ear to ear. He said: 'Thank you, Mother. It's wizard. I love it.'

That night, before Margo tucked him up, he came downstairs and he kissed me on the cheek.

When I went to check on him later, he was sound asleep with the car in his hand.

## 91

I slip the maxi-dress over my head; the peach polyester crackles with static. I hold my arm up to admire the sleeves, they're impractical really, but so pretty.

Getting out of those dreary old clothes has been like shrugging off a heavy overcoat. I feel lighter like this. Stronger, I suppose. Ready to enter this new age.

That confidence is still with me, deep inside me, when I leave the flat. I take large strides with my head held high. I enjoy the way the maxi-dress billows round my ankles. The sun is shining, it's cold and clear. I came out without my coat but I'm warm.

I arrive at the house at noon on the dot. I ring the doorbell and Alice answers. She takes a step back when she sees me. 'Golly, Gilda? Is that you?'

Her smile is wide and she hugs me like she really means it. She hugs me, really hugs me, like I haven't been hugged since Leo. She says: 'Well done, you. I love your hair. You look wonderful!'

And I blush and say: 'Thank you, Alice.'

She's made rather less of an effort. She is wearing some sort of peasant dress.

She leads me into the house and I am greeted by the smell of roasting chicken. She shows me into the living room. It's tidy and slick with polish.

I look round: 'Where's Reuben?'

She pauses for a second, her expression rather stiff. 'I'm so sorry. He was called in to work. There's been some emergency to do with the printers. He's terribly upset to be missing you.'

Mute with disappointment, I slump down on the orange sofa.

Alice puts a hand on my shoulder. 'I know it's sad. It's just one of those things. We can still have a lovely lunch, can't we?'

I nod but the day has been ruined.

She goes to the kitchen and returns with a bottle of Bristol Cream Sherry. She pours a decent amount into two little glasses and hands one over to me.

She talks about the house and my clothes and my new hairstyle. She tells me about Reuben's work and how terribly busy he's been. I'm feeling slightly better by the time she tops up my glass again.

The telephone rings and at first she ignores it. It keeps on ringing, the caller won't give up. Alice wrinkles her nose. 'Sorry, Gilda, I'm going to have to answer that.'

I get up and explore the bookshelf while she's gone. Most of the titles are Reuben's science fiction but the books about design must be hers.

She is absent for several minutes. I'm over near the door so I catch the odd sentence.

'Why does it have to be? – she's lonely and she cares about you – so what? – a few hours – for God's sake, you need to grow up!'

When she comes back into the room she looks calm and un-flustered. She smiles. 'I hope you're hungry. There is rather a lot for just us two.'

Alice says we'll eat in the kitchen at the little folding table she's set up in the corner. It is simply arranged – just knives and forks on red Formica. There's a large wooden salad bowl in the centre.

I take my seat and watch her get the chicken out. She spears it with two forks and transfers it to a carving dish. Then she lights the hob and puts the roasting tray on and sets about making gravy.

I am struck by how competent she is as she stirs in flour and slugs in wine. She tastes again and adds salt and pepper. All the while she's chatting to me. She tells me about some wallpaper she saw in the Habitat on Fulham Road. I think how very long it's been since I had a conversation with anyone but Margo.

When she's finished she pours the gravy into a little jug with one swift, clean movement. Then she gets the carving knife and sets about the chicken. 'Breast or leg or both?'

The plate she puts before me is piled high with meat. Three roast potatoes sit glistening on the side. 'Help yourself to salad,' she says as she pours us both a glass of red wine.

'To your fabulous new look,' she toasts me.

I wish Reuben was here, of course I do, but the chicken is delicious, I have to say. The roast potatoes are crisp and golden and I can't get enough of the gravy. I tell Alice she's an excellent cook. She shrugs: 'I just shoved it in the oven.' She tilts her head. 'Do you cook, Gilda?'

'No. I never really learnt.'

'Well then, perhaps I could teach you?'

I smile. 'That's kind, but you're busy with work?'

She toys with a bit of lettuce on her plate. 'No. Not any more. The shifts – it wasn't really fair on Reuben.' Her cheeks flush pink and she doesn't meet my eye. 'We don't need that disruption in our lives.'

Alice has made chocolate mousse for pudding. She serves it up in gold-rimmed coffee cups and we both eat it daintily with teaspoons. We talk about Margo's toe operation and she tells me about her mother's arthritis. The conversation is stilted now and there are silences we struggle to fill. Alice resorts to talking about the weather. 'It's nice for this time of year.'

In desperation, I admire the little coffee cups, they're quite ostentatious really. Not what I'd expect. Alice says: 'Yes, they are rather grand. A wedding present from Berta and Frank. Italian, I think.'

I remember the ugly cups Berta gave me and I laugh out loud at the contrast. Alice asks what's funny so I tell her all about those cups. How cheap they were, from Woolworths. What an ugly shade of yellow.

She smiles and shakes her head. 'That doesn't sound like Berta at all. I've always thought of her as such a generous woman. She speaks very highly of you.'

# 92

I was thirty-one when I married Leo. That's not much older than Reuben when he got married to Alice. But I'd already been through so much by then – had a son, an ex-husband, a past.

We got married in Islington Town Hall in the June of 1948. Margo and Zelda Ward from the refugee centre were there. I'd wanted Reuben to be there too but Frank said he had to stay in school.

Leo looked handsome; tall and smart in his borrowed three-piece suit. I wished we had more guests there so that I could show him off. The outfit I wore was nothing special – a cream linen dress which I'd had since before the war. But I felt beautiful because Leo told me I was beautiful.

Margo gave me a bouquet of pink roses to carry. It was the only wedding gift we got.

The ceremony was over in half an hour. We said our vows and Margo cried. We signed some forms and Zelda took a photograph. Then the four of us went out for lunch.

Afterwards I remember feeling so full of joy. We'd made it, Leo and I. We were finally husband and wife. Later he insisted on carrying me over the threshold of our flat. I was drunk and tired and happy so I let him.

That wedding night was so different from my first. It was warm and familiar; a body I already knew. I remember thinking: *This is how it should be*. I thought: *This is it now. Forever.*

Frank was very generous with the settlement. I don't know why – he didn't have to be. He insisted on giving me some money from the house, though really none of it was mine. He said he just wanted things resolved. We moved from Leo's studio to a decent-sized flat in Swiss Cottage.

Leo got himself a job in a school, teaching elementary German three days a week. He grew up near the border so he knew the language well. We didn't have much but we had enough to enjoy ourselves. Enough that we could have the odd treat.

I began to realise how lonely I'd been, at last I had a real companion for cafes and visits to the cinema. Leo would make up stories about the people around us: the woman with a secret Mexican lover; the old man who was clearly a Soviet spy. We would sit and talk and the hours flew by like minutes.

The first time Reuben came to stay with us I was so on edge I made Leo's life a misery. He had to repaint the spare room twice, because I didn't think my son would like the colour. I bought Reuben a *Boy's Own* adventure book, which I laid out on his bedspread with a bag of pear drops. I got him some Robinson's barley water and a box of Sugar Puffs for his breakfast.

His father brought him up on the train and Leo and I went to meet him at Finchley Road station. We stood at the ticket barrier – I was so nervous I couldn't keep still. Leo was chattering on about a woman he'd seen with hair like Churchill's poodle. I snapped: 'Will you just be quiet please?'

Eventually I spotted Frank and Reuben on the stairs. They were walking hand-in-hand. Frank leant down and whispered something. Reuben nodded, his face was pale and serious. Neither of them smiled when they saw us.

Leo stepped forward as they came through the barrier and put out a hand for Frank to shake.

Frank said: 'I won't stay long.' And to Reuben: 'You behave for your mother.'

My son looked down at his shoes. Frank gave him a quick hug, then left us together. Reuben turned to watch his father go. The three of us stood in silence.

Finally, Leo sprang to life. 'Hello, young man, your mother's told me so much about you. I used to have a little boy your age. He liked fruit and nut. I bet you do too. I happen to have a bar in my pocket.'

Reuben hardly said a word as we walked home but Leo kept up a steady stream of chatter. My son ate the square of chocolate Leo gave him and he nodded when asked if he liked cricket.

He wouldn't let us carry his suitcase. I could see it was heavy, he kept shifting his grip on the handles. I said: 'Go on, darling, why don't you give it to Leo?'

Reuben looked panicked. 'I promised Father I'd take good care of it.'

Leo laughed. 'Quite right, Reuben. You're a sensible boy, you shouldn't trust strangers. Why don't we carry it together?'

He patted my son on the head and took one side of the case. I was so grateful, I could have wept.

I didn't see Reuben as often as I wanted to but he came to stay with us in the school holidays. We spent that time together, the three of us, and I felt we were becoming a family.

We'd been married just short of a year when I heard the news about Frank and Berta. Reuben told me: 'Daddy's getting married.' I guessed it was Berta straight away.

She and her husband had been friends of Frank's from before the war. They used to come for dinner sometimes but Berta's husband was a bore. She was vibrant and witty back then and I remember thinking she didn't belong with him. When he died so suddenly it was terribly sad but I thought it might be better for Berta.

After she was widowed I saw a lot less of her but I knew she and Frank had stayed in touch. I thought he felt a duty towards her, she was childless and she was alone.

I remember she came once for afternoon tea. Things were very strained between Frank and I. She'd gone over the top with a garish floral dress, but she's always been showy like that. She was older than me – is still older than me – and I suppose I felt a bit sorry for her. I remember thinking: *She is past her prime.* She must have been at least thirty-five.

So when I heard that Frank was getting married, Berta's was the first name I thought of. I admit to a stab of jealousy – she'd move into my house, sleep in my bed. I wondered how it had come to this: this woman would be living with my son.

But actually, given time, I was pleased for them. Frank deserved to have somebody too. I thought perhaps it would make my life easier. That Frank being happy would take away some of my guilt. I thought perhaps he'd let me spend a little longer with Reuben. I thought Berta would want children of her own.

# 93

It's three in the morning and I can't get back to sleep. I've been doing this a lot of late, lying here staring into darkness. It's strange because I used to sleep so well – with Frank, with Leo – even with things at their worst. But something has changed in me. I'm different now.

Once I'm awake my head starts whirring, I try to stay calm but it doesn't seem to help. I pull at threads, I pick at scabs, I make things worse than they are.

Tonight I can't stop thinking about the coffee cups – my mind draws back to them over and over. I try to distract myself with happy thoughts of peaceful places. It's no good, they're all I can think about.

I need to find those cups. I kept them, I'm sure I did. I rack my brain for where they might be – I know I didn't throw them away. And even though it's the middle of the night and I should be fast asleep because I've got things to do tomorrow, I get up out of bed and into my slippers. I need to find those cups right now.

I go to the kitchen and switch on the light. The brightness makes me wince but I don't falter. I head for the cupboard under the sink; it's been years since I last looked down there. It's deep and dark and extends right into an awkward corner. It's where I keep the things I don't use. It's where I keep the things I have no place for.

I approach the cupboard gingerly, expecting junk to come clattering out. But actually it's so packed full that when I open the door nothing stirs. Most of it is taken up with pipework and there's a strong smell of damp that I'm sure I should investigate. I spot Windolene and a rusting pot of Vim and a basin my Reuben was once sick in.

I struggle to pull the items out – they're wedged in like stones in a wall. Behind them is a stack of Leo's old ashtrays. There's a pair of his thick-lensed spectacles, all dusty, on the top. I find some bicycle clips and a porcelain soup terrine. It hasn't been used since my marriage to Frank. It comes from another world entirely; I know I'll never use it again.

My back hurts from stooping so I sit on the floor. The cold tiles chill me through my nightdress. I reach blindly into the cupboard's furthest depths. Those cups are in here somewhere, I'm sure they are. I find a broken white candle, a milk jug with its handle missing, a Brillo pad, a thermos flask and a booklet on how to work the oven.

Finally my fingers touch a small cardboard box. I have to put my head in the cupboard in order to reach it. It's right at the back. It's grey and flimsy. When I bring it out I see the price tag on the top. My heart is in my throat.

I open the little box carefully and they are all still there, nestling in the cardboard. Six of them, still that same ugly yellow. Still the cheapest, chunky china that Woolworths ever sold.

But what strikes me as I sit in the kitchen is how small they are, like dolls' cups really. Not big and brash like Berta at all, but the kind of cups a child would choose.

I take the little box over to the light. It's late and I'm tired, but

I know I need to do this. I put on my reading glasses and study it closely.

And that's when I see it. Grey pencil on grey cardboard. Four words in childish handwriting. *From your loving son.*

## 94

It was the little things I noticed at first. Reuben had a haircut that was not the way I liked it. He wouldn't wear the purple scarf I gave him because 'Berta says mauve is for girls'. He tried to stop me smoking cigarettes: 'Berta says they're bad for your health.' His blue toy car was no longer his favourite and he swapped it for a big red truck.

I could see that I was losing him. He was slipping away from me like when he was a baby. There was nothing I could do to keep him close. He was changing; I felt powerless to stop it.

When I got Frank's letter saying they were going to Switzerland for the holidays I knew straight away that Berta was behind it. Frank said she had a cousin in Zurich and the fresh air would do them all good. I could tell it wasn't his idea, it was Berta's way of taking my son. They were going away for a whole six weeks. Six weeks of mountains and fun. I got three days with Reuben that summer.

Leo hated to see me cry so I was sitting at my dressing table trying to repair the damage. We were going out that evening the three of us – me, Leo and Reuben, to the theatre. It was supposed to be our holiday treat. A celebration that we were together as a family.

But all I could think of was how soon it would be over. How little time I had with my son.

When Reuben came into the room I was putting on my earrings. I'd redone my mascara twice but my face still looked smudgy and bruised.

He must have been excited about his holiday. His eyes were bright beneath his too-short fringe. He looked different standing there. Taller. Older. He'd finished his first year at senior school. He was wearing a pair of ugly brown shorts that were not the ones I'd bought him.

He was holding a gift wrapped in tatty tissue paper. He didn't say anything. Just handed it over. I looked at him and he looked down at his feet.

When I opened it I saw six ugly coffee cups in a Woolworths box with its price still on. I could see straight away they'd come from Berta. *Bought in haste,* I thought. *Bought by someone who doesn't care.*

So I told Reuben exactly what I thought of those cups: their cheapness, their ugliness, their stained-urinal yellow. I didn't hold back; I let it all out. I voiced all of my anger and all of my pain, as if Berta was standing there in front of me.

I said: 'I don't want anything from that woman. She can keep her stinking gifts. She isn't your mother, never forget that. You're my son and you belong to me.'

I saw Reuben's face as he ran from the room. I saw his strained expression, the tremble in his lip. He was quiet at the theatre later. He barely spoke for the next two days.

And then he left for Switzerland and that was it for the rest of the summer.

# 95

It's still too early – I should have thought – nobody's opened their curtains yet. All the houses are shrouded in darkness. The sun is just pinking the sky. There's frost on the ground, but I'll have to wait. I should have dressed properly, not left in such a rush. I pull my coat more tightly round my nightdress and I lean against the wall beneath the trees. I close my eyes, just to rest them for a minute. My sockless feet are numb inside my shoes.

I haven't slept since I found the cups, I've been going through what happened over and over.

Those things I said to Reuben, none of it was meant to hurt him.

He loved me when he bought those cups.

He loved me.

When I open my eyes the street is lighter. It's raining slightly but I'm sheltered by the oak. A bowler-hatted man leaves his house. I watch him struggle with his black umbrella. I need the loo. My mouth is very dry. I wish I'd brushed my teeth.

I flick the bits of dead leaf from my coat and I stamp my feet to warm them. I tie my headscarf tighter round my hair. As I step out onto the pathway, I feel wobbly and exposed. I raise a hand to shield my face – I don't look up, keep my eyes on the ground. An engine revs on the road outside. I walk quickly to the house and press the bell.

There are footsteps inside but the door doesn't open. Eventually I hear the bolt slide across and Reuben is there in his work clothes.

'Mother? What are you doing here?' His face is pale. Frowning.

'Reuben!' I go to hug him. He steps backwards, just out of reach. 'What's going on? Why are you here?'

His voice is all wrong. This isn't how I planned it. And suddenly I know I shouldn't have come here. Reuben hasn't got his shoes on yet. 'It's too early. I'm sorry, darling. I just – I should come back later.'

Reuben puts his head in his hands. I glimpse anxious eyes through his fingers. He doesn't ask me to go away but he doesn't ask me inside.

'The cups. I didn't realise.' The lump in my throat makes it hard to speak. 'I got it wrong. I thought they came from Berta. I thought – I was so sure that Berta had bought them.' My nose is running. I can't find a tissue. I dab at the mucus with my hand.

Reuben slowly shakes his head, his eyes are points of black staring just past my shoulder. His voice is quiet but I can hear the strain behind it. 'Mother, go home. I don't know what you're talking about. I can't do this now. I've got work.'

I try again: 'The coffee cups—'

He cuts me short: 'Go home.'

He turns back inside and leaves me there on the doorstep. I'm freezing cold and desperate for the loo and a tissue to blow my nose. I know I mustn't stay but I can't go home like this. I stand there for a minute and cry. I don't know what else to do.

Alice comes out in her dressing gown. Her face is still puffy with sleep. 'Gilda, what's happened?' She hugs me. 'You're freezing.

Come inside, you poor thing. Look at you, you're shivering. Come in quick before you catch a chill.'

I start to speak but my whole body's shaking. My teeth are chattering and I can't get the words out. Alice tries to take my coat but I pull away and keep it on.

'I'm getting you some hot tea. Has something happened? What's wrong?' I tell her I need the loo and she leads me to it.

I hear murmured conversation and the front door slams. Reuben has gone to work. My face in the mirror is the face of a mad woman. I am here, in their house, in my nightdress.

I walk out slowly, past the kitchen. Alice is pouring the tea into mugs. She calls to me: 'Gilda, come in and sit.' For a second I almost do. Her voice is full of warmth. It would be so nice just to sit and tell her everything. I think she'd be gentle. She'd understand, I think.

## 96

Leo was very kind to Reuben and he tried his best to love him. Sometimes it was hard for him, I know. It's different when it's not your flesh and blood. Reuben was 'a great boy', 'a clever clogs', 'a champ', but he could never be what Leo wanted. He could never be Leo's true son.

And though I adored to see them together, I was always aware of that lack. It made me more protective of Reuben. Made me love him even more.

My son had just turned ten when Leo offered to teach him chess. I was thrilled and went straight out and bought a set – a smart one in ebony and boxwood.

We unpacked the pieces from a baize-lined box; the heavy brass-hinged board smelled of varnish. We laid it out on the kitchen table. Reuben came alive with excitement.

Leo said it was a Staunton set. He lined up all the pieces, the black and the white. He asked my son to choose his favourite. Reuben shyly pointed to the horse.

Leo picked it up. 'Of course – yes – the knight.' He stroked its wooden mane with a finger. Then he put it on the chessboard and showed Reuben how it moved. 'Like this – in an

L-shape. It's special because it can jump.'

Reuben nodded, gravely serious, and Leo moved on to the next piece. He went through all of them one by one and then put them back in the box.

'So,' said Leo. 'Now it's your turn to show me. I'm going to pick the pieces and you can tell me all about them.'

Leo the teacher. I could hardly breathe in case I spoilt it. My son was solemn, determined to get it right. Bottom lip between his teeth, he studied each piece that Leo gave him. He spoke in almost a whisper, as if reciting a spell. 'This one's the rook, he moves across or down. This one's the bishop, he goes in a diagonal line.'

'Bravo,' said Leo. 'You'll be a grandmaster in no time.'

Reuben beamed from ear to ear and hugged me without being told to.

Their games became a routine when he was with us. They'd sit opposite each other on Sunday afternoons. It moved me to see the two of them like that: heads bowed deep in concentration.

I'd sit and watch them play for hours. I could see Reuben's confidence building. Leo was patient: 'Careful, Reuben, are you sure?' My son would hesitate, look for clues from his stepfather. 'Won't that put your king at risk? Maybe the rook would be better.'

One evening after Reuben was in bed, I told Leo how much the matches meant. We were sitting at the table with a glass of wine, they'd been playing chess all afternoon. My two boys together; my family. I could see their relationship growing.

I said: 'He really looks up to you, Leo. He's happy – it's wonderful to see it.'

I remember Leo's smile then, how the love shone out of his eyes. He said: 'Did I ever tell you I taught my own son chess, back in Poland before the war? We used to play in the evenings while Katya cooked us dinner. He was really good, Gilda. He beat me every time. I thought he'd join a league when he was older. He . . .'

262

He swallowed, tried to clear his throat. 'It's . . . these games with Reuben remind me so much of that time. Sometimes I even forget who I'm playing with. Sometimes I think my son's alive.'

# 97

The faint metallic taste from the sleeping pill I took last night is still in my mouth as I pour out the whisky. I swallow it straight and pour out some more. There's no reason now to hold back.

It's hard to know how long I've been sitting here. I can hear the tick of the living-room clock but I can't make out the time. The light from the hallway casts shadows on the wall. The curtains have been drawn all day. For all I know it's dark outside.

I've been thinking about Reuben – his face on the doorstep. I keep going back to it, over and over. What kind of mother am I, that my son can't even look at me? What kind of mother am I, that he had to tell me to leave?

And I think of all the other times I've got it wrong. I think how often I've let him down, how I failed him and chose the wrong thing. Right from the start he deserved so much more than he got from me.

I dropped Reuben once. I've never told anyone this, but I dropped him and I could have really hurt him.

His nanny was late bringing him in that evening and I'd had a second whisky. Perhaps I'd been a little generous with the measure, but I wasn't drunk. I was not drunk.

She handed him to me and then she left to get his blanket. She was worried he'd be cold so she left me with my son. When Reuben saw her go he started wriggling and kicking and struggling on my hip.

He caught a bit of my hair in his fist. He twisted it and pulled it. And I was holding him in my one arm and trying to release my hair with the other and he strained again and he – somehow he just pitched back.

There was a dull thud as he landed on the carpet. He lay there still and silent. For a second I thought the very worst had happened. For a second I thought both our lives were over.

But then he got some air in his lungs and he screamed louder than I'd ever heard him scream.

By the time the nanny returned I had my son back in my arms. He was still making so much noise that she came running over. 'Goodness me, Reuben. What's all this fuss about? Hush now, little man. Here's your blanket.'

I didn't tell anyone what happened; I thought they'd take him away from me. But after that, whenever Reuben cried I handed him to someone else.

# 98

Reuben was a shy, sweet boy, but he turned into a sullen adolescent. He hardly spoke when he came to stay and only mumbled in answer to our questions.

Leo tried to draw him out with offers of football, movies and chess but my son would rather stay in his room and read, he made that very clear. When we forced him to put his book away at mealtimes he ate quickly, forgetting his manners. By the time Leo and I had poured ourselves some wine, Reuben had emptied his plate.

Frank said he was in trouble at school. He'd struggled to make friends and his work had slipped. It hurt me to hear that, I wondered if it was my fault. If I'd been a better mother, if I'd made some different choices, maybe things would have been easier.

Frank and Berta were on holiday that fortnight, so I was the one the headmaster rang. He said Reuben had had an accident and needed to come home straight away.

I froze. 'Is it bad?'

'It's nothing terribly serious. He's hurt his arm, but he'll mend.'

I asked how it had happened.

'Youthful high spirits. You know what boys are like.'

Youthful high spirits didn't sound like Reuben at all.

We got to the school as fast as we could. When we arrived a boy was sent to fetch my son. Reuben came down with his arm in a sling – his face was colourless. I went over to hug him but he flinched.

Leo talked to the headmaster and tried to get to the bottom of things. Reuben had been fighting but the headmaster wouldn't say why. 'One of the boys knocked into him. There was a bit of a scuffle and your son fell over. They were playing a game. Boys will be boys. I don't think any harm was meant.'

All the way home in the back of the taxi, Reuben slept wrapped in a blanket. I could see how fragile he was, an injured bird. His poor arm clutched to his chest.

When we got home he went straight to his bedroom. Leo took him supper but he hardly touched a thing. The next day, again, he stayed in bed and wouldn't eat. I was scared for him and called the doctor in.

He was a kind man with a gentle face and said Reuben just needed rest. 'Try not to worry, Mrs Zubek. It's hard for boys to open up to their mothers. He'll talk when he's ready. Perhaps his father might do better?' We decided Leo should have a go. 'Be patient,' the doctor said.

I was making a pot of tea when I heard Reuben shouting. I ran to his room. My son was wild-eyed and hysterical. He was sitting on the bed with Leo beside him. He pointed at me. 'Get out! I hate you! It's all your fault!'

Leo shook his head. 'Gilda, go back to the kitchen.'

I did as I was told. I poured my whisky with shaking hands. My husband stayed with Reuben and tried to calm him down.

They were in there together for almost an hour. Reuben refused to talk at first. Then, slowly, slowly, Leo got it out of him. The boys at school had been bullying my son. They'd made his life a misery for years. They picked on him because he was Jewish and

267

they picked on him because his parents were divorced. They told him Leo was a dirty Pole, they called me a slut and a tart. When he tried to stand up for me they pushed him down a flight of stairs.

It was three days before Frank and Berta got home. Reuben stayed in bed and refused to speak at all. He ate his meals from a tray in his room. When I came to say goodnight he turned away.

Leo said I shouldn't worry, Reuben would come round. He told me not to take it to heart. 'He's your son and he loves you,' he said.

But I saw my Reuben's face when Frank arrived to collect him. He heard his father's voice and came running out of his room. He clung on to his father. He grabbed him round the middle with his one good arm. My son was sobbing, he couldn't get his words out.

Frank's voice was soft and low and soothing as a lullaby. 'I'm here now, my brave boy. It's all right. I'm here now.'

# 99

The concierge brings the whisky upstairs and I feel myself blush as I take it from him. He doesn't linger but he looks me in the eye and says: 'You take care, Mrs Meyer.'

I close the door and open the bottle. This time I don't see the point in decanting it. I pour a slug of it into my glass. I'll try and make this bottle last.

I haven't been well, these past two days. I haven't been quite myself. I've been finding it hard to figure out what's real and what is not. I wanted so badly to mend things with Reuben. I wanted to make it right. But it's too late, I've hurt my son too much. I can never make up for what I've done.

I think perhaps I need to talk to someone. Sometimes you just need to talk. I dry my eyes with my dressing-gown sleeve. Leo didn't like it when I cried.

I hunt for my address book and find it on the hallway table. I flick through all the pages – from the front right to the back. Eventually I spot the entry but the number is an ink smudge, impossible to focus. I hold the page at arm's length but the figures refuse to align.

I pour a little more whisky in my glass and I sit on the floor to concentrate. I lean my back against the hallway wall. The skirting board is hard against my spine.

When I open my eyes, the place is in darkness, my address book is still in my hand. I am stiff and shaky as I clamber to my feet. I have no idea of the time.

I switch on the lamp and locate my spectacles. I turn back to the page and now I can read it. I reach for the telephone and pick up the receiver. My finger is clumsy in the dial.

The ring is long and foreign. She isn't going to answer. One hand hovers over the plungers – I can hang up at any time.

I count ten rings. Eleven. Twelve.

'Hello? Who is it?' That fake American accent. 'Hello? Hello? Is anyone there? Hello? Gilda? Is that you?'

I sip my whisky and it helps a little. I manage a whisper. 'Yes. It's me.'

'Are you all right?' She sounds wary. Suspicious. 'Is something wrong? Why are you calling? It's not like you to call.'

A tear slips into the mouthpiece. 'I just – I wanted to speak to you, Lena.' The words come out strangled. It's hard to breathe. 'I wanted to talk, that's all.' In the silence the receiver crackles. 'I'm fine.' The lie echoes back at me.

She's quiet for a second. 'You've been drinking.'

I quickly put my glass down. 'No. Just a little. It's fine.'

'I thought you'd stopped all that.' She pauses. 'You said you'd stopped it.'

I press a hand against my forehead to cool it. 'There's no need to worry. No need.'

'I'm your sister, of course I worry. I just wish you were happier, darling. I want to know what's going on in your life. When are you coming out to see me?'

Her kindness is so unexpected that something comes loose inside me. I crouch down and clutch the receiver to my chest, the telephone cord stretches tight. I breathe in deep, gulp at the air. Then I sob my pain into the handset.

Her words are soft beside my ear: 'Gilda, what's wrong? What is it?'

When I finally speak my voice is small. 'I've been so blind. Such a bloody stupid idiot. It's too late. My poor son. How could I not have seen?'

She's silent for a fraction too long.

'Lena?'

She sounds hesitant. 'No, darling, hush. It wasn't your fault.'

'But it was my fault. I'm a terrible mother. I should have known. I should have. Because that was it, wasn't it? That's when it all went wrong.'

'No,' her voice is urgent, she speaks quickly, firmly. 'We all heard the rumours but Father didn't want you to know. Frank was too important to him. He was worried about his business.'

My head is bursting. My forehead throbs. 'I've messed it all up. It's too late.'

'I did try to warn you but it was all so complicated. I could see it was bad, but by then you were with Leo—'

I'm suddenly exhausted. My sister never listens to me. 'Reuben, Lena. I'm talking about Reuben.' My words come out slurred. 'The coffee cups.'

# 100

I knew that Leo wanted children of his own. We'd talked about it when we first got married. He hoped that it might help him move on: heal the wounds from what had happened in Poland. And you can't say no to something like that. You can't say no if you think someone might leave you.

So I told him: 'Maybe one day.' And he accepted it. He didn't push me. He said: 'Yes. Maybe one day.' But I could see all the hope in his eyes.

There were a million selfish reasons why I didn't want a baby. I was scared of giving birth again. I knew I'd been a failure as a mother. Still I would have gone through with it. In those early days, I would have. I would have done anything to make him happy.

But as time goes on things change in a marriage. After five years a baby felt just as far-fetched as the mansion Leo dreamt of or the car he hoped to drive. We talked about it from time to time. I never said no, but I never said yes. I thought we could just let it slide for a while. Middle age felt like a haven.

The night things came to a head we'd dropped Reuben back at school after a half-term week full of silence. We were both of us exhausted, both of us strained to breaking point. I poured myself a drink. I wanted to blot out the day.

When Leo said we needed to talk, my first thought was that he would leave me. He sat me down at the table in the kitchen and he said: 'This can't go on.'

He said he needed more from our marriage. 'I've tried my best, but it isn't enough. Gilda – I want a family with you. Now, before it's too late.' And that hurt because I thought we were a family. Me, Reuben and him.

He reached over the table and he took hold of my hand and he said: 'Gilda, I want to be a father.' And I thought: *But aren't you already a father?* And I thought: *He's given up on my son.*

We'd been married nearly six years when I found out I was pregnant. Leo guessed before I knew myself. When I refused my coffee and felt queasy at breakfast, he put down his toast and he grinned. He said: 'Gilda, d'you think you could be?' His eyes were shining. He leant over the table and kissed me on the lips and my heart sank like a stone.

I didn't go to the doctor, though Leo kept trying to make me. I spent the next weeks certain nature would take its course. Every little cramp, every flutter saw me rushing to the toilet, a mess of hope and fear. I was thirty-seven, too old to have a baby. Women miscarry all the time.

But gradually, my feelings shifted. I thought about the first time I held my son. I found I could recall every tiny detail – each papery fingernail, each vein beneath his skin. I remembered the rush of overwhelming love; the knowledge that I was his mother.

At night I lay in bed beside my husband who was so full of hope, so sure. He said: 'This will be a fresh start for us. Our own baby – I can't wait to meet it.'

And I thought perhaps things would be different. We weren't at war. I knew what to do. I'd be a better mother this time.

*

I was only nine weeks gone when Leo told Reuben. We'd both agreed we would wait until later but Leo simply couldn't keep it in. He made the announcement while we were sitting in the living room. 'Reuben, we've got something exciting to tell you. Guess what? We're going to have a baby!'

My son didn't lift his head from his book.

'A little brother or sister, Reuben. We'll be a proper family. Isn't that wonderful?'

Reuben kept reading.

I said: 'Darling, please answer Leo.'

My son lowered his book a fraction. I could see the tension in his jaw. 'Why are you even telling me?' His eyes bored into me. 'You don't give a damn what I think. You never have.'

Leo snatched the book away. 'Apologise to your mother!'

'No. She doesn't care about me. If she did she'd still be with my father!'

Leo didn't think before he threw the book. The hard-back cover flapped as it hurtled the short space between them. I didn't see the impact, I hid my eyes, but I heard the thud. When I looked again my son was white-faced. The book was splayed out on the floor.

Leo was horrified. 'Oh God, Gilda – darling, I'm so sorry. I didn't – I'd never – you know I'd never hurt him on purpose.'

And it's true, he'd never hurt my son on purpose. I could see he was a good man and he'd been through too much pain. But I knew he'd never love my son in the same way he'd love a child of his own. He wanted us to make a fresh start with the baby; be a family, just us three.

And though I loved Leo – love him still in many ways – I couldn't make a fresh start. I couldn't let my son be pushed out.

When I left Frank I was given a choice. I chose Leo and Reuben paid the price. This time I had to make the right choice. This time I had to choose my son.

# IOI

In my dream it is a school bell, summoning me in to an exam I haven't prepared for. I'm sweating, heart pounding; I know I'm going to fail. The bell keeps ringing. Nobody warned me about this test. It rings and rings long after it should stop.

Something in it drags me back to consciousness, though I'm exhausted and I just want to sleep. I realise it's the doorbell. My head is splitting, my mouth is dry. I reach for the bedside clock and it's almost noon.

I slowly put my feet to the floor, feeling every single one of my fifty-three years. I take my gown from the hook on the door and trail it as I shuffle to the hall.

I clear my throat a couple of times. 'Yes. Who is it?'

'Gilda, it's Alice. Can I come up?'

I grope through the fog in my brain. I can't think what she's doing here. It's been three days now since I've left this flat and the air is thick and stale.

'Please let me in, Gilda. I need to know you're OK.'

My daughter-in-law – did I invite her? Yesterday is a big black hole. I move my tongue around the sourness in my mouth. I shrug and buzz her in.

I walk back to the bedroom thinking I should put some clothes on. I check my face in the mirror but it's too far gone to fix. I'm bra-less, in my nightdress. I pull on one of Leo's old sweaters. I run a comb through my bleached-out hair, which is lank and dark with grease.

Her knock is so gentle I almost miss it. A tiny little tap. It takes all my strength to open the door. She's standing there, neat and clean.

'Gilda, thank goodness.' She tries to hug me but I know I haven't washed. I lead her into the living room, I'm not sure where else to take her.

The carpet is a mess of ashtrays and glasses. The curtains are closed and she opens them. Leo's old records are scattered on the floor; Reuben's baby pictures on the table.

She says: 'I kept trying to ring you. I was worried when you didn't answer.' I remember the telephone did ring once or twice. I thought it was Margo and left it.

Standing drains me so I sink into my armchair. Alice moves an ashtray to sit on the sofa opposite. I reach for the bottle and I ask her if she'd like one. 'Whisky?' My voice is a croak.

'No, it's a little bit early. Why don't you go and run a nice hot bath while I make things comfortable out here.'

Alice has told me to run a bath. This is all so strange and my brain is very slow. It's an odd instruction – I still can't think why she's here. But her voice is strong and her orders are clear so I go and run the bath like I'm told to.

It takes a while for the tub to fill. I sit on the loo seat and wait. I hear Alice moving around outside: the clink of crockery, the bang of a cupboard. The sound is comforting. I've been on my own too long. I feel like a small child again.

There's a walnut-shaped bruise near the top of my right thigh. I think I might have bashed it on the hallway table. I was talking on the telephone. To – to Lena? Did my sister call? A memory flickers then evaporates.

When the bath is full of steaming hot water I lower myself into it slowly, slowly. I watch my flesh turn from grey to pink. I rest my feet between the taps.

I duck my head right under the water and stay there as long as I can. *I told Lena about the coffee cups. Didn't I?*

When my lungs are bursting I come up for air. Then I sink into the warmth once again.

# 102

I'd heard horror stories about backstreet butchers but I would have gone to one, done anything. In the end I asked Zelda Ward for advice. Somehow I knew I could trust her.

She wasn't shocked and she didn't judge me. She asked me if I was sure. Then she gave me the number of a doctor and I called him the very same day.

I turned up alone and on foot at a red brick house near Wandsworth Common. It wasn't grand but it was far from down-at-heel. It was middle-class, comfortable, genteel.

My heart was in my throat as I walked up the path. The door was answered by a man in his sixties. He had a bank-manager's face – professional, unsmiling. He spoke to my shoes. 'Follow me.'

He led me down a corridor to what looked like a family living room. He said: 'It's best you pay up-front. It might not be practical later.'

I used Lena's fifty dollars, the money she'd sent me when I left Frank. I handed it over in a pale blue envelope. He took out the cash and counted it.

He smelled of lemons, I remember that. Aftershave or disinfectant, I couldn't be certain. He wore a check shirt, a tie and a Harris tweed jacket – there was no reassuring white coat.

He took me upstairs to the bedroom he used as his surgery. There was a narrow couch covered with a faded yellow blanket. He spoke briskly as if I were a tiresome child: 'Underclothes off and lie down, please.'

He washed his hands in the small white corner sink and he dried them on what looked like a tea towel. Then he said: 'Right. Down to business.' He took off his jacket and rolled up his shirt-sleeves. I lay there, shut my eyes and tried to be somewhere else.

He didn't speak during the procedure. He opened my legs. Put something cold inside me. I felt a searing pinch and that was it.

Afterwards he told me to sit up. He gave me some pills and a glass of water. He gave me some more pills for when I got home. The water tasted of rust.

I took a taxi back to the flat. I was aware that the driver was talking to me – something about the traffic, the coronation and fish for tea. I couldn't reply, I kept my eyes on my lap. I could feel the giant pad the doctor gave me.

It started in the early hours of the morning. The cramps woke me from a troubled sleep. I stumbled to the bathroom and sat shivering on the loo. I gripped my knees with clammy hands. I counted the tiles on the floor.

I told myself I'd done the right thing. *I had to do it. I did it for Reuben.*

I'd been in there for I don't know how long when I heard Leo's footsteps outside. 'Darling, are you OK?' He tried the handle but I'd locked the door. 'Darling, you've been in there ages.'

'I'm fine. I'll just be a minute.'

He rattled the handle. 'Let me in, please – I'm worried.'

I cleaned myself up as best I could and opened the door a crack.

'What's wrong? What's happened?' He looked so young in his striped pyjamas.

'I can't—'

'Oh God. I'm calling an ambulance.'

I grabbed his arm. 'Leo, don't.'

He pulled away and took the telephone from the hallway table. 'My God Gilda, why didn't you wake me?'

I watched helpless as he picked the receiver up; stood frozen in the bathroom doorway as he dialled.

'My wife. I think she's having a miscarriage—'

'Leo, stop!' I lurched forward and grabbed the telephone from him.

'What are you doing?'

'I can't go to hospital. It's my fault. I did it. I had to. For Reuben.'

'Did what?' His eyes stretched wide.

I put my hand on my stomach. 'I – had – to.'

He lurched backwards. 'What have you done? You killed it? Gilda, what have you done?'

I thought he was going to hit me. Instead he punched the doorframe. I flinched as his knuckles connected with the painted wood. Then he turned and went back to the bedroom.

I followed him in. I was too weak to stand so I sat against the wall. He opened the wardrobe and started throwing things into a suitcase. He was shouting, sobbing. 'Our baby? How could you?' He pointed to the blood on the hem of my nightdress. 'You're a murderer. You murdered our child!'

# 103

Alice calls from the living room: 'Gilda? How are you getting on?'

I am standing in my underwear trying to find some clothes. Everything I pull out is lurid and skimpy. The colours make my eyes hurt. I dig around towards the back of the wardrobe and find an old pair of navy-blue slacks. Then I throw on Leo's sweater again and run a comb through my hair.

When I walk into the living room, all the ashtrays and glasses are gone. Leo's records are back in their covers. The photographs are stacked in a pile. The window is open and the air is almost fresh.

Alice says: 'There now. That's much better, isn't it?'

And she's right, it is better.

My daughter-in-law tells me she's warmed some soup and she brings a little bowl in from the kitchen. I try a smile: 'Thank you, Alice.' It's the first hot food I've had in days.

I sit in my armchair with the tray on my lap and Alice sits opposite and watches me eat. The soup is Campbell's cream of chicken. I don't remember buying it. I spoon it up quickly. It's bland and easy to swallow. Alice nods approval with each mouthful. I don't pause until the bowl is empty.

She picks up the little stack of photographs and points to the top one. 'Look at the two of you.' She holds it up so I can see. 'God, you were beautiful. I've never seen you look so happy.'

It was taken just after Reuben was born. He's swaddled in my arms, gazing up at me blindly. My eyes look soft and full of love.

She says: 'You were terribly young.'

'I was twenty-three, the same age as you.'

She stares at the picture for a minute. 'Do you ever wonder what your life would have been like if you hadn't had children?'

My thoughts flick back to the other baby. But she doesn't know – of course she doesn't know. I shake my head. 'I couldn't begin to imagine it. I wouldn't want a life without Reuben.'

She puts the picture down and touches my arm.

'You know, we were really worried about you.'

I flinch at the memory – his face on the doorstep – but I notice she said 'we' and it cheers me.

She says: 'You still don't seem quite yourself. Are you all right? Is there anything else I can do? I'll pop in and see you tomorrow if you like.'

I'm not sure how to answer. It's as if she didn't see the empty whisky bottles. 'I'm starting to feel a little better now. Thank you.'

She gets up from the sofa and puts on her coat. I feel a stab of panic. The grown-up is leaving. She stops and rests her hand on my chair-back. 'I'd like to think we could talk to each other. We can talk to each other, Gilda, can't we?'

Alice's departure drains the life from the flat. I reach for the whisky bottle, then think, no, and put it back down.

Instead I pick up the pile of photographs and look again at the girl with her son. She has thick, glossy hair, she has dark eyes and smooth skin. I'm as far away from her now as Reuben is from that baby. It doesn't change the fact that the girl was me. I'm shocked to realise she was beautiful.

# 104

I heard nothing from Leo for several weeks and I thought that was it. Marriage over. But then he rang and said he had something he needed to ask me. I convinced myself he wanted to talk things through; at least to give it a try.

He said we should meet at the flat but I insisted on Luigi's. I wanted to remind him of happier times. I reserved the table we always sat at, the small one in the corner with the view of the whole restaurant. I booked the hour we always dined at. Eight. Not too early, not too late.

I dressed carefully for our meeting, wore the glass pearls he gave me on our first anniversary. I had my hair set, bought lipstick, tidied the flat, changed the bed sheets. I stocked up on his favourite Lyons coffee and his full-strength Capstan cigarettes.

I told myself he really would be coming home with me. Perhaps we could start again. I knew I'd done the worst thing possible, but there was just enough hope to make me try.

Leo was already waiting at the restaurant, he didn't smile or get up to kiss me. The room was crowded – the hustle and bustle of a busy Friday night. He ordered a bottle of cheap red wine before I'd even taken my coat off.

I could tell he'd been drinking all afternoon. He knocked over the salt pot as he reached for his spectacles. He stared at me through bloodshot eyes. I wanted to run away.

We knew the menu off by heart but I sat there in silence and studied it intently. I hid behind the peach-coloured card so I didn't have to meet his hostile gaze. When the waiter came Leo didn't order *saltimbocca*. He said he felt like trying something different. 'The lobster, I think, for a change.'

The waiter said: 'Good choice, sir.'

I ordered the chicken I always ordered. I felt queasy as the waiter walked off, he was friendly and I wanted him to stay.

When it was just the two of us again, Leo ploughed on with the wine. He was downing it quickly, as if it were water. He topped up his own glass but left me to fill mine myself.

I could see he was making the nearby diners uncomfortable. I tried to ease the tension. I talked about the flat; told him about a play I'd like to see. I stayed away from the difficult subjects, the ones he'd come to talk about. He said nothing, just knocked back more wine.

The lobster arrived with a flourish from the waiter. A celebration dish; the finest Luigi's could offer. Half a lobster all pink and warm and curled up on the plate like a foetus.

The waiter put it down in front of Leo and my husband didn't wait for my meal to arrive. He took hold of a spindly lobster leg and he twisted it off with a flick. Then he put it to his mouth and he sucked out the flesh. He tilted his head back and sucked.

He set about that lobster with grim determination. He tore at it with his fingers. He shattered its shell with needless force. Flecks of juice splattered his crisp white shirt.

I forked up a mouthful of lukewarm chicken Milanese but my throat closed tight at the thought of it.

In the end it was me who brought up the baby. I wanted him to know how sorry I was. I thought I could make him understand if I could only find the right way to say it.

I spoke quietly, anxious no one else should hear. 'Leo, you know I never wanted to hurt you. I was frightened for Reuben. He's been so confused, so angry with us both. I was scared we might lose him altogether.'

He shook his head. A smudge of grease glistened on his chin.

I tried again: 'He's my son. I had to protect him.'

Leo's voice was loud. 'What about our baby? Or isn't that important now? Was that a boy? A son?'

I whispered: 'I don't know.'

'It was a boy, I'm sure of it.' His face seemed to crumple. 'I can't stop thinking about him. What did I do to deserve this? That's two sons I've—'

'No, Leo. Hush. We don't know that. We can't know. I might have lost it anyway. I'm older now and—'

'You killed him!'

Panic fluttered in my chest. 'Don't talk like that, Leo. Not here.' The other diners looked then turned away. We were the subject of every conversation.

When Leo's glass went crashing to the floor I couldn't tell if he'd thrown it or dropped it. He looked so distraught, I reached out to comfort him. But he pulled away from my touch as if it burnt.

He said: 'Reuben is a cold child. You're wasting your time with him. You love him but he'll never love you back.'

And everyone was staring at us as he got up from the table. Everyone watched as he walked out. He left me there in that crowded restaurant blotting my tears with a dark blue linen napkin.

That was the last time I went to Luigi's and the last time I ever saw Leo.

# 105

Margo is in an awkward mood because we've had to go to a different cinema. Our usual one has tricky timings on Sundays and she likes to be home before dark. This new place doesn't sell the choc-ice Margo likes and there's a funny smell of mothballs that gets right up her nose. Worse, the usherette doesn't hear her back-row request and we end up plonked somewhere in the middle.

Afterwards we find a cup of tea and Margo says the cafe is charmless. We're the only customers in here yet we still have to wait to be served. Margo complains the cake looks dry and there's not enough icing or cream. Then she orders a slice and moans about the portion size. The subtext is: it's all my fault. I should never have changed our weekly ritual.

She asks me yet again why we couldn't see our film on Saturday as usual. And I tell her yet again: 'I was busy.'

'But busy doing what?'

I'm not up to this today. I haven't had a drink since Alice's visit. I'm tired and I still can't think straight.

'Busy doing what?'

'Reuben needed help buying Alice's Christmas present.'

Margo folds her arms. 'Did he? It's only October. Tell me, what did he get her?'

I stumble on. 'A – one of those – a Teasmade. We went to Peter Jones and found one straight away. Reuben seems to think she'll be thrilled with it, though—'

She cuts me off. 'Gilda, don't.'

'But really it's a silly gift. Even I know how to boil a—'

'Gilda, please.' She shakes her head. 'I've had enough now. I'm not a fool. Why can't you just tell the truth?'

The cafe slides into sharpest focus: the scratched Formica table top; the dark brown crust on the condiments. There's a fork behind Margo's chair-leg, lying prongs-up on the floor.

Margo reaches over and touches my hand. 'I'm not angry, darling, I'm not. But I need you to be honest with me. I bumped into Reuben at the shops earlier – I hardly recognised him it's been so long. I said how much you'd enjoyed his birthday meal and he looked at me like I was mad.'

'I—'

'No, Gilda. Don't. It's difficult, I understand. But we've known each other nearly forty years. If you can't talk to me, you've got no one.'

# 106

I was with my son on the morning of his wedding. For a minute it was just the two of us, waiting for the others to arrive. We were standing outside the registry office and he was all dressed up in that dreadful brown suit. He was so grown-up and so young all at once and I just wanted him to be all right.

I remember I was feeling at odds with the day already. I'd been dreading seeing Frank and Berta. Dreading going through it alone. I knew my outfit was too tight and too white because when Reuben saw me in it, he didn't say he liked it. I wanted to go home and change it. Start again in something better.

It was just the two of us, me and my son. He was standing shivering beside me on the steps. He looked so fragile and it made me feel fearful for him. I said: 'Poor darling, are you all right?'

And he said: 'Yes. Just a little bit nervous, I think.'

That's when I should have hugged him. I know that now.

He said: 'I can't believe I'm actually getting married.'

I should have told him I loved him; that it's natural for a groom to be scared. Instead I said: 'Marriage isn't easy, darling. People change and feelings don't always last. I don't want you to make the same mistakes I've made. It's not too late if you're having doubts

288

about Alice. If you've changed your mind, it's not too late.'

I saw my son's expression and I knew I'd got it wrong.

Then Frank and Berta arrived and both of them hugged him. They admired his ugly suit and Frank said he was proud. And I stood on the side and I looked at the three of them. I marvelled at how easy they all found it.

I heard Berta tell Reuben he'd make a lovely husband. She said: 'We think Alice is super. You've got yourself a good one there.'

The sun shone right in her face as she said it and lit up her wrinkles like a spotlight.

And then my Reuben went and married that girl. He said his vows in front of all of those people. He stood on those steps in his ugly brown suit and he held her hand like it was a trophy.

And I knew he really loved this Alice and I knew that I should be happy. But I also knew something had shifted between us.

# 107

I've been lying to Margo for thirty years, pretending things with Reuben are fine. Now she knows the truth and she's quiet, which isn't like her.

She's staring down at the scratches on the table top, her chin is almost to her chest. She's pushed her half-eaten cake aside. I wonder if our friendship will survive.

And I realise now what losing Margo would mean. She's the only one who's stayed with me: through school, through motherhood, through both failed marriages. She's the only one left who really knows me.

I reach over the table and cover her hand with my own. She doesn't look up but she doesn't pull away. 'It was stupid, Margo, but I wasn't trying to trick you, I was lying to myself as well. I didn't want to admit how bad things were. I wanted you to think well of me.'

The waitress comes over and clears our plates. My throat feels tight and I ask her for a glass of water.

'The fact is, Margo, I've never been good enough – I let him down again and again. We were close when he was small but then I got so many things wrong. I can't even begin to make it right.'

The waitress returns with the water. Margo sniffs but she doesn't look up. I'm exhausted. I've lost her. 'Talk to me, Margo.'

Finally, she looks at me. 'It's been more than twenty years since you left Frank. Reuben is a grown-up now, he's got a house, a job and a wife. He's got his own life and it's a good one. He can't keep punishing the people who love him.'

She lowers her voice and leans over the table towards me. There's a fierceness in her eyes I haven't seen before. 'D'you want to know what I really think? He's behaving like a spoilt little shit. Yes, you made mistakes, Gilda, but that's what humans do. You've apologised. You've served your time. I know you tried your best with Reuben, I was there. Remember? That summer in Dorset? I saw how you were with him.'

The cafe is empty and the waitress wants to go home. She comes over with the bill and Margo pays it.

She pauses for a second as she's putting on her coat. 'You seem so certain that all of this is your fault. Do you think Frank was really that innocent? Haven't you wondered in all these years at how convenient it was for him and Berta?'

# 108

If I'm honest, I always pitied Margo. Poor old Margo who never had a man. Leo and I used to joke about it. 'The spinster' he called her, or 'your old maid friend'. It was cruel and I should have put a stop to it, I know. It helped me to have her to look down on.

So really it served me right when I found myself alone. Dear old Margo, she offered me a shoulder to cry on. She was gentle and patient with me. She let me talk and she listened. She said: 'Gilda, you've had enough sadness in your life.' I knew I was lucky to have her.

I didn't tell her about the baby, I never told anyone about that. I said Leo had met someone else. She said she'd never thought he was good enough. 'He wasn't kind. He was out for himself. There was something I didn't quite trust about him.'

She offered to help me with the practical things; the painful boring business of getting through the day. And I needed her help, I was feeble at the start. I'd been married for nineteen years in total, from teenage to middle age, my prime years, I suppose. From home, to school, through both my marriages I'd never had to fend for myself.

I'd never changed a fuse, driven a car, carved a slice of bread or paid a household bill. I'd never queued for rations or cooked a meal from raw ingredients. Living through the war had taught me precious little. I didn't have a chequebook or a bank account.

I had to learn it all from scratch and at first I found it quite beyond me. Every noise in the flat made me startle: the footfall of a neighbour; the scrape of the letterbox. I felt swamped by the blankets on the empty bed. I had to take pills with my whisky.

When the light bulb in my living room went I sat in darkness for days. The evening gloom went well with my mood; I told myself I deserved it.

But Margo was having none of my nonsense. She spotted a problem and she fixed it. She got Leo's stepladder out of the loft and climbed right up to the top. The old bulb was out and a new one was in and the room was brightly lit before I knew it.

I remember thinking how strong she was, how much I envied her self-sufficiency. I said: 'You really are something Margo,' as she clapped the dust from her hands.

She said: 'Darling, you don't have to be afraid. The truth is you can do anything you want now. Your life's your own. It's up to you.'


I put off telling Frank about the split. I was sure he'd be triumphant. I pictured Berta's smug expression as she squeezed his knee in quiet celebration.

The truth came out when they turned up to collect Reuben. He'd been silent all weekend as usual – didn't mention his stepfather once. But Berta walked through the door and asked: 'Where's Leo?'

She took me by surprise and I stuttered for a second. I said: 'He's gone. He left me.'

Frank said: 'My God, are you all right?'

Berta shook her head. 'Of course she's not all right.' She took off her coat and put down her handbag and left Frank and me together while she made us both tea.

And actually, they were kind to me. Both of them were very kind. There was no 'you had it coming'. There was no 'I told you so'.

Frank seemed a bit uncomfortable, kept looking at the door to the kitchen. But he said how very sorry he was and I could tell that he honestly meant it. 'Berta and I just want you to be happy. We've only ever hoped for the best for you.' I think I knew then that he was very happy with Berta. I think I knew for certain then that he'd never been happy with me.

He asked if they could help in any way. 'You must call us if there's anything we can do.' And I thought what a good man Frank was and how strangely things had turned out.

Then Berta came back in with the tea, which was far too strong and far too sweet. 'Leo's a schmuck,' she said. 'I always thought so. I have no doubt you're better off without him.'

When Leo first left me it felt like a serious illness. I was shaky and off-kilter. It was hard just to get through the day. But actually as the months went by I found out I was all right on my own. I had money from Frank – enough to live on – and Margo helped me with the practical things. I met her often for lunch or coffee and on Saturdays we went to the cinema.

Reuben came to stay in the holidays and it was fine, just the two of us, as long as he had his books. Conversation was stilted but I thought that was just his way.

I learnt to appreciate that peaceful time. For a while the flatness suited me.

It was the year I turned forty-two, the year of our tenth wedding anniversary, that Leo finally wrote to me and asked for a divorce.

It was a good letter, I thought. Not emotional but not cold either. He'd met someone, they'd had a daughter together and now he wanted to marry.

It helped me that he didn't say he loved her. He'd wanted a child and I was pleased he'd made that happen.

I did think, just for a little while, about the baby we would have had together. And I wondered, just for a second, whether that really was another boy. But then I locked those thoughts away and I rang my lawyer and gave Leo what he asked for. No point in digging up the past. No point in making it harder.

We were divorced on the grounds of his desertion in the spring of 1959. My father died in the summer and my mother the following year.

So at the age of forty-three I was just Gilda Meyer again. I was twice-divorced and middle-aged and nobody's wife any more.

# 109

It was Alice's idea to go for this walk. It's a clear crisp day and it feels good to be out. The cold air rasps my throat, much like my cigarettes. I squint against the afternoon sun, I lift a hand to shield my eyes.

She takes my arm as we set off up the street towards Primrose Hill. It is very strange to be walking beside her. I glance at her profile, she has freckles I hadn't noticed before. Her astrakhan coat smells warm and slightly lamby. Her blonde head moves in time with mine.

We hardly talk, the two of us, we walk in companionable silence. Now and again she points to something: a girl on a bicycle, a man with an overweight dachshund.

The hill is busier than I was expecting and I remember it's the half-term holiday. Children kick through leaves on the path ahead of us. A boy in a duffle coat chases his sister.

The breeze picks up as we make our ascent. It pulls at my head-scarf, so I take it off and put it in my pocket. Alice asks if I'll be warm enough. I'm too out of breath to answer her. When we reach the crest I make straight for the bench. My daughter-in-law sits down beside me. We stay quiet for a while and just look at the view. A man in a Grenadier Guards' jacket flies a kite.

Alice opens her mouth and I think she's going to tell me something, but then she shuts it without saying anything. She shakes her head – just a little but I notice. Then she opens and shuts her mouth again.

On impulse I reach to pat her hand, which is resting on the wooden slats between us. It's the briefest of touches: a fleeting softness. But the rush of affection warms me.

She takes the gesture as a sign of my impatience. 'You're freezing, Gilda. Let's get you home.'

'No, I'm fine.' I touch her hand again. 'It's just – I wondered – are you all right?'

Her smooth face creases. She shakes her head.

'What's wrong?' My stomach lurches. 'Is it Reuben?'

She tries to smile but it doesn't reach her eyes. 'No, Gilda. Reuben's fine. Everything's running like clockwork as far as he's concerned.'

A tear slips from the corner of her eye. She takes out her handkerchief and blots it.

'But you're upset about something.'

'It's nothing. I'm just being foolish.' She sniffs. 'I've been missing my job a bit, that's all. It was nice to make new friends, it felt like I was learning something. I thought I might open my own shop one day – Reuben said . . . well, it's a silly dream, isn't it? I don't even know what I'd sell.'

I could imagine my daughter-in-law with a shop of her own. I think she'd be rather good at it. I remember her design books, their orange sofa, the zigzag curtains. I could pop in and have a cup of tea sometimes. I start to tell her: 'Furnishings maybe?'

But she stops me with a hand on my arm. 'Come on. It's cold. Let's go home.'

# IIO

I wake up with Margo's question in my head. '*Haven't you won-dered in all these years at how convenient it was for him and Berta?*' It niggles away like the start of a blister and by lunchtime it's hard to ignore.

I spoon some cottage cheese onto four Ritz Crackers. I unfold *The Times* and try to focus on the headlines. The Tories are well ahead in the opinion polls; the public is confused by the seven-sided fifty pence coin. *Frank is a good man. He's always been a good man. Is it really possible? Surely not.*

I finish my crackers but I'm still a little peckish so I open the packet of ginger nuts I keep in the cupboard for Margo. I take out two or three and eat them with a cup of tea. *Frank moved on to Berta so quickly – why wasn't I surprised when Reuben told me? That time she came to visit us for tea, she was dressed like she was going to a nightclub.*

I am midway through the crossword when I remember Frank's spectacles. I'm stuck on a very difficult clue and the thought comes out of the blue. It has nothing to do with Seven Across, perhaps it is the light from the window that triggers it. Perhaps it is the broadsheet newspaper itself, the way I've spread it here on the table.

The memory is so clear that I stop and put my pen down. *Berta handed him his reading glasses without him having to ask for them.*

# III

I'd forgotten she was coming that afternoon and my dress had sweat-patches under the armpit. It was a pre-war tea dress in faded primrose cotton that didn't flatter me in any way.

I came downstairs and she was standing in our living room, dressed up to the nines in vibrant floral silk. I'd been arguing with Frank since early that morning and was desperate to go and meet Leo.

I forced my face into a smile. 'Berta, how lovely to see you'.

'Gilda, you look charming,' she said, though I knew I most certainly didn't.

She was standing in front of the large bay window and I studied her face while we waited for Frank. Her husband had died at Dunkirk. Frank went to the funeral by himself.

She was still quite attractive, but the vertical lines on her forehead were new. I thought: *She will struggle to find someone now.* I thought: *She is past her prime.*

I called up to Frank: 'Darling, Berta's here!' I was anxious to get proceedings underway. The sooner we drank our tea, the sooner I could go and meet Leo.

My husband came down and the maid brought a tray in. She served us all with such painful slowness, I almost grabbed the teapot myself.

Berta rattled on about the news of the day – she's always had a lot to say for herself. Frank was particularly charming and I felt cross that he was encouraging her. 'What's your view on it, Berta?', 'What d'you think about that?'

When he brought out his newspaper to show her an article, I thought we'd be there all night. He opened the broadsheet and straightened it, then spread it out on the table. The light from the window made patterns on the newsprint. *Berta handed him his reading glasses without him having to ask for them.*

And just in that moment – just in that second – she was his wife and I was the outsider. But then they started talking about Attlee's government and that thought got lost along the way.

The three of us sat there for over an hour and Berta showed no sign of leaving, though she must have seen me checking my watch. The teapot stood empty on the tray, we'd eaten all the cakes. The concert was due to start at half past six; Leo might simply go without me.

Eventually, I couldn't bear it. 'Berta, forgive me. There's somewhere I have to be this evening. I need to go up and change.'

I looked at Frank expecting fury. But he smiled at Berta and waved a hand in my direction.

'I'd get a move on if I were you. You'll be late.'

## II2

My brain feels itchy with thoughts, as if it's crawling with tiny insects. I'd like to lift it out of my skull and rinse it clean under the tap. I imagine cool water on delicate pink. The lightness, the relief of it. Nothing has changed, yet all of it's changed. Everything I thought I knew is different.

Gullible fool. My face burns with the shame of it. How could I have walked past so many signs? How could I have been so naive? All those fleeting doubts I dismissed as paranoia. Margo guessed it, my sister, my parents – everyone, it seems, but me.

The maid in the background when I spoke to Frank from Brighton; at the time I thought it cruel of him to hang up so quickly. He must have spent the night with Berta, my phone call probably woke them. I begged my husband to let me come back while she was lying naked beside him.

Poor cuckold Frank and his childless widow – they watched me from a distance, their reputations intact. I signed the confession papers. I told the court I'd committed adultery. I lived with the gossip and the sideways glances. I lost my social standing, lost people I'd thought were my friends. I accepted the punishment for the bad things I'd done. I handed over my son.

I made it all so easy for them, I went along so meekly! I was touched that Frank was generous with the settlement – when he helped us buy the flat, I was grateful! No wonder they were kind when Leo left, I bet it pricked their consciences to see me so unhappy. I lapped up their sympathy and comforting words. I thanked them for the titbits they threw to me!

That phone call with Lena makes sense now. '*We all heard the rumours but Father didn't want you to know.*' Father couldn't afford to fall out with Frank so he turned his back on the facts. I bet he banned all talk of Berta. He had to protect his business. Better to see his own daughter shamed. Better to cut me off.

But my mother, my sister? They heard the rumours too. Imagine how different my life would have been if they'd simply had the nerve to speak up.

Mother was very distant when Reuben was born and lost contact altogether after I left Frank. At the time I thought she was angry with me. Now I wonder if she wasn't just ashamed; afraid perhaps of letting something slip.


I've never been in charge, I realise that now. I've been jostled, talked into things, told what to do. My parents, my husbands, my sister even – all of them did it. The truth is I never tried to stop them.

I thought I was making decisions on my own. I thought the mistakes were all mine. But the choices I made were never really choices: I only had half of the picture.

I've blamed myself for everything; every little flaw in Reuben's life. I've carried that guilt alone for more than twenty years. But that's it, I've had enough. I need to get my son back.

Margo was right, I've served my time. It's Frank and Berta's turn to carry that burden now.

## 113

Their house is not nearly as grand as I'd imagined, a post-war semi in Hampstead Garden Suburb. Their privet hedge is overgrown and its stems stand on end like it's shocked by our arrival.

'I'm not going in with you.' Margo hangs back as I step through the gate. 'I'll be here when you come out. Good luck, darling.'

Their front door beckons with peeling paint and a rusty letterbox. I walk up the path and ring the bell. I look back for Margo but she's already out of sight. I hear footsteps inside and the door swings open. I can't think what to do with my face.

Berta is wearing a tangerine twin-set. She says nothing at first, then her eyes stretch wide. 'My God, Gilda, I didn't recognise you!' She puts her hand over her mouth then drops it to her chest. 'Your hair! You look so different!'

'I need to talk to Frank.'

She hesitates for just a fraction of a second. Then she says: 'Do come in.'

The entrance hall is covered with photographs. Reuben as a teenager skiing in Switzerland; aged twelve with his head in a book; a large family portrait with Berta in the middle; Reuben in his graduation gown. There are also several pictures of Berta as a younger woman: jaunty by a tennis net and waving from an open-topped car.

She says: 'I'll go and tell him you're here.'

She is gone for quite some time and I study each photograph.

When she returns her smile is nervous. 'Come with me.' She leads me through a glass panelled door into a narrow living room. Frank sits at the far end in a leather wingback chair. He has a rug over his knees and a newspaper open on his lap.

'Gilda?' He looks pleased to see me, but he doesn't move to stand up. As I get closer I notice his skin is tinged yellow. His voice is warm. 'Sit down and Berta will make us some tea.' He gestures to the sofa opposite him.

'So,' he says. 'What brings you here?'

I glance round the room, more photographs of Reuben: astride a bicycle; in cricket whites; with an elderly woman who, I'd guess, was Berta's mother. There's one of Berta and Frank together in Hamburg. The pair of them look young and happy. Frank has a full head of hair.

I point to it. 'When did you first meet Berta?'

Frank takes the newspaper off his knee and folds it. His voice is calm, his movements unhurried but I notice his trembling hands. 'Her parents were friends of my parents. She was part of my set in Hamburg.'

My throat is very dry. I wish I had some whisky. 'Frank, did you always love her?'

He nods. 'Yes. I always loved her.'

'Then why didn't you just marry her in the first place?'

His half-smile wavers. He looks down at his lap. 'We were engaged but she broke it off. She found out she couldn't have children. She knew how much I wanted them so she married someone else. It was painful but I understood. We didn't see each other for a long time after that. I came to England and that's when your father approached me.'

'He knew you'd been engaged?'

'All of Hamburg knew I'd been engaged. I came to London partly to escape that.' He shifts position, his frame seems to shrink into the chair. 'By the time Berta turned up here we'd all moved on. We were both of us married to other people; you were pregnant with Reuben. You might find it hard to believe now, but I honestly thought we were happy.'

Berta comes in with a tray of tea. She pours it without looking at me. She says: 'Help yourself to milk and sugar.'

Frank waits for her to leave.

I hold his gaze. 'When did you and Berta decide that you were not in fact happy married to me?'

He looks flustered for the first time in our meeting. For a few seconds neither of us speaks.

'I tried to make it work, Gilda. When Reuben was born, I was desperate to make it work. I thought, you know, that being a father – I thought I would be able to forget her. But then you took to your bed for so long and I needed someone I could talk to. Berta always understood me best. When I saw her nothing had changed.'

My head throbs, the start of a migraine. A ring of tightness presses on my skull.

Frank looks scared. 'Nothing actually happened between us to begin with. We didn't – not until after her husband died. You and I were living separate lives by then. We were all of us so unhappy. I just needed some comfort. You did too. With Leo. Didn't you?'

'But I was honest about Leo from the start. You and Berta lied to everyone – to me, to our friends, the courts, our son. You let him think it was all my fault, watched as he turned against me. Even now after all these years, you could put a stop to it and you don't.'

Frank shakes his head. 'I wanted us to stay together, Gilda. Despite it all, I wanted us to be a family. You were the one who left.'

'You wanted to protect your business! It had nothing to do with saving our marriage! You didn't want a scandal, you didn't want my father to find out! You never wanted me, you wanted Berta from the start – you were just too much of a coward to admit it!'

He reaches over and touches my knee, his brown eyes weak beneath watery grey. 'It was a terrible time for all of us. You were drinking too much. You weren't stable, Gilda. You were always out with Leo. We were worried you wouldn't manage on your own, I was afraid you might become ill again. I spoke to your father about it – we agreed we had to do what was best for the boy.'

Berta returns to collect the tray, I get up and reach for my bag.

Frank says: 'Gilda, it was all such a long time ago. Does any of this really matter now?'

I stand very straight, shoulders back, chin up. 'You got your little family, didn't you? It worked out just the way you planned it. You raised your child with the woman you loved. The two of you stole my son.'

# 114

I was thrilled when Reuben went off to study at Cambridge. The day of his graduation was the proudest of my life.

Frank and Berta invited me, which was kind though I wished my son had thought to do it. We went to Cambridge together, we three; me, my ex-husband and his wife. And actually it was fine. We all behaved impeccably. The three of us were terribly civilised. We're terribly civilised still.

The morning of the ceremony we collected Reuben from his room. His set, he called it, like a badger's sett. I'd been expecting something grander, with a bathroom.

All of us had made an effort to look our best. Reuben was wearing a dinner jacket under his gown. Frank was in his wedding suit, and even Berta looked OK.

I wore a blue dress, which I'd bought for the occasion. Reuben told me he liked it. He said: 'Mother, you look nice.'

I felt elegant as we walked together to Senate House. For once I felt I looked just right.

Our seats were near the back of the hall. Tiny figures in mortarboards trooped one by one up to the stage. Frank nudged me when it was Reuben's turn. We clapped until our hands hurt.

Berta said she was proud of him and I didn't answer because he's not her son. This was my day, my celebration. My son's Cambridge degree.

Afterwards we went and had lunch at a carvery. The four of us together for the first time.

At the end of the meal Frank took out the speech he had folded in his pocket. His voice was formal, the one he kept for public speaking. He over-defined his words like a radio announcer.

'Reuben, you've become a very fine young man. You've worked hard and it's paid off and we're all as proud as can be.' He raised his glass. 'I know it hasn't always been an easy road. But, Reuben, you've steered it with aplomb.'

And we all stood up and toasted my son because it really was quite something what he'd done.

Then Frank sighed and he sat back down. When he spoke again his voice was softer. It was quieter. Almost a whisper.

He said: 'What a funny little boy you were, Reuben. It feels like it was yesterday. You always had your head in a book. I can't believe what a long way you've come.'

There were tears in Frank's eyes, though it might have been the wine. He said: 'I've seen you grow through all of it. It's been the joy of my life.'

Then he patted his son on the shoulder and Reuben's eyes were shining too. And I just sat there and I didn't say anything because Frank had taken all of the words.

Later, alone in my guest house, I went back over the day. I thought about Frank's speech and I was glad he'd said those things out loud.

And I realised I'd never told Reuben how I felt. That thought was like a light coming on. How could he possibly know how much I loved him if I'd never found the words to say it?

I drained the last of my whisky and I shoved some clothes on over my nightgown. I slipped on my shoes and I went out into the

309

dark. I walked as fast as I could on the cobblestones. Suddenly it seemed so important to say it. I had to get to Reuben and tell him.

It took me an hour to find his college and by that time it was very late. I asked the porter for help and he was kind and concerned about my welfare. He walked me up to Reuben's room and he waited while I knocked on the door.

And I was surprised because a young woman answered. A pretty young girl with a wineglass in her hand. I heard laughter and music and the chatter of people behind her. I thought I'd got the wrong room.

But then I saw my son in the background. He was drinking and swaying to some jazz. He didn't see me standing at the door. He was tipsy and happy and young.

I thought about how I must look, with my nightgown on under my coat. And I realised it wasn't the right time to tell him. He wouldn't want to hear the things I said.

So instead I told the girl: 'It's nothing, I'm sorry. You youngsters need to make the most of your party. I can talk to Reuben in the morning.'

She smiled. 'Are you sure? His parents are here – you wouldn't be the odd one out.'

## 115

I've practised the lines I have to say but I am nervous as I pick up the telephone. My palm is clammy on the handset.

The receptionist answers and asks who's calling.

I say: 'It's Mrs Meyer, Reuben Goodman's mother.' She tells me to hold. The line goes dead. I listen to my breath against the mouthpiece.

My son is rather abrupt with me, he doesn't like it when I call him at work. He says he's terribly busy on deadline, he's only got a minute to spare.

My voice is stiff as I say the words. 'Darling, I was wondering if you'd have dinner with me after work on Thursday? I thought just the two of us for a change. I'm going to cook.'

'Why?'

'Can't a mother ask her son to dinner?'

He's silent and I imagine his brain ticking over. I shut my eyes, braced for his excuse.

'Yes, of course. It's just—'

There's a rustle of movement in the background and a colleague yells something I can't make out. Reuben sounds hassled. 'OK, yes, fine. I'll be there. Sorry, I've got to go now.'

I put down the receiver and lean against the hallway wall. My pulse is racing like I've run up the stairs.

He said yes. I can hardly believe it.

# 116

There's something familiar about the handwriting. I stare at the envelope as I go up in the lift. The slant of the letters, the curl of the 'G' in Gilda. The penmanship is loose and flamboyant. I've seen this writing somewhere before.

I'm almost at my door when I realise it's Berta's. The post-mark reads *Hampstead Garden Suburb*. I picture her licking the back of the stamp, her pink tongue emerging from too-bright lipstick.

I tear it open as soon as I get in. I scan the page, it is scarred with crossings out. When I hold it to my nose it smells of her.

> *Dear Gilda,*
>
> *Frank doesn't know I'm writing this, he'd tell me I had no right, but I can't just sit and do nothing. He hasn't been well this past year – I'm sure you noticed how fragile he was. He tries to put on a brave face but your conversation upset him greatly. He hasn't slept since your visit; he hardly eats.*
>
> *Frank is a good man. It wasn't his fault that I couldn't have children. Perhaps I shouldn't have ended our engagement but it's easy to say that in hindsight. When I heard he'd married you, I told myself that was an end to it. He was so happy when Reuben was born, I thought I'd done the right thing.*

*But then my husband died and you got ill. War makes you realise how short life is. Frank and I both needed someone to talk to. We got close again. You know the rest.*

*Even so, he always said he'd stay with you. He was adamant that Reuben needed his family. He didn't want a divorce and I understood that.*

*But – I'm not blaming you – it turned out that Leo wasn't a gentle man. Frank couldn't risk a scandal. Things couldn't go on the way they were. So we did what we thought was for the best at the time. That's true for all of us, isn't it? Reuben was such a troubled little boy. He needed a home that was stable and calm. Frank and I knew we could provide that for him.*

*It wasn't fair on you, the way things turned out. We aren't proud of it. We've tried over the years to repair some of the damage. But you're right, we haven't done enough.*

*Frank's son means everything to him. It would kill him if Reuben ever learnt the truth. Please don't say anything that might harm their relationship.*

*I know you've always tried to put your son first. I'm asking you to do that once again. You are a good mother Gilda. Please – for Reuben's sake.*

*Berta*

I refold the letter carefully and put it back in its envelope. She's trying to protect her husband, I don't blame her.

It's too little, too late, that's what I think. I'll do what's best for Reuben and me. For Reuben and Alice and me.

## 117

The doorbell goes at half past ten and I'm cleaning up the kitchen in a brand new pair of Marigolds. I tug off a glove and press the intercom.

'Gilda, it's me. Are you ready?'

I glance behind me into the living room where sunlight streams through freshly washed windows. Alice and Reuben's wedding portrait stands proud on the bookshelf in its silver frame. I smile and buzz her straight up.

My daughter-in-law is carrying a large cardboard box. 'I thought we'd make steak and kidney pie. It's one of Reuben's favourites.'

She leads the way into my little kitchen and sets the box down on the floor. Then she pulls her frilly white apron from inside and loops it over my head. She gestures for me to turn and ties it in a bow behind my back.

She lays the ingredients out on the counter. I've never seen so much food in this room. She laughs. 'Don't worry, it's a very simple recipe.'

There's a measuring scoop, a pie dish, a rolling pin and a mixing bowl. My own kitchen equipment is an ice-cube tray and a soda syphon.

I wonder if I'm up to it after all? Perhaps I'll just stand here and watch. I've never made any sort of pastry before. I've never cooked a steak or a kidney.

She says: 'Right, let's get started. Roll up your sleeves.' Then she points me to the mixing bowl and tells me to measure out the flour.

She is very much in charge, my daughter-in-law. She shows me how to use the sieve and cuts some butter into little gold nuggets. Then she drops it into the bowl and tells me to rub it in.

She demonstrates the movement and I watch her closely. When I fail to reproduce it, she touches my hands to guide me.

I'm clumsy to begin with but after a while I'm a child in the sandpit. I press flour and fat into powdery flakes. I pick up a handful, like Alice showed me, and watch it cascade through my fingertips.

'That's perfect,' she says. 'This pastry's going to be great. Food always tastes better when it's cooked with love.'

I nod. All you need is love.


When the pie is prepared we make chocolate mousse. Alice breaks the chocolate into cubes and shows me how a bain-marie works. I study my daughter-in-law, she seems a little less tired. I ask her if she's feeling any better.

She sighs. 'I'm sorry, Gilda. My moods are all over the place, you mustn't take too much notice. One minute I'm laughing, the next I'm in floods of tears. It's ridiculous, I should pull myself together.'

She hands me the wooden spoon and I stir the chocolate. She watches over my shoulder as it melts. She reaches round to turn the heat down.

I speak slowly, carefully, measuring each word. I need to get this absolutely right. 'I remember when I was pregnant with Reuben, I was so worried about the future. Everyone told me I was supposed to be happy but all I felt was scared and alone.'

316

I glance back at Alice. She's very pale, unmoving. Her eyes are fixed on the gas ring.

'The thing is, when he was born I loved him more than I thought was possible. I loved him more than life itself. Through everything, through all the stupid things I've done, it's the one thing I've never regretted. I'm so glad Reuben's in the world. I'm so very glad I had him.'

She tries to smile but her face is tight with worry. 'Gilda – please – you won't tell Reuben, will you? I was – it's come as a bit of a shock. I just need a little more time to get used to it. It's not – I'm not ready, that's all. Please. He can't know yet.'

I nod. 'You'll let him know when the time is right.'

I go back to stirring the chocolate.

# 118

I don't know what woke me that particular night, but I sat up with a start. The blackout blinds made the darkness complete. My heart was racing out of my chest and I knew I had to go to my son.

I took my torch and tiptoed down the corridor, past Frank's room, past the nanny's room. I opened the door to the nursery.

He was standing in his cot. His blankets were scrunched up under his feet, I could see in the dim glow of torchlight that his cheeks were wet with tears.

'What is it, darling? What happened? I'm here now. Did you have a bad dream?'

My son reached out to me and I lifted him over the bars. His chest was heaving in his vest. 'There was a baddie. He tried to get me.'

'No, Reuben, no. It's just a dream. There's no baddies here.' I carried him over to the chair and sat down with him. He clung to my shoulders with hot little hands. I stroked his damp hair from his forehead.

'There was a bad man. I saw him.'

'No, darling, no baddies. Mummy won't let any baddies get you. Mummy's here to protect you. Mummy will keep you safe.'

# 119

My head is aching and my shoulders are stiff. My feet hurt from too much standing up. What I need is a long hot soak in the bath; to stop the clock and unwind. A little glass of whisky. A sit-down in my armchair. I yearn for the familiar routine.

But there's no time to rest, there's too much at stake; it's not just me and Reuben now, there's Alice and the baby. Everything needs to be absolutely perfect. All our lives depend upon tonight.

I go to the bedroom and check my hair in the mirror again. My daughter-in-law is right, it does look better. I wasn't sure when I saw the packet but now I'm pleased I let her do it. It's less harsh, perhaps a little kinder to my skin-tone; less Myra, more Marilyn Monroe. I look less like my sister, which can only be a good thing, perhaps a little more like myself.

I'm wearing the outfit Alice picked for me: my new purple blouse and the bubblegum pink skirt. She told me I looked beautiful in it. She said: 'I think Reuben will love it.'

She brought me a special scarf for good luck. She tied it in a band around my hair. I like the feel of the silk behind my ears, soft against the sensitive skin there.

I go into the dining room to check that everything's just as I left it: the polished oak table set for two. The decanter of Reuben's

319

favourite wine. The silver candlesticks gleam in the half-light and I find a box of matches and set it beside them. I switch the chairs so my son's will be comfortable. The napkins are folded in the glasses.

The smell of steak and kidney wafts over from the oven. I go in and check on it, just like Alice told me to. I look at the chocolate mousses in the fridge and they're set, just like she said they would be.

I go into the living room and give it one last tidy. I plump the sofa cushions and straighten the rug.

Then I go to the cabinet in the corner of the room, the tall one where I keep my special things. I reach up to the very top shelf and I take out the little cardboard box. I bring it down – holding it carefully, carefully – and I carry it to the kitchen.

When I open the box they are all still there – all six of them. They are still that ugly stained-urinal yellow. Still the cheapest chunky china that Woolworths ever sold.

I gently pick two from the cardboard and I set them on the coffee tray with their saucers and two teaspoons. They are small and plain and lacking in charm, but these cups are the most precious things I own.

# 120

Twenty minutes is nothing. I know it's nothing. No one is punctual these days. He's probably been held up at work. Perhaps the trains are giving him trouble. Twenty minutes isn't even late. It's fine. He'll be here. I must be patient.

Only each minute feels like an hour to me now. My nerves are all on high alert. I perch on the straight-backed chair in the living room. I count to a hundred with my eyes closed. I think how much a little whisky would help.

I reach in my pocket for Berta's letter.

*We've tried over the years to repair some of the damage. But you're right, we haven't done enough.*

The doorbell goes and my stomach lurches. I rush to the intercom. 'Reuben, is that you?'

'Yes, Mother, it's me.' He sounds tired.

I shove the letter back in my pocket and go out to the corridor to meet him.

The lift clunks deep in its shaft and I breathe through my nose to calm myself. Its hums and clicks grow louder as it nears my floor. Finally the metal doors slide open. My son is standing stiff and unsmiling.

I go to hug him and he moves just out of my reach as usual. His eyes are fixed on the carpet as I usher him into the flat.

I lead him to the living room. 'Sit down, darling, you've had a long day.'

He takes off his hat and puts it on the coffee table. He shrugs off his coat and drapes it over the armchair.

At first I think I must be dreaming, but no, I look again and it's true: my son is wearing his forest green shirt. Yes, it's a little bit creased, but then he's had it on all day; yes, it's a bit on the large side but at least there's room to grow. That green does bring out the hazel in his eyes. I turn away quickly, in case I embarrass him. I want this too much. He mustn't see it.

I walk over to the cabinet and fix him a whisky. I drop a cube of ice in a cut-glass tumbler. My senses hone in on the smell, the noise as the liquor leaves the bottle. The amber dances as I pass it over. I make myself a soda and lime.

He takes his drink and sips it slowly. His eyes dart round the room: at the table, the bookshelves, his wedding photograph.

Finally he looks at me. 'What have you done to your hair?'

I touch a protective hand to it. 'I felt like a change.'

He nods but doesn't say he likes it.

I ask him how his week's been.

'Fine.'

'Tell me, how's work going?'

'Fine.'

His house is also 'fine' and his wife is 'fine' too.

We sit there in silence while I try to think of another question. The clock ticks towards eight. Reuben asks me nothing.

At eight on the dot I get up to take the pie out. I tell my son to go through to the dining room. 'I've cooked you one of your favourites.'

I'm pink with pride as I set it on the table. Steam rises from its golden crust.

Reuben raises an eyebrow. 'Did Alice make this?'

The question stings but I manage a smile. 'She helped me a little because I've never made pastry before. I wanted to cook you something special.'

I pick up my son's plate and serve him a nice big slice. He looks wary as he takes it from me. I pour him a glass of wine.

He eats too fast; swallows without chewing; lifts fork to mouth like a clockwork drummer boy. He smothers the pie in salt and pepper; wipes his chin with the back of his hand.

I ask: 'Is it all right, darling?'

He mumbles: 'Yes, it's nice.'

He's racing towards the finish line and I can't think how to slow him down. There's so much we need to sort out between us, so much we need to talk through.

The scrape of cutlery is the only noise in the room.

All too soon, his plate is empty. I offer him a second helping of pie. He shakes his head, no, he's full. I get up and clear both our dishes away though I'm not even halfway through mine.

I go back to the kitchen and bring out the two chocolate mousses I made. Each one is dainty in a crystal goblet. Each one topped with a cocktail cherry. Each one perfectly smooth.

I say, 'I hope you've left space for dessert,' as I place his on the table in front of him.

He eats the entire mousse in three large spoonfuls. I taste a bit myself. Eggy sweetness sticks in my throat.

I feel foolish collecting up the goblets when I've only just put them out. Reuben keeps glancing at his watch. I check my own and it's eight twenty-five.

*

I walk back into the kitchen and fill the kettle. I light the gas and put it on the hob. I measure the Lyons grounds into the coffee pot and I give the teaspoons one last polish.

# 121

We were side by side at the mirror in my bedroom when Alice pulled the scarf from her bag. She looked almost shy as she handed it over.

'It's only a token. I thought it might bring you good luck.' A narrow band of silk in a soft coral pink. 'I know how much this evening means to you.'

She wrapped it round my head with gentle hands and tied it in a knot beneath my hair.

'He does love you, Gilda. He may not show it, I'm not even sure if he knows it himself, but it's there. I see it all the time.'

I held my breath. 'When do you see it?'

'In little things. He hates it when other people criticise you. Berta once said your coat was old-fashioned and Reuben almost blew his top. He's kept an old toy car you gave him and won't let anyone touch it. Also, whenever I come off the phone to you he wants to know you're OK. He sees how close I am to my mother . . .'

She picked up the brush and neatened the back of my hair. 'You know, it takes a lot of effort to stay angry with someone for so long, I don't think he could sustain that unless he loved you.'

She put a hand on my shoulder and pointed at my reflection in the mirror.

'Gilda, you look beautiful. Don't stop trying with Reuben, will you? He won't make it easy, but don't give up.'

# 122

The silver tray is heavy and difficult to walk with, cups topple on their saucers, teaspoons rattle. I hold my gaze on the tall pot of coffee. I move slowly, one inch at a time.

I set the tray down gently in the centre of the dining table. The cups look almost pretty in the candlelight. I take my seat and pick up the pot. Under my breath I pray.

My son is silent as he looks at the tray, he's waiting for me to serve him. I try to keep my voice light but my hand starts to tremble as I pour.

'Reuben, do you remember these cups?'

His face is blank, impossible to read. I pass him his coffee. He leaves it on its saucer to cool.

'They're the ones you gave me when you were a little boy. Do you remember?' I can feel the desperation building inside me. 'I hardly saw you that summer. Your father and Berta – I thought Berta was trying to take you from me. I got it all mixed up. I was sad and confused. I thought these cups came from her.'

He says nothing, just stares at his cup.

'Reuben, I know the truth now. You saw these cups and you saved for them and you bought them to try and make me happy. I'm so sorry for the dreadful things I said that afternoon. I was all in a mess and I wasn't thinking clearly. If I could go back, I'd do it all so differently. I love these cups because they're from you.'

He picks up his cup. It is tiny in his hand. He turns it and examines it, twists it side to side. He doesn't add milk or sugar. He doesn't take a sip. My own cup stands empty still. The silence stretches.

'It was the summer—'

'Yes. I remember.'

My throat is very tight. 'I was upset and I got it wrong.'

My son shrugs his shoulders like all of this is worthless, as if it hasn't touched him at all.

His voice is flat. 'Is that it? Is that your apology? Why now, that's what I want to know. Why now I'm married? It's been twenty years – you've never bothered before.'

He isn't being fair, he doesn't know how hard I've tried. I want to tell him. I need to explain. But his face is dark with anger and I can't find the words. Berta's letter sits folded in my pocket.

He says: 'You're selfish, that's what I think. You're afraid of getting old on your own. You're jealous of Alice and the time I spend with her. It's pathetic. I couldn't give a damn about these cups!'

He slams the cup back down on the saucer. Hot coffee splashes onto polished oak. He moves to mop the spillage with his napkin but there's too much.

I stumble back to the kitchen. I shut the door behind me. Then I stand at the sink and let the water run.

# 123

Reuben's friends were doing some sort of dance, shaking their hips and flinging their arms up. The parquet floor pulsed with drowning swimmers. Energetic but hardly romantic.

I was fifty-two years old and every part of me ached. I'd been rooted to the spot for several hours. I'd stood there through the speeches and the telegrams and the toasts, through all the stilted small talk and the photographs and the wedding cake. I'd been on my feet all day in those clamped-on little court shoes and I needed, for a minute, to sit down.

So I drained my glass of whisky, it was just a very small one, and got myself another for the walk to the ladies' room. The chatter and clink of the party receded. I walked slowly, taking my time.

It felt nicely out of bounds to be leaving the reception – a schoolgirl tiptoeing through hallways during lessons. I trailed one hand along the cool, smooth wall. Before I knew it, my whisky glass was empty.

The ladies' room, when I eventually found it, was a silk-lined sanctuary with a smell of Elnett hairspray. It was calm and empty and no one there was judging me. I didn't have to smile any more.

There was a velveteen chaise longue beneath a giant gilt-framed mirror. I perched on the edge of it and peeled off my shoes. I massaged my soles and flexed my swollen toes, which felt stiff and stuck together in my stockings.

I put my feet up for a minute or two – maybe more, it's hard to know. And I thought about the wedding and I told myself I had to let go.

I thought: *What does anything matter really, as long as Reuben is happy?* And I thought: *She's not so bad, this Alice. Perhaps we could even be friends.* And I thought: *This could be a fresh start for me.* And I thought: *I could leave the past behind.*

And I let myself believe that things would be different when I got back to the party. I'd be warmer, wittier, kinder to Berta. I'd find Alice and say something nice.

I sat up straight and smoothed the creases from my skirt. My head still felt heavy but clearer somehow. I crammed my feet back into my shoes and I was ready to return and join in.

As I strode down the corridor I saw Frank and Berta coming towards me. They were arm-in-arm, the two of them. They were laughing together, which was nice. Some strands of Berta's hair had come loose and they fanned round her jawline like feathers. She seemed softer like that. Younger, I thought. Frank looked exhausted but happy.

He gave a little nod as I approached so I smiled and said a jaunty: 'Hello there.' I beamed especially brightly at Berta, who tucked her hair back as if I'd made a comment.

Frank said: 'You've just caught us, we're getting our coats. We thought we'd leave the young ones to it.'

And I wondered if I'd misheard him because surely they couldn't go yet? No one leaves the party before the bride and groom, not when it's their own son's wedding.

So I asked: 'Have you said goodbye to Reuben? He was busy on the dance floor when I saw him.'

Frank looked confused. 'But – we've all just waved them off. All those tin cans tied to the car, don't say you missed it?'

I tried to keep smiling because this was my fresh start. I told myself to feel different and I told myself to let go.

Berta put her hand on my arm. 'Don't be sad, darling. It's been such a lovely day. They'll be back in a week. They had to get their flight. I'm sure they didn't miss you on purpose.'

Frank shuffled his feet and passed me a neatly pressed handkerchief. 'People are looking, Gilda. Please don't cry.'

# 124

'Mother?' His voice cuts through my thoughts. He's sitting at my dining room table and he's waiting for me to come back. But I'm tired and my make-up is smudged and I don't have anything left to give him.

He calls: 'Are you OK in there?'

I do not answer.

I love my son, but he isn't a kind man. Perhaps it's my fault – I try too hard. He's too sure he's right; too black and white. There's no room for compassion or forgiveness.

Would he love me any more if I showed him Berta's letter? He'd surely love Frank less, there'd be some justice in that.

*Your father betrayed us both.* It would feel so good to say it out loud. *He was unfaithful long before I was.* It would feel so good to tell the truth.

His eyes are on me as I wipe up the coffee. His face is softer now. He leans forward a little in his seat and then back again. I carry on wiping though the table is clean.

Chin down, he mumbles into his shirt. 'I probably shouldn't have said all that.' The chair creaks as he gets to his feet. 'I should go now. Alice will be waiting.'

My fingers tense on the cloth. I have a fleeting urge to throw it at him.

'Sit down.' I'm shocked by the force in my voice. 'Sit down, Reuben. I haven't finished yet.'

He hovers for a second, every muscle reluctant, then slowly sinks back into his chair.

I drop the cloth and dry my hands on my skirt. A knot of righteous anger tightens in my stomach. I pull out my own chair and sit opposite my son. 'There's something else you need to hear.'

I reach in my pocket and take hold of Berta's letter. A sudden sense of vertigo, of lives about to change.

I whisper it: 'Berta wrote to me.'

The colour drains from Reuben's face. His eyes stretch wide. For a second I think he knows what's in the letter. But when he speaks, his voice is small. 'Is it Dad? Is he ill again?' He covers his mouth with his hand.

And all I can see is his love for his father. So much love I can hardly bear it. It's the love I saw when he ran to his dad with his arm in a sling. It's the love I saw at lunch on his graduation day.

I want to say: *He doesn't deserve it!* I want to say: *He lied to us both!* But Frank is shelter and safety to Reuben. I've never had that.

And I curse myself for being weak because just like that I know I can't do it. I shove Berta's letter back down in my pocket. I am a good mother.

I take a deep breath. 'No, darling – hush. Your father's going to be fine.'

'He's OK?'

'Yes. He's OK.'

'Oh God, I thought—' A tear slides down his cheek. He swipes at it. 'But he's OK.'

For a moment neither of us speaks.

I glance at the coffee cups, still empty on the silver tray. The bowl of sugar lumps, the polished teaspoons. I think: *That's it then. Nothing's going to change.*

Reuben frowns. 'What was the letter about? Why would Berta write to you?'

I feel myself flush as I stumble for an answer. 'She was worried about Alice – we both were. She's seemed a bit unhappy lately.'

'She's fine.' His voice is gruff. 'She's just tired.'

I think about my daughter-in-law: her warmth and her kindness; I think about her dream of owning a shop; I think about the baby. I think of all the ups and downs that she and Reuben have ahead of them. I want so very much to be a part of that.

I say: 'I wasn't sure about Alice when I first met her. Perhaps you're right, I was a little jealous. But Reuben, I've got to know her now. I can see how special she is. You two are lucky to have found each other. If she wants to work, you should let her work. She's your wife. You can trust her. There's nothing to fear from it.'

Reuben rests his forehead in his hands. 'I want to trust her. It's hard.' He shakes his head. 'I'm scared she's going to leave me.'

I move to touch his arm but my courage fails. I touch the table beside him. 'No, darling, no. She loves you, she'd never do that.'

He looks at me. Really looks at me. Meets my eye for the first time this evening. His voice is very quiet. 'You did. You left.'

And that's it, isn't it? That's the truth. Nothing I can do or say can change it. Not Frank, not Berta's letter, not Alice, the baby, the cups, a new blonde hairdo. I'll always be the one who walked out.

And the strange thing is, it doesn't kill me to hear it. It's part of me, part of who I am – something I did long ago. I made mistakes. I wasn't the only one. One day my son will understand that. But right at this moment it really doesn't matter – we have other things to think about now. More important things.

I get to my feet. My shoulders are stiff. I say: 'Please don't punish Alice for my mistakes. She needs a husband who trusts and supports her. If you can do that, it's simple: you love each other and that's enough. The two of you have so much to look forward to. Let her be the person she needs to be. She isn't going to do what I did.'

I follow my son into the living room. I watch him as he collects his coat from the chair. I watch him as he slides his arms into the sleeves and does up the buttons one by one.

He's silent as he puts on his brown leather gloves. He looks at his hands, he doesn't look at me. I think perhaps I see him nod, just once, as he straightens his grey felt hat.

His hand is on the door when he turns to me. He is stiff and awkward. 'Thank you, Mother.'

I manage to say: 'My pleasure, darling.' I manage to say: 'See you soon?'

I lean in to kiss him on the cheek and his skin, very briefly, touches mine.

The front door closes quietly behind him. I hear his footsteps on the hallway carpet. I hear the lift doors open and shut.

I go back to the dining room and sit down at the table. I look across at his empty chair. I pick up the ugly yellow coffee cup from my saucer and fill it with the lukewarm coffee left in the pot.

The cup is small but it's solid in my hand.

I lift it to my lips and take a sip.

# 125

The photographic print is rather larger than I'd envisioned. I had to buy a special envelope for it: it is stiff manila with a cardboard back, red letters read *Do Not Bend*.

I take out my pad of Basildon Bond and brush my fingertip over the watermark. I make myself a fresh cup of tea and sit down at my desk to compose.

I move my pen slowly, make every letter plump and perfect. I space the words so they span the notepaper. If I make a mistake, I start again.

I wait a full ten minutes for the ink to dry and read it three times before I put it in the envelope.

> *Dear Berta,*
> *Thank you for your letter. I enjoyed my recent visit to*
> *your house, it was nice to see where you live at last. So*
> *many photographs! You and Frank have built a good life for*
> *yourselves. How fortunate my son could be a part of it.*
> *I noticed, though, there's something lacking from your walls*
> *— there's not a single picture of Reuben as a baby. He was such a*
> *sweet little boy, you missed out on all that. Those early years are*
> *so important, aren't they?*

*This photograph, then, is my gift to you. Consider it a symbol of our mutual understanding. It was taken just after Reuben was born. I was only twenty-three years old — my family was on the other side of the ocean. I think I look happy, though. I was so very proud of my son.*

*I trust you will find somewhere prominent to display it.*

*Gilda*

I put on my coat and walk to the postbox. I feel a sense of rightness as I drop the letter in.

I stride back down the road with my head held high and I make my way to the cafe where Margo is waiting for me.

# ACKNOWLEDGEMENTS

Thank you to my brilliant editors: Arzu Tahsin who saw what this book should be and had the talent to get it there and Jennifer Kerslake who took up the baton with such intelligence and sensitivity. I'm deeply grateful to the entire W&N team, especially Steve Marking for his stunning cover design, Craig Lye, Rebecca Gray and Cait Davies. It's been a joy.

Huge thanks to my wonderful agent Felicity Blunt for her unwavering support and editorial insight; to Lucy Morris, Jessica Whitlum-Cooper, Melissa Pimentel and all at Curtis Brown; to Sam North, whose belief in Gilda took me through the first draft and to Joanna Briscoe and my fabulous Faber Academy classmates.

Thank you also to my early readers, advisers and friendly ears: Amanda Smyth, Helen Little, Kate Myers, Ursula Milton, Adam James, Sally Kennedy, Melanie Garrett, Carol Barnes-Burrell, GZ Mughal, Chloë Mayer, Elisa Lodato, my partner in writing travails Susan Allott and long-suffering German consultant Matthias Hoss.

Finally to my folks. Mum and Dad, you've been utterly amazing. Nick, Suzy, Nat, Joe and Sam, this book would be nothing without your encouragement, enthusiasm and comedy title suggestions.

I'm a poor historian and apologise for the many liberties I've taken in telling this story. That said, I learnt much from letters and first-hand accounts, as well as the BBC's incredible online archive. There are a few books I'm particularly indebted to: *From the Edge of the World: The Jewish Refugee Experience through Letters and Stories*, compiled and edited by Anne Joseph; Norman Longmate's *How We Lived Then, A History of Everyday Life during the Second World War*; and Sheila Hardy's *Women of the 1960s*. The mistakes are all my own.

# In conversation with Francesca Jakobi

**When did you start writing *Bitter*, and could you tell us a little more about your grandmother, whose story provided inspiration for the novel?**

I started writing *Bitter* in my late thirties – a classic 'now or never' moment. It was a short story at first, inspired by a photograph of my grandmother at my parents' wedding. Like Gilda, she had an affair in the 1940s and lost custody of my father. I'd grown up hearing that she was a weak and selfish woman, but I adored her and could see how much she loved my dad. I wanted to consider an alternative point of view.

**How did you approach the balance between truth and imagination?**

I didn't know many of the facts around my grandmother's divorce so *Bitter* is mostly imagination. My gran was a gentle character and would have been appalled at Gilda's antics. That said, the two do have similar backgrounds and my grandmother also lived in a smart Swiss Cottage flat. Both were elegant women and, even in her eighties, my grandmother was justifiably proud of her legs.

**Did you have a strong idea of Gilda's voice from the outset? She can be prickly and unkind at times – do you think it's important for a protagonist to be likeable?**

Yes, Gilda's voice was prickly right from the start. I know some people struggle with unlikeable protagonists, but I love them as long as I can understand what's made them that way. I enjoyed the challenge of getting readers to care about Gilda, even if they didn't warm to her.

***Bitter* is set between Germany before the Second World War and London in the forties and sixties. How much research did you do for the novel? Did you visit any of the locations?**

I've always been a reluctant researcher – it reminds me of my dreaded history homework as a teenager. Luckily there are lots of fantastic films and novels set in these periods, so I didn't have to read too many hefty tomes. I loved looking at old photographs and letters both in online archives and in the Imperial War Museum. I also spent a very enjoyable afternoon lurking in Harrods beauty hall and walked up and down Finchley Road imagining myself as a stalker. I didn't go to Hamburg; to me those chapters have a dark fairy-tale quality that I was keen to hold onto.

**Although Gilda is suspicious of Alice to begin with, she is won over by her daughter-in-law's generous, kind nature and her loyalty to her son. Do you think the mother-in-law/daughter-in-law relationship is a tricky one to traverse?**

It can be, especially if one side is jealous or insecure. There's often a power struggle between different generations with different ideas about how a wife/mother should be. Luckily Alice is close to her own mother and wants that for Gilda and Reuben.

**Do you have a favourite author? What book do you most recommend to friends?**

I have a terrible memory and I'm very fickle, so my favourite author changes all the time. I tend to love strong voices and books set in the mid-twentieth century. The novel I've recommended most recently has been *Life After Life* by Kate Atkinson.

**Do you have any writing rituals, and what are you working on at the moment?**

When I was writing *Bitter* I used to work in my local coffee shop. After writing for an hour I'd reward myself with a slice of cake. Sadly, that had to stop due to the expansion of my posterior.

I'm in the early stages of writing a second novel with a strong central character very different to Gilda. It's going quite slowly. Perhaps I need more cake.

**What's the best piece of writing advice you've been given?**

Just keep going and don't show it to anyone too soon. It will take as long as it takes.

# Discussion points for reading groups

1) Gilda's voice can be sharp and biting, particularly when she makes judgements about those closest to her. Do you find her hard to like, and if so, does this affect your reading experience? Does your impression change over the course of the book?

2) How important are physical appearances in *Bitter*? Consider Gilda's attitude towards Lena and Alice, both of whom are neat and small, and her own attempts to alter the way she looks through new clothes, hair and make-up.

3) 'It was difficult to juggle so many lives: a teacher, a lover, a mother, a wife' (p.197). Examine how far Gilda's identity is determined by the roles she performs and the expectations of others.

4) Do you think Reuben is justified in his treatment of Gilda?

5) 'They're so hopeful standing there, so full of fairy tales and happily ever after . . . It doesn't last that feeling' (p.7). To what extent does Gilda's attitude towards marriage change?

6) Explore the theme of loneliness in the novel.

7) Gilda is both betrayer and betrayed. How much responsibility does she bear for her fate?

8) 'He says she taught him how to love; that she taught him what love could be. And I can't look at him because he didn't learn about love from me' (p.4). Discuss the relationship between love, guilt and bitterness in the novel.

9) Francesca Jakobi was inspired to write *Bitter* by the experience of her grandmother, who was sued for adultery after the Second World War and lost custody of her son as a result. Does knowing this affect your response to the novel?

10) Do you think Gilda subverts or conforms to the mother-in-law stereotype?

11) Gilda can be described as an unreliable narrator in that it isn't clear whether she is relating events in a truthful manner. How does her viewpoint impact on your understanding?

12) The story unravels in the past and present – with sections set in Germany and London in the 1940s and in London in the 1960s. How does this dual narrative help to build tension?

13) What do you make of Gilda's letter at the end of the novel? How do you envisage the future for Gilda, Frank, Berta and Reuben?

14) 'If I'm honest, I always pitied Margo. Poor old Margo who never had a man' (p.292). Do you think this pity is justified? How does Margo view Gilda?

15) The law changed in 1969, the year *Bitter* is set, to allow couples to divorce without blame. How much was Gilda a victim of the times she lived in? Does this affect her attitude towards Alice?